Sorcery, Swords & Scones

A COZY ROMANTIC FANTASY

TALES FROM THE TAVERN
BOOK TWO

T.L. STONE

BROADMOOR BOOKS

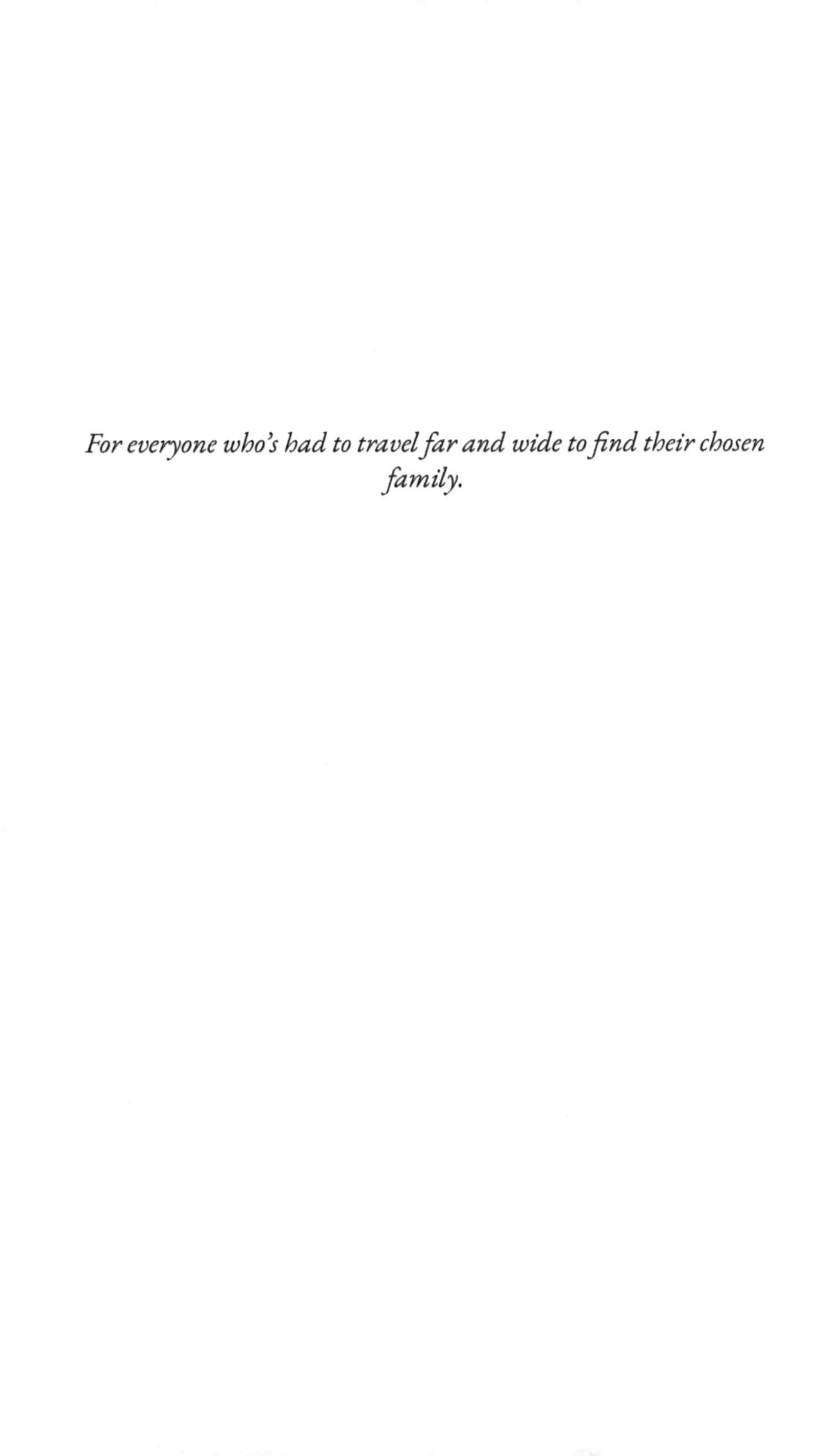

For everyone who's had to travel far and wide to find their chosen family.

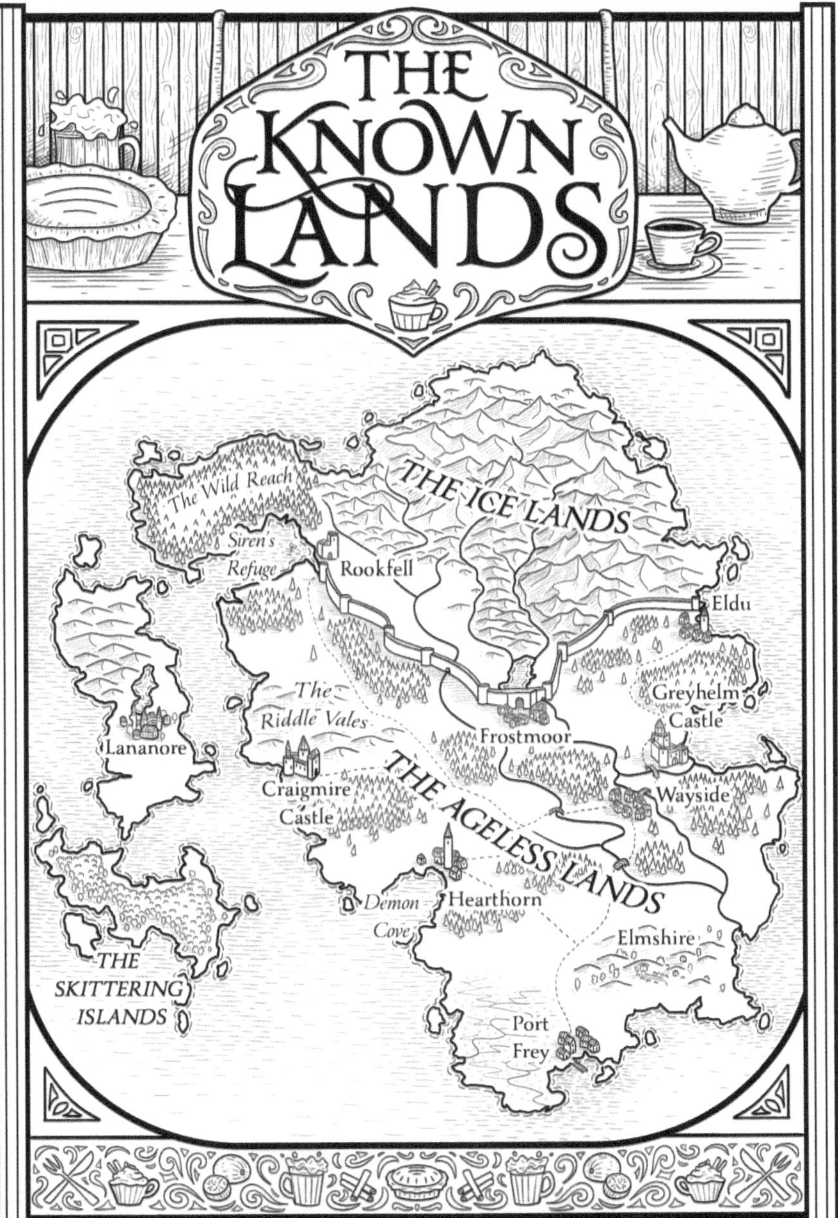

THE KNOWN LANDS
The Wild Reach
Siren's Refuge
Rookfell
THE ICE LANDS
Eldu
Greyhelm Castle
The Riddle Vales
Frostmoor
Lananore
Craigmire Castle
THE AGELESS LANDS
Wayside
Demon Cove
Hearthorn
Elmshire
THE SKITTERING ISLANDS
Port Frey

SASS WIPED the back of a hand across her forehead as she pushed through the swinging doors into the tavern's kitchen. "Grognick's beard, it's boiling in here."

Lira glanced up from pulling a tray of golden-brown, crescent-shaped pastries from the oven and grinned at the dwarf. "Well, I have been cranking out meat pies since the dinner rush started."

"And the rush is nowhere near done." Sass tossed her long, dark braid off her shoulder and leaned gratefully against the wooden table in the center of the room as she drew in a ragged breath. Her feet ached and begged for her to sit, but she knew that would only make it impossible to heave herself up again, and since she was the only server they had, resting wasn't an option.

"I think this is called beware of what you wish for," Lira said, as she blew an errant strand of auburn hair from her eyes. "We wanted The Tusk & Tail to be busy again."

Lira was right, of course. This was what they'd wished for, although Sass sometimes thought they might have wished *too* hard.

When she and Lira had first laid eyes on the tavern, the building had been entombed in cobwebs and grime, and the odor of decay had run roughshod over the place. The kitchen had been dank and cold, with teetering stacks of pots and pans festering on the counters and threatening constant collapse.

Sass took in the copper pots gleaming proudly overhead and the new cast-iron stove that hummed along without belching smoke. "I remember when our ornery old oven either burned food or refused to heat."

"And don't forget that the place smelled of dead troll."

Sass wrinkled her nose. "How could I forget?"

Now the air was laden with the promise of buttery pastry and braised meat, which was a welcome change.

Even as she took in the warm, inviting kitchen, Sass sighed. "Would it be wrong to admit that I sometimes miss the days when we had no business?"

The half-elf cook straightened and slid the baking pan onto the table, dropping the orange knitted potholders beside it. "After all our work to spruce up The Tusk & Tail and attract a devoted clientele?"

Sass dabbed at the beads of sweat that clung to her hairline. "We might have spruced too well." The dwarf jerked a thumb toward the great room. "The place is packed, and I've got enough orders for your meat pies to keep you elbow deep in pastry all night."

Lira's long hair was pulled up in a high ponytail with curly wisps escaping from the nape of her neck. Her slightly pointed ears were exposed, a sign that she wasn't as hesitant to reveal her elvish lineage anymore. She tightened the tail of hair with a tug and cut a glance to the white, winged stoat perched on the windowsill. "Did you hear that, Crumpet? No more scraps for you tonight."

Crumpet wiggled his whiskers, his inky eyes darting to the pastries and then to Lira. He chattered indignantly.

"Crumpet says he liked it when it wasn't so busy, either." Sass shoved up the puffy sleeves of her blouse. "Isn't that right, Crump?"

Lira's twitch of the lips slid all the way to a smile. "First, you hated the idea of Crumpet staying here, and now you're his translator?"

Sass sniffed. "I'm not one to get on the wrong side of an enchanted wee beastie." She thought about how much the flutter-stoat had become part of their tavern family and how tough he'd proven himself to be. "Besides, Crumpet is the bravest little guy I know."

Lira reached over and scruffed the fur on the top of his head. "That he is—and an excellent judge of baked goods."

Sass put a hand to her belly. "Speaking of food, I haven't eaten a bite since breakfast."

"Speaking of breakfast, those lemon sweet rolls didn't last long."

Sass ignored the obvious reference to how many of the yeasty, gooey rolls she'd eaten. "See? That's the problem with Pip's pastries; they don't keep well."

Lira's brows lifted. "As if we'd have any way of knowing that."

Sass paid no mind to that comment either. It wasn't her fault that the village's halfling baker created pastries so delicious that they never lasted much longer than the brief walk from his bakery to the tavern.

Lira plucked a small, blistered crumb from one of the meat

pies and handed it to Crumpet. "I would offer you a leftover scone, but there are none left."

Sass eyed the crumb in the flutterstoat's paws longingly. "I'm also rethinking my afternoon scone break idea."

Lira slid the hand pies onto a pewter tray with quick hands. "Because it's been so successful that there are no extra scones for us?"

Sass gave her friend a side-eye glance. "I suppose I have no one to blame for this but myself and perhaps your baking."

Crumpet chittered as he daintily wiped his paws, unfurled his wings, and flew to the copper pots hanging above.

"And your taste-testing skills, Crump," Sass added with a wry smile, then swiveled her head around the kitchen. "What happened to the recipe you were working on for the Harvest Festival? Anything left from that?"

Lira's brow pinched, and Sass regretted reminding her that the festival to celebrate the coming harvest season was mere days away. Not that she had any doubt that Lira would come up with a delicious recipe the tavern could showcase, especially since her friend now had her gran's recipe book.

"The apple crumble bars? I'm still working on the perfect apple to cinnamon ratio."

Sass scanned the kitchen for the large leather-bound recipe book that contained much more than recipes. "I thought you were using one of your gran's recipes."

"I am." Lira glanced at the flutterstoat. "But my gran's measurements for recipes weren't always precise. I'm still working out what her version of a sprinkle, a pinch, or a handful is, which means lots of trial runs. Right, Crumpet?"

Sass straightened and put her hands on her hips. "Are you telling me that the wee beast ate everything?"

"Like you said, he's excellent at taste-testing."

Before Sass could register another complaint about the

enchanted stoat eating better than she did, the kitchen doors that only took up the middle part of the doorway swung open.

"If there's any taste-testing to be done, I'd like to be considered for the job."

Sass and Lira both turned as Korl stepped into the kitchen. The tall orc guardsman wore quilted chest armor over dark pants and had his black hair tied back. His skin was dusky green, with small tusks that peeked from his lower lip. Muscles bunched his arms and shoulders, which were currently free of weapons.

Lira's face lit up at the sight of her fiancé. "You're done with work?"

He nodded, his dark eyes flashing as he took her in. "Guardsmen work, at least."

Korl had recently taken over the old tinker's workshop, although he was still working as a guard until he was ready to open for business. Despite his imposing appearance, the orc preferred fiddling with gadgets to swinging a sword. But above all things, he preferred Lira, which was clear in the way he looked at her and the way his cheeks splotched dark every time she walked into a room.

Sass tried not to envy the couple. After all, Lira was her best friend. But it was hard not to want someone to gaze at her with that doe-eyed infatuation. Especially a certain someone, Sass thought, her eyes flitting to the kitchen door as if willing the blonde guard to walk in behind Korl.

When she didn't, Sass wagged a finger at the orc, making him take a step back although he was twice as tall as her. "Don't even think of coming in and distracting my cook with those smoldering orc looks."

Lira stifled a laugh. "Smoldering orc looks?"

Sass narrowed her gaze first at her friend and then at the guard. "You know what I mean." She took another step toward Korl. "Now go out to the great room, and I'll see if I can commandeer one of her meat pies for you."

"Much appreciated, Sass." Korl winked at Lira over Sass's head but dutifully backed away, leaving the half-doors creaking in his wake.

"You need to set a date for your wedding, you know," Sass said once the orc had left.

Lira held up her flour-dusted palms. "I can't add one more thing to my plate until the Harvest Festival is over."

Sass tapped one toe impatiently. "You're sure you're not putting it off?"

Lira scoffed at this, but dropped her gaze back to the work-table. "Why would I do that? I'm crazy about Korl."

Sass twitched one shoulder. She didn't know the answer either, but she could have sworn that Lira had been avoiding the topic every time she brought it up. "All I know is that it's going to take a bit of time to pull together a fancy wedding, so the sooner we start planning, the better."

Lira's eyes became slits as she placed the final crescent on the tray and sent it across the wooden table to Sass. "Who said anything about a fancy wedding?"

"I have—to everyone."

Lira's eyes went skyward. "As long as I don't have to think about this fancy wedding until after the Harvest Festival."

Sass tried to keep the triumph out of her smile. "I suppose it can wait, although I might have already talked to Tin about color palettes."

"Are you adding wedding planner to your list of talents?"

"How hard could it be? Not harder than whipping this place into shape, that's for sure."

"There's no denying you did a miraculous job fixing up the tavern. It's the beating heart of the village again, and a lot of that is down to your hard work."

Sass cleared her throat, which had become unexpectedly thick. "Go on with you."

Lira looked to the flutterstoat. "It's true, isn't it, Crumpet?"

The flutterstoat bobbed his tiny head up and down and emitted a torrent of animated chittering.

Lira wiped her hands on her dough-smudged apron, looking very pleased with herself. "See? He agrees with me."

Sass snorted and flapped a hand at the pair. She didn't want to admit how much good it did her heart to hear that, but it was hard to ignore the warmth spreading in her chest. "Folks are happy with what we've both done with The Tusk & Tail."

"Which is due, in large part, to your hard work and eye for sprucing up even the dingiest places." Lira swept her arms wide, and bits of flour flew into the air. "It wouldn't matter what I served if folks had to eat it in a grimy, depressing hovel."

Sass thought back to the state of the place when she'd arrived. Then she thought about the state she'd been in when she'd arrived in Wayside—tired, hungry, desperate. Truth be told, she had been in little better shape than the gritty old tavern.

She shrugged off those memories, reluctant to dwell on the truth behind why she'd been so desperate, why she'd ended up in Wayside in the first place. "I suppose you're right, but it was your idea to fix it up."

"A bit of quick thinking so I'd have an excuse to stay and a place to bunk down." Lira walked over and threw an arm around Sass's shoulders, and then walked them both out of the kitchen so they could stand and observe the bustling great room.

A fire roared in the hearth at the far end of the room, casting a glow across the patrons filling the long wooden tables. Tankards thumped, forks clinked, and laughter bounced off the beamed ceiling. The sharp scent of peat smoke was softened by the savory aroma of meat pies and only the faintest hint of ash and spice that floated over from the Hellkin bartender.

Lira gave the dwarf's shoulders a squeeze. "Not bad for a reformed rogue and a failed burglar."

Sass groaned at the reminder of the night they'd met and at her bungled attempt at robbing the tavern's till. "Not everyone can be an expert lock picker."

The former rogue held out one hand and wiggled her fingers, which now kneaded dough instead of picking locks. "Still, my gut told me I could trust you, and my gut is rarely wrong."

Sass's own gut churned as she stood beside Lira and looked at so many of the villagers who'd become her friends. She should tell Lira the truth. She should have told her from the beginning, but with every day that passed it was harder and harder to admit why she was there. The *real* reason. Now, so much time had passed it felt impossible.

Maybe it wouldn't matter, she told herself for the hundredth time. Maybe her past would never catch up with her. Maybe she'd finally found a safe haven in Wayside.

The truth will always come out, Sarsaparilla. She could hear her mum's voice as clear as day in her head. *Just like a glittering jewel hidden beneath layers of stone, the truth will always reveal itself.*

Sass hoped that, for once, her mum's mining wisdom wouldn't prove itself to be true.

Two

"ANY CHANCE of getting some of those meat pies at the bar?"

Sass jumped and pressed a hand to her heart at the low, rumbling voice coming from behind them.

Lira was the first one to spin on her Hellkin friend and swat him with a dishrag. "You've got to stop doing that, Vaskel."

Her former crew mate gave Lira a wolfish grin that Sass knew was more mischievous than truly wicked, despite his red skin and the pointed horns sweeping back from his forehead. "Do what?"

Lira huffed out a breath and granted him a reluctant smile. "Sneak up on people."

Usually, he wouldn't have been able to creep up on them without the faint scent of ash masked by sandalwood giving him away, but the tavern was such a cacophony of smells that it was hard to parse his distinctive aroma from the rest.

His icy blue eyes flashed more kindness than heat as he cast a look back at the polished wood bar. Patrons crowded the length, perching on stools or using the bar to prop themselves up, and Sass noticed more than one female eyeing the bartender who'd stepped away. "Some of my customers could use some food to counteract the ale."

"So you aren't plying your fans with drink?"

The Hellkin cocked the dark slash of a brow with the scar running through it. "Are you implying I need to?"

Lira tapped one foot on the wood plank floor. "You know the rule we agreed to, Vask. No seducing the patrons."

Sass wondered if it was considered seduction if the women were more eager than he was. It was hardly his fault that seduction was as natural to Hellkins as swinging an axe was to dwarves.

"I've seduced no one."

Lira leaned back to sketch a gaze over the buxom milkmaids and starry-eyed shop girls at the bar who were tracking Vaskel's every move, then she eyed her friend. "You know that not everyone is as immune to your charms as Sass and I are."

Vaskel's laugh was a velvet chuckle as he wound one arm around Sass's shoulders and his tail around one of her calves. "Who says Sass isn't secretly in love with me?"

Sass's cheeks warmed, but she elbowed Vaskel playfully. "Go on with you. You know you aren't my type."

Vaskel shrugged and slid his gaze toward the hearth and the blonde guard sitting in one of the overstuffed and oversized armchairs next to it. "Speaking of your type, don't you have a date tonight?"

"It's not a date," Sass said hurriedly. "At least, I don't think it is."

Lira's head snapped to her. "Wait, you and...?"

"Val agreed to stay after closing tonight." Sass didn't meet Lira's eyes as she shifted from one foot to the other. "But it's not what you think. She's going to teach me how to knit."

"Ah, yes, knitting," Vaskel said, disbelief oozing from his words. "Too bad I didn't think of that one before."

"Well, I think it's great that you and Val are hanging out," Lira said brightly, "even if it is as two friends knitting. The best things start with friendship, right?"

Vaskel wrinkled his nose, clearly ready to challenge this idea before Lira shot him a look.

He cleared his throat. "Absolutely. Look at Lira and me. We've been nothing but friends, and there are few people I adore more than her." He lowered his voice. "Not that I would let her bruiser of a fiancé hear me say that."

Both women laughed at the thought of Korl being a bruiser or being threatened by Vaskel. The orc was a gentle giant if ever there was one.

Lira's face softened into a smile. "Is that why you're still hanging around Wayside?"

Vaskel folded his arms across the leather vest he left unbuttoned at the top. "Wayside was supposed to be only one stop in my search to locate everyone in the old crew. I was planning to continue my search for Rog before you two begged me to stay because your barkeep up and left."

"That is true," muttered Sass, "and he's a vast improvement on Durn."

She and Lira had a lot of reasons to be grateful to the tavern's former owner, but no one could argue that the surly man had been a big draw. Not only did Vaskel seem to attract patrons like a fairy moth to nectar, but he took particular pride in keeping the bar spotless. A trait that Durn had never possessed.

Lira's brows pinched. "What I wouldn't give to see Rog again and know he's safe. I'm thrilled that you and Cali stayed in Wayside. It's made it feel more like home than ever, but not knowing about Rog worries me."

"I've put out feelers," Vaskel said. "If he's out there, I'll find him."

"If he wants to be found." Lira held up a finger. "Our gnome friend might not be quite as stealthy as Cali, but he's good at staying hidden."

Vaskel grunted his agreement then glanced at the bustling great room. "Speaking of our Pantheri friend, where is Cali?"

Sass had been so busy getting food out to the patrons, refilling tankards of ale, and worrying about her not-a-date with Val that she hadn't clocked that Lira's other former crew mate wasn't occupying her usual perch at the bar.

"You know Cali," Lira said with an airy wave of one hand. "She probably got wrapped up in the latest pirate romance Iris found for her."

"How is it I haven't scored an invitation to the apothecary's secret book stash?" Vaskel asked.

Sass tilted her head at him. "You read?"

The Hellkin's expression was arch as he peered down his nose at her. "How do you think I learned so much about females if not by reading their deepest, darkest fantasies? The best books are romances."

Lira gave him a playful shove back toward the bar. "Go take care of your customers, and we'll get some pies out to you."

Sass watched Vaskel saunter back to his post, his pointed tail swishing behind him. "He was joking about reading romance, right?"

"Oh, no. Vaskel would never joke about that. He might have read more romance novels than Cali."

Sass opened and closed her mouth. Well, the Hellkin never ceased to surprise.

Lira wiped her hands on her apron as she turned toward the kitchen. "If you want to take off a bit early, that's fine by me."

Sass already regretted mentioning knitting with Val, and she could feel heat climbing up her neck. "There's no need..."

"Go on, Sass," Lira said, her voice quieter. "You've worked hard enough. It's okay to live a little."

Sass didn't have a chance to respond before Lira had ducked through the swinging doors leading into the kitchen, but she couldn't stop the heavy breath that slipped from her lips. Her friend was right. She deserved to enjoy herself, even if she and Val were only friends.

As much as the woman intrigued her, she hadn't been able to let herself imagine anything more. At first, when she didn't know if things in the village would work out, it had seemed too presumptuous. But now that she'd settled into a nice life at The Tusk & Tail, she should be able to imagine more.

If only...

Sass pushed aside the fears that tickled the back of her brain, assuring herself that the growing sense of dread was all in her mind. She had nothing to worry about. She had a cozy place to lay her head, good friends, and honest work to keep her occupied. Not to mention the striking blonde guardswoman who'd caught her attention from the first moment she'd walked through the doors.

If only she could get a read on what Val thought of her. Despite the guard's friendly demeanor, she still didn't know if Val considered her anything but a friend. Did the woman like to play her cards close to the chest, or had Sass been relegated to the friend zone?

She glanced toward the fireplace, where Val was knitting and laughing at something Korl had said from where he sat in the chair across from her. Even the sound of Val's laugh made happiness bubble inside her. Lira was right. She deserved this. All of this.

Then she caught sight of the figure hunched over a small table in the back corner. A hood sagged over his eyes, and his face was bathed in shadow, but Sass would know the silhouette of a dwarf anywhere. She stumbled back, her breath caught in her throat, and all thoughts of a happy future fled her brain.

She didn't know how he'd found her, but she was certain why he had.

Three

SASS BACKED AWAY, her steps wooden. Maybe he hadn't seen her. Maybe he wasn't here for her. It was possible he was simply passing through, wasn't it?

Before she could remind herself of the absurdity of a dwarf traveling from the Ice Lands without a good reason, a voice snapped her from her thoughts.

"Sass here can settle our argument."

She glanced down at the halfling and gnome sitting across from each other at the end of a long table. Tinpin Thistledown, the village haberdasher, and Pip Brambleheart, the baker, had taken to meeting up at the tavern for the occasional dinner and more than occasional pint.

As usual, Pip's wiry gray hair stood on end with flour-frosted tips, and his dough-smudged clothes wore the battle scars of his day in the bakery. By contrast, Tin's impeccably tailored waistcoat and high-buttoned jacket were pristine, and he'd slicked his hair neatly to one side.

Nerves frayed Sass's smile, but she couldn't be rude and ignore her friends. Besides, it would seem suspicious, and the last thing the dwarf wanted to do was appear jittery. "Don't tell me you two are arguing."

"It's not a real argument," Pip assured her with a flickering grin.

"Because it's no contest. No contest at all." Tin straightened, puffing out his small, ascot-embellished chest. "Gnomish recipes are far and away superior. Far and away."

Pip's laugh was tight. "But no one can bake them like halflings. Everyone knows that if you're searching for the best baking in the Known Lands, you go to Elmshire."

The gnome shifted in his seat. "Only because gnomes keep our villages secret. Very secret indeed."

Sass had little interest in who came up with the recipes or even if it was a gnome or a halfling that baked them. In true dwarf fashion, all she cared about was the eating.

"Did the recipe for your lemon sweet rolls come from a gnome?" she asked, her stomach rumbling at the thought of the yeasty rolls slathered in sweet, gooey icing.

Pip's eyes flared with indignation. "Bite your tongue. That recipe was my creation, as is my special creation for the Harvest Festival."

"Then I'd have to side with Pip. If there's anything more delicious than those lemon sweet rolls, I haven't tasted it." Sass also knew that whatever the halfling whipped up for the festival would be equally addictive, and her stomach growled in anticipation.

The halfling crossed his arms over his chest and gave his gnome friend a satisfied smile. "Then it's settled."

Tin braced his hands on the table and leaned forward, his eyes glinting merrily. "Not by a long shot. Not by a very long shot."

The pair were so focused on their good-natured debate that they didn't seem to notice Sass stepping back and drifting toward the bar. She slipped behind it to join Vaskel, who was back to pulling pints and chatting with the patrons.

He cut his gaze to her, clearly surprised to see her behind the bar instead of weaving her way around the tables or talking with Val near the crackling fire. "You get lost?"

Sass snorted out a laugh. "I'm just taking a wee break, is all."

Vaskel plucked a pewter tankard from the shelf tucked beneath the bar. "Since when do you take breaks?"

Sass knew she needed to act like everything was normal, but her heart was racing. She wiped her sweaty palms down the front of her apron and attempted to steady her breath. "Aren't you the one encouraging me to live a little?"

He nodded as he spun the tankard in the palm of his hand. "I am, but not if it's going to make you a wreck."

"I'm not a wreck." Sass flipped her braid off her shoulder and stole a glance at Val, which made her stomach do a flip. "Just a touch nervous."

Val chose that moment to meet her gaze and send her a bright smile, which did nothing to calm Sass's nerves or assuage her guilt at hiding secrets from her friends. Not that the dinner rush was the time to come clean.

She turned to the Hellkin, deciding to lean in on his assumption that she was nervous about Val. "Could you do me a favor?"

Vaskel's usually wicked smile faded, replaced by an earnest expression that did nothing to banish the guilt gnawing at Sass. "Anything. You know that."

She mustered her best smile. "I need a few moments to freshen up. Can you cover the floor for me?" She jerked a thumb toward the table nestled in the corner. "Especially that table. I didn't make my way to that fellow yet."

Vaskel flicked his gaze over her head, his crimson brow bunching. "The round table tucked in the back?"

Sass didn't dare look as she bobbed her head. "Aye, that's the one. I didn't take his order yet."

Vaskel craned his neck before cocking his head to one side. "Who's order, Sass? There's no one at that table."

Sass whirled around, popping up onto her toes to get a clear view of the table. Where there had been a cloaked dwarf, there was now only an empty chair and a single burning candle with wax puddling in the copper holder.

Her breath stuttered in her throat as she swung her head from side to side and scanned the great room. He'd been there; she was sure of it. She hadn't imagined him. She wouldn't have imagined him. Not when she knew what his presence would mean.

Fear trickled down her spine and sent a shiver across her skin. But if he had been there and was there no longer, where had he gone? That was even more worrying.

"You need a break if you're seeing things," Vaskel said with a grin that Sass tried, but failed, to return.

A hundred scenarios ran through her mind as Vaskel patted her shoulder, but none of them ended well for her. And in none of them did she keep her happy new life at The Tusk & Tail.

Four

"ARE you sure I'm doing this right?" Sass eyed the snarl of yellow yarn in her lap and then the neat square Val had knitted.

She was sitting in Val's usual chair by the hearth, where the crackling fire had burned down to a smoldering mound that spit out the infrequent spark. The rest of the patrons were long gone, and Vaskel had mysteriously vanished from behind the bar. Only the occasional sound of clattering dishes emerged from the kitchen, a sign that Lira was still cleaning up.

She and Val hadn't been at it for long, but it was clear that Sass was not a natural. Not that she didn't want to learn to knit, but most of her interest lay in the blonde guardsman and not in scarf-making. Still, Sass was sure she could have made a better showing if she hadn't been so distracted.

"Don't be too hard on yourself," Val said. "It took me a while to learn."

Sass looked up and caught the flash of amusement in Val's eyes. "I doubt that."

Val put one of her large hands over Sass's smaller one and squeezed. "Even the most skilled knitters started with the first loop. You can't become a master of anything without being awful at it first."

Well, that was true. Sass hadn't been skilled at axe-throwing with her first toss. In fact, she'd almost taken off her grandmother's foot.

Sass let her gaze lock onto Val's hand covering hers, and all thoughts of knitting flew out the window. Maybe this hadn't been such a bad plan, after all. Not that she'd intended to be so bad at yarnwork, but she couldn't argue with the results.

The slam of a door made them both jump, and Val jerked her hand off Sass's, moving it instinctively to the hilt of her sword. When no one came in the main door, both women released long breaths and nervous laughs.

"It must have been the kitchen door." Sass shot a frown toward the back, even though Lira could hardly register her annoyance.

Val took in the empty great room. "Are we the only ones left? I must have lost track of time."

Sass opened her mouth to argue that it wasn't so late, but a yawn came out instead. She slapped one hand over her mouth, but it was too late. Val was already grinning.

"That means I've definitely overstayed my welcome."

"Not at all," Sass insisted as Val tucked her knitting needles and yarn in the basket by the side of her chair.

"I think this was a good first lesson, but I really should get some sleep. I'm on duty tomorrow morning."

Sass reluctantly stood and dropped her knot of yarn. She'd hoped that the pretense of a knitting lesson would make it easier to tell Val how she felt about her, and Sass was sure there had been a moment between them, but what if Val thought it was nothing but a lesson? What if the heat in Val's gaze had only been the warmth of friendship?

"Thanks for taking the time to teach me," Sass said, forcing herself to keep her smile neutral.

Val rested a hand on the dwarf's shoulder and gave it a brief squeeze. "I'm always happy to bring another knitter into the fold."

Well, that didn't sound romantic.

Sass mustered a smile. "I don't think we can call me a knitter yet."

Val assessed the tangle of yarn in the basket. "Maybe not." She winked at Sass. "That just means you need more lessons."

Wait, did Val mean lessons or lessons? Sass had never considered herself thick, but she couldn't for the life of her figure out if Val's smiles were merely friendly or if they meant something more.

Val gave her quilted chest armor a tug and tossed her blonde waves off her shoulder. "Tomorrow? Same time, same place?"

Sass let relief wash over her that Val wanted to see more of her. That was a good sign, wasn't it? "Aye. You can find me right here keeping the fire warm and the ale cold."

As soon as the words had left her lips, she stifled a groan. Why had she said that? Of course, she'd be here. She was here every day. She lived here. Why did being around Val make her sound like a simpering idiot?

At least Val hadn't seemed to notice. Or if she had, she didn't look at Sass like the dwarf had sprouted a second head.

"See you tomorrow, then."

Sass walked Val to the door and waved her off into the night. She lingered in the doorway for a moment, breathing in the cool night air and listening to the chirping of the insects and the gurgling of the nearby stream. Once Val had melted into the darkness, she stepped back inside the tavern and closed the heavy door behind her.

For a first date that wasn't actually a date, that could have gone worse. Of course, she still wasn't sure if Val liked her in the way she liked Val. Lira assured her that Val did, but how could Sass trust the same woman who had taken so long to realize that Korl was into her? The orc had literally built Lira a stove, and she still hadn't been sure.

But what if Lira was right? It was easier to see things when they weren't happening to you.

"Am I just as clueless as she was?" Sass whispered to herself. That wasn't a pleasant thought since Sass prided herself on her well-honed dwarf instincts.

With a shake of her head, Sass turned and towed the errant benches and chairs back under the wooden tables, humming her favorite sea shanty to herself. When a flutter of movement in the corner caught her eye, she stiffened, her hands curling around the top of a chair. Her knuckles went white as a figure materialized from the shadows in the corner.

Sass held her breath as the dwarf pushed back his hood to reveal the bushy brows, hooked nose, and black pointed beard she knew so well.

"I've been looking for you for a long time, Sass."

Five

"THRAIN." Sass exhaled the word on a sigh. "How did you find me?"

She'd been wrong about which dwarf had found her, and the relief that it was Thrain almost buckled her legs.

The dwarf took a few steps forward and threw one leg over a bench, sitting down and motioning for her to do the same. "Do you forget how well I know you?"

Sass uncoiled her hands from the top of the chair and pulled it out with a scrape. "I have forgotten nothing."

Thrain stroked the point of his beard and let out a harrumph. "You want to rethink that last answer?"

Sass's gut churned as she glanced over her shoulder toward the kitchen where Lira continued to clang the occasional pot. She didn't worry that Thrain was a threat to her friend. It was more likely that his presence threatened everything she'd built.

When she turned back to the dwarf, she sat up straighter. "I'm not surprised they sent you to find me, but I am surprised you agreed to it. I thought you, of all dwarves, would understand."

His eyes became slits that almost vanished beneath his shaggy brows. "Understand?" His voice cracked. "You let me think you were dead. Me! Your best friend since we were crawling."

Sass opened her mouth again and closed it just as swiftly. Why did it have to be Thrain? Any other dwarf sent by her family, she would have no trouble dispatching or misleading. But she couldn't lie to him.

Which is why he's the one they sent.

Sass steadied her breath and her nerve. "I didn't intend for anyone to think I was dead."

"You didn't think we would assume the worst when you vanished? You didn't count on us believing the mountains had taken you when the only thing you left behind were tracks in the snow that ended at the edge of a cliff?"

Sass worked the tail of her braid as she thought back to her escape from the Ice Lands and the brutal trek across endless snow. If she were being honest, she'd hoped they would consider her lost to the swirling storms, but she'd never staged a fall off a precipice. "If there were tracks ending at a cliff, they weren't mine. I took the southern route and wound through the base of the mountains."

Thrain made another sound of disbelief, but Sass slid a hand across the table that separated them. "I never meant to scare anyone, least of all you. I thought if anyone would understand what I did, it would be my best friend."

The dwarf shifted on the bench and cleared his throat gruffly. "I knew you weren't happy with the arrangement, but I didn't know you were desperate enough to run away."

Sass kept her gaze on the frayed end of her braid as she ran her thumb over it again and again. "You know my family would have never listened to reason. Our clan was obsessed with making an alliance with King Trollbane."

Thrain grunted, which was as much agreement as Sass knew she would get.

"It was all moving too fast, and no one cared what I wanted," Sass continued, the sensation of being trapped resurfacing as she thought about why she'd left home. She tugged absently at the neckline of her blouse with her free hand as she wrestled that feeling back down.

"So you thought running away from everyone you loved and who loved you was the best plan?"

"I'm sorry if I hurt anyone, especially you." She tossed her braid over her shoulder and folded her arms across her chest. "But you know better than anyone alive that I couldn't marry Florin."

Thrain shrugged off his cloak, exposing the silvery fur lining that must have kept him from freezing on the journey from the Ice Lands. "You're the daughter of a dwarf ruler. You always knew your duty, and the future planned for you. You'd been promised to Florin since you were no taller than an axe blade."

Sass glared at him. "I decided to make my own choice."

Thrain scraped a hand through the dark hair that hung in long tangles over his shoulders and swiveled his head to take in the tavern. "And this is your choice? Working as a tavern wench in the South?"

"I'm no tavern wench, Thrain. I'll have you know I own half of this successful establishment." She smiled at the smoldering hearth and the polished tables, warmth bubbling up in her chest like a pot of simmering chai. "It might not be a dwarven mine or a mountain palace, but it's my home now."

Thrain wrinkled his prominent nose. "How could this ever be home for a dwarf princess?"

Sass bristled at the mention of her former title. "I'm not a princess anymore. Not if it means I have to marry who my family says and live a life of someone else's choosing." She pressed her lips together and glared at her former friend. "So you can go back to the mountains and tell everyone that you failed at your task, because I'm not coming back with you."

A weary sigh escaped Thrain's lips. "Your family didn't send me, Sass."

That made her sit up. She didn't know if she was relieved her clan hadn't sent out a search party or outraged. "They didn't?"

Thrain shook his head. "I came looking for you on my own. Partly to find out if you were truly alive and throttle you if you were."

Sass couldn't help but laugh. "Now that sounds like the Thrain I know."

A shadow of a smile twitched at one corner of his beard. "I'm glad to find you alive, Sass, but I haven't forgiven you for leaving me like you did."

Her heart squeezed with regret and affection. She stood, crossed to his side of the table, and put her hands on his shoulders. "My only regret in leaving was that I didn't take you with me."

Thrain's dark eyes shone. "You aren't just saying that because you know I can best you in a fight?"

Sass dredged up a grin, a weight lifting off her chest. "No. I wished you were with me a thousand times during my journey, and I wondered what you were doing under the mountains."

"I wasn't under the mountains." He made a face. "I was tracking you all over this flat, sweaty land. For a dwarf who'd never left the Ice Lands, you didn't make yourself easy to find."

"If you were the only one searching for me, maybe I shouldn't have bothered covering my tracks."

Thrain's broad shoulders sagged. "That's one of the other reasons I came. I'm not the only dwarf looking for you."

Sass tilted her head in confusion. "I thought you said my family didn't send a search party."

"They didn't." The dwarf drew in a long breath and held Sass's eyes. "But the fiancée you left behind did."

A shiver ran through her. Florin Trollbane, future ruler of the Black Ridge, wasn't someone to be trifled with, and Sass had a sinking feeling that her former intended would not be nearly as forgiving as Thrain.

Six

SASS STOOD QUICKLY AND PACED. "Why would Florin come after me? Why would anyone want to chase down the dwarf who ran out on them? She still can't want to marry me."

But Sass knew very well why someone like Florin would want to find her—punishment, revenge, retribution for the humiliation Sass had inflicted when she snuck away in the dead of night.

Thrain crossed one leg over the other at the knee as he watched her stride back and forth. "She claims you took something when you ran off."

Sass stopped pacing and spun to face her friend, her blood running cold. "This is about the amulet?"

"If that's the engagement present Florin gave you and you kept, then yes."

Sass fought the urge to glance up toward her room above the tavern. As much as she trusted Thrain, she didn't want him to know that she'd stored the valuable jewel under her saggy mattress all this time.

Sass thought back to the opulent engagement party her parents had thrown for her and Florin. The palace beneath the mountains had been aglow with hanging lanterns, and music had echoed off the glittering black stone that surrounded them. Tables had groaned under the weight of the feast, with spiced mead as sweet and free-flowing as a summer stream.

The Thornshields and Trollbanes had toasted and cheered their upcoming alliance, the royals thumping their axes and pounding their fists. Sass hadn't spent more than a handful of moments with Florin. Only time enough for gifts to be exchanged —an exquisite silver amulet for her and a jewel-encrusted ring for Florin—and a brief kiss shared as the crowd cheered.

But the kiss had been enough to tell Sass that she couldn't go through with it. If you could call the perfunctory brush of cool lips across hers a kiss. Sass grimaced even now as she thought of the hard, calculating look in Florin's eyes and the smug, possessive smile. Even with her fiancée's amulet encircling her neck, the silver prickling as if it was marking her as Florin's property, Sass had decided then and there to run.

"If that's all Florin wants, I'll give it back."

Like all dwarves, even one who'd run far from her ancestral land, she appreciated finely crafted jewelry. There was no question that the glittering amulet boasted exceptional design and intricate metalworking. One reason Sass hadn't left it behind was its value. Who knew when she might need something worth trading on her journey?

But it had been exactly that same value that had kept her from pawning it, even when she'd been desperate. It had felt wrong to sell something that she knew had been artfully crafted by skilled dwarf metalworkers. No one in the Ageless Lands would have given her what it was truly worth. Now she was glad she hadn't exchanged it to the bandy-legged sailor in Eldu who'd offered her passage to Port Frey or the trader near Greyhelm Castle who'd assured her that the eggs he wanted to trade would hatch dragons.

Sass put her hands on her hips and faced Thrain. "I'll give you the amulet, and you can return it for me without ever revealing where you found me. Everyone wins."

"Were it only that easy, Sass."

"What?" Sass threw her arms wide and let her voice rise. "Why can't it be that easy? Florin wants the amulet. I can relinquish the amulet and stay here. Everyone gets what they want."

She suspected her family would not be getting what they wanted, which was a valuable alliance with the Trollbane clan, but she couldn't dwell on that. It wasn't like anyone had considered her happiness when they'd made the deal to marry her off to someone as cold as Florin.

"Do you remember when Florin visited our mountain when we were children? She lost a game of dwarf runes and tossed all our rune tiles into the deepest trench in the Ice Lands."

Sass's heart plummeted. She remembered losing her beloved runes all too well. It was one of the reasons she'd never played any game with Florin again. The dwarf princess was not a gracious loser.

"It's not only the amulet that Florin wants back, Sass." For the first time since he'd arrived, Thrain's expression teetered toward sympathetic. "The Trollbanes insist that you honor the marriage pact."

Sass spluttered her protests. "Why? Who would want to marry someone who crossed the Ice Lands to get away from them?"

But she knew the answer to that. The Trollbanes were known

far and wide for their tenacity, their ability to pursue a vein of precious metal embedded in unforgiving rock for as long and far as needed. She shouldn't be surprised that they would refuse to release her or her family from the engagement. It wasn't about what she wanted. It was about what had been promised.

Never cross a Trollbane.

She'd grown up hearing that repeated like a mantra. And what had she done the first chance she'd gotten? She'd crossed a Trollbane.

Thrain scraped his fingers through his beard. "It also may have something to do with her mother's failing health. Florin needs an alliance to shore up her power, especially since certain Trollbanes favor her sister."

"And what if I refuse?" Sass could hear the shake in her voice, and she despised it.

Thrain slammed a hand on the table as he stood, his cheeks reddening. "It's not that simple, Sass!" His bellow rattled her bones and made her rear back. "The Trollbanes claim that they will take retribution on our clan if you don't return with the amulet and marry Florin."

Retribution from the Trollbanes could never be good. Could Sass live with herself if she caused such strife for her family?

"I didn't know," she said, more to herself than to Thrain.

The tension drained from his body as he released a heavy breath. "I know you didn't."

She swept her eyes around the tavern again, as if to imprint the overstuffed chairs, the stone hearth, and the wood-beamed ceiling in her mind. As much as The Tusk & Tail had become her home, she couldn't abandon her clan to the Trollbanes' wrath.

Her breath hitched in her throat as she felt the dream she'd been living in Wayside slip through her fingers like the finest gold dust. "If that's the only way to save—"

Before she could finish, the kitchen doors swung open and Lira ran out with a copper pot in one hand and a rogue's blade in the other, Crumpet riding on her shoulder with his wings flared wide and the hair on his back abristle. The high-pitched scream from Lira and the screech from Crumpet were enough to make Thrain stagger back, upend the bench, trip over it, and land sprawled on his back—half on the bench and half on the stone floor.

Lira came to a stop next to Sass, and they both stood over the moaning, fallen dwarf.

"You okay?" she asked Sass, the pot still held overhead and clearly ready to be used as a weapon. "I heard shouts."

"Never better." Sass fought the urge to laugh as she leaned over Thrain. "You okay down there, Thrain?"

Lira dropped her arms, and Crumpet's fierce chittering faded. "You know him?"

"Aye, he's an old friend from home."

Lira quickly put the pot and blade on the nearest table and rushed to the prone dwarf. "I am so sorry. I had no idea."

Thrain pushed himself to his elbows as he stared at Lira, whose hair was wild around her face, and the winged stoat on her shoulder, who held up tiny paws as if he was preparing to box. Then he slid his gaze to Sass. "Grognick's beard. What kind of tavern is this?"

Seven

"AGAIN," Lira said as she handed Thrain a steaming mug of chai, "I'm so sorry about the screaming demon impersonation. I thought you were an intruder."

"No damage done." Thrain brushed off his brown pants and the wool vest that topped it with one hand before he took the earthenware mug, his gaze fixed firmly on the flutterstoat riding Lira's shoulder. "What do you call that thing again?"

Crumpet let loose a torrent of chattery protests.

"Crumpet is a flutterstoat."

Thrain's expression told Sass that the explanation hadn't cleared things up. "And they're common around these parts?"

Lira turned her head to grin at Crumpet. "Oh, no. As far as I know, Crumpet is the only one of his kind. My gran enchanted him and gave him wings. Accidentally, we think."

Thrain's eyes flared for a beat, but he didn't ask Lira to elaborate further on how any of that happened when magic was frowned upon in the Known Lands. Instead, he took a sip of his chai, his dark eyes shifting from Lira to Crumpet and finally to Sass. "You've taken up with an elf *and* an enchanted beast?"

"Half elf," Lira corrected, clearly ignoring the suspicion dripping from Thrain's words.

"She's half human," Sass said, feeling odd that she had to say that or that it mattered. "But most importantly, she's my friend."

Sass thought back to the days when she'd been wary of elves simply because they were elves. She couldn't fault Thrain for his misguided opinion, since she'd also grown up hearing that all elves were arrogant and disloyal.

Thrain nodded, sizing up Lira. "I suppose you don't look too elvish." He cleared his throat. "And any friend of Sass's is a friend of mine." He bit his lower lip and cut a questioning look to Sass. "That is, if Sass still considers me a friend."

Lira cocked her head at Sass, handing the female dwarf her own mug of chai. "Is he a friend?"

Sass avoided meeting Lira's eyes, although she knew she couldn't hide her past for one second longer. She took a wee sip of the drink and allowed the warming spices to soothe her nerves. "I wasn't lying about Thrain being a friend. We were as thick as thieves for most of my childhood, and as surprised as I am that he found me, I'm happy to see him."

Thrain muttered something about Sass having a funny way of showing it, but she ignored him as she faced Lira and tilted her head to lock eyes on the woman. "It's everything else I lied about."

Lira tucked a strand of hair behind a pointed ear, her face still flushed from an evening spent over a hot stove. "What do you mean?"

Goblin's spawn, this wasn't easy, Sass thought as she took a significant gulp of chai. It was as if she teetered on a precipice. One word would tip her over and drag her from the cozy life she'd created and the family she'd found. Then again, if everything could disintegrate so easily, was it ever real?

Sass stared into her mug. "You know I told you I left home and traveled here on my own?"

Lira bobbed her head cautiously.

"Well, all that was true." The words spilled from Sass as if saying them faster might lessen their impact. "What I didn't tell you was why I left or what it might mean if the wrong dwarf found me. I lied when I said there was no one looking for me."

Lira stiffened as her brow bunched with wrinkles. Crumpet unfurled his wings and flew back toward the kitchen, as if uninterested in all the talking and perhaps sensing the conflict brewing. Part of Sass wished she could follow him. Instead, she drained the last of her chai and set the mug on the table with a thunk.

"I didn't tell you that my family rules one mountain in the Ice Lands or that I left because I didn't want to go through with an arranged marriage. I didn't tell you there might be search parties looking for me or that I ran off with an engagement present that my former fiancée apparently wants back."

Lira's mouth fell open. "Why...why didn't you tell me? I told you about my past and my secrets," she bobbled her head from side to side, "eventually."

"And I was planning on telling you—eventually." Sass wrung her plump hands. "But with every day that passed, it got harder. Then things were so good here that I feared ruining it, and I convinced myself that I was safe and that my past wouldn't catch up to me."

"But it did," Lira said quietly with a furtive look to Thrain.

Sass's heart twisted when she heard the hurt in her friend's voice. Why hadn't she trusted Lira with the truth when she had the chance?

"I'm so sorry I didn't tell you. I should have. Every day I thought about it, and every day I made up an excuse not to do it." Sass waved a hand at the great room. "I've never had something like this — some place where I truly belong. I was afraid to do anything to break the spell, because to me The Tusk & Tail is magical."

Lira stared hard at Sass before quickly closing the distance between them and grabbing both of the dwarf's hands. "Why did you think I would care about your past? We all have secrets. Orc's blood, you know the secrets I kept from everyone when I first came back to Wayside. I'd be a pretty big hypocrite if I got mad at you for not spilling all of yours to me."

Sass's throat thickened. "You're not mad I didn't tell you?"

Lira hitched one shoulder. "I'm shocked, but I understand not wanting to spoil a good thing. I know the feeling of wanting to protect a happiness that feels so fragile it might shatter in your hands." She threaded her fingers through Sass's. "As long as you don't expect me to call you Princess Sass."

Sass laughed. "Please don't."

Lira released her hands and curled an arm around her friend's shoulders. "We've dealt with unpleasant blasts from the past before. We can handle this one." She glanced at Thrain, who was eyeing the pair over the top of his mug. "No offense intended."

"None taken," Thrain grumbled. "By the way, what do you call this funny tea?"

"Chai," Sass said quickly, "and it's one of our best sellers."

Thrain took another tentative sip and tipped his head back and forth as Sass twisted to face Lira. "The unpleasant blast from the past won't be Thrain. It will be Florin Trollbane."

Lira repeated the name with raised brows. "Your former fiancée?"

"Along with what will most certainly be an armed search party," Thrain added after swallowing a gulp of chai.

"This fiancée sounds like a peach," Lira said under her breath.

"A peach who blinded her own sister in one eye because she thought the dwarf was prettier than her." Thrain pointed to his left eye. "She's not one to be crossed lightly."

Lira's face paled. "And this is all about an engagement present you ran off with? Can't you just return it?"

Thrain sighed. "Like I told Sass, it's not that simple. Florin wants the amulet Sass took and is insisting she come home and go through with the wedding."

Lira held Sass at arm's length. "You aren't going to do it, are you? If you ran away to escape the wedding, why would you go back?"

Sass blinked rapidly at the thought of leaving everything she'd built with Lira. "I don't want to go, but Florin is threatening retribution on my family if I don't."

Lira looked at Thrain, as if for confirmation.

He nodded grimly. "That's why I tracked down Sass on my own. I had to tell her that Florin's search party is closing in on her."

Both Lira and Sass cut their eyes to the door, as if a horde of angry dwarves would burst through at any moment, boots stomping and axes swinging.

"This is ridiculous. No one can force you to marry them." Lira then dropped her voice and gave Sass a questioning look. "Can they? Is this a dwarf thing I've never heard about?"

"There was a marriage pact, which would create an alliance between the clans," Thrain said, "but the Thornshields wouldn't force the issue if Florin wasn't threatening retribution."

Sass's shoulders slumped. "I can't let that happen. As much as I hate the idea of marrying Florin, I can't subject my family and friends to the Trollbanes."

Lira whirled around and started pacing her own small circle

across the tavern floor. "I think better when I'm baking, but I'm not firing up the oven again tonight." After a few more turns, she stopped and clapped her hands. "I've got it. Instead of option one —you go back home and marry someone against your will—or option two, you stay here and cause trouble for your family, we pick secret option three."

She was smiling so brightly that Sass hated to ask. "What's secret option three?"

"We negotiate, of course." Lira bounced on her toes as she rubbed her hands together. "When this armed search party arrives, we use our best powers of persuasion to convince this Florin to accept something other than you."

Thrain shot Sass a look that said he wasn't impressed by secret option three. "Powers of persuasion?"

Sass remembered what she'd helped Lira recover — the leather-bound, moonstone-embellished recipe book that was also a spell book. "By persuasion, do you mean magic?"

"Magic?" Thrain swung his head from woman to woman. "Like the kind that gave that little weasel wings? Since when is that allowed?"

"Flutterstoat," Lira corrected before she gave them both a mischievous grin. "Technically, it's not allowed, but those rules were created to stop the spread of dark magic, not cozy magic like enchanted beasts and protective charms, right? And maybe I don't mean magic at all. Maybe I mean the healing powers of hot chai."

Thrain peered at his mug and muttered to Sass in a low voice. "I hope she means magic."

Eight

"I DIDN'T TAKE offense at your friend's comment about my chai," Lira said the next morning when she bustled into the tavern with the thick, leather-bound spell book tucked under her arm and a paper bag in one hand.

Sass paused in her task of straightening the chairs she'd left akimbo the night before and grinned, grateful that her friend wasn't holding a grudge about the secrets Sass had kept from her. She was less concerned that Thrain was slow to warm to Lira's chai.

"You can't take anything Thrain thinks about food to heart. He was always a picky eater, even about dwarven fare."

Lira glanced at the fire that was already crackling and the cushions in the armchairs that were freshly fluffed. "Someone's been up early."

"I couldn't sleep well," Sass admitted. "Cleaning has always calmed my mind, so I thought I might as well give the place a good spit-and-polish."

It had been a bit more than that, but Lira didn't need to know that she'd swept all the floors to within an inch of their life, rewashed all the tankards behind the bar, and polished the tables until there wasn't a hint of the frothy ale and meat pie filling that had been dribbled on them the night before.

"Then you deserve one of these." Lira unrolled the top of the paper sack, and an intoxicating aroma of yeast, citrus, and sugar wafted from it.

Sass's stomach had been silent all morning, but now it let out an ornery grumble as she reached into the bag for one of the sticky treats. "Pip's lemon sweet rolls make all the work worth it."

"The best baked goods do." Lira plucked out a gooey roll and put it to her nose, inhaling deeply and moaning before continuing to walk toward the kitchen. "That's why I'm trying a new recipe today."

Sass hadn't even taken a bite of her roll, but she hurried after her friend. "You're trying something new? Aside from the apple crumble recipe for the Harvest Festival?"

Lira backed through the swinging kitchen doors since she didn't have any free hands, and Sass slipped in behind her. The half-elf dropped the paper bag of sweet rolls on the wooden table that took up the center of the room before gingerly lowering the heavy book to the surface. Then she held up a finger and took a bite of her iced roll.

Sass followed her lead, letting her teeth sink into the pillowy dough and closing her eyes as the lemony sweetness exploded on her tongue. She nearly swooned as she chewed and swallowed, taking another bite and then another before she was licking the last drizzle of heavenly icing from her fingers. When she opened her eyes, Lira had polished off her roll and was wiping her hands on a dishcloth.

"Now that we've gotten the most important thing out of the way," Lira grabbed her apron from a wall hook and tied it around her waist, "I suppose I should put the chai on to heat."

Crumpet was slowly uncoiling himself from the nest of blankets Lira had made for him on the corner of the counter, stretching his tiny arms and legs and shaking out his wings as a sleepy yawn twitched his whiskers. He glided to the table where Lira handed him a bit of sweet roll, and he cooed his appreciation as he nibbled it delicately.

"Morning, Crumpet." Sass hopped onto a stool and let her feet dangle, as Lira plunked a copper pot onto the stove. Her gaze lingered on the leather book with the glittering moonstone embedded in the cover. "What about the new recipe?"

Lira snapped her fingers. "Right. Sorry, I let Pip's sweet rolls distract me."

"Easily done." Sass was grateful that the sweet breakfast had taken her mind off her bigger worries, and she had no desire to return to them.

Once Lira had poured milk into the pot and added the chai spices, she ran her hand over the worn leather of her gran's recipe book. The recipe book was also a spell book since her gran had once been a mage.

"After I left you last night, I went home and started thinking about ways we could keep your ex-fiancée from finding you or making you return to the Ice Lands." Lira flipped open the book. "There are spells in here for obfuscation, but they aren't permanent, and I'm not sure how long you'd want to walk around unseen."

Sass wrinkled her nose at this. Sure, she'd run from Florin once, but did she want to hide forever?

Lira looked up at her and nodded. "Exactly. That's what I thought. I also found a spell that can bewitch someone into forgetting you, but it would have to be cast on a lot of dwarves if an entire search party is descending, so I'm not sure that will work either."

"One question." Sass cocked her head at Lira. "I know you have your gran's book, but she was a mage and you're not. Do you have any idea how to cast any of these spells?"

Lira took a moment to pull her long hair into a high bun, and she jabbed a wooden skewer through it to hold it in place. "Not exactly, which is why I stopped looking up spells and started reading recipes. That's how I found my gran's crumpet recipe."

Sass cut her gaze to the white, winged stoat, who was fastidiously licking his paws clean. "Crumpets are food?"

Lira laughed. "Of course they are. Where do you think I got Crumpet's name?"

"Crumpets aren't part of dwarf cuisine. I assumed it was just a cute name you made up."

Crumpet flew to Lira's shoulder and let out what the dwarf would have sworn was his version of a laugh.

"I know." Lira shared a look with the tiny creature. "I can't believe it either."

Sass held up her palms. "Laugh all you want, but are you going to tell me more about these crumpets or not?"

Lira turned a few pages of the book until she grinned. "Here it is, Gran's crumpet recipe." She let out a wistful sigh. "I don't know how to describe them. They're more savory than sweet, but once you slather a hot one with butter and jam, they're nothing short of addictive."

Even though Sass had just eaten a sweet roll, her stomach rumbled at the thought of anything slathered with sweet butter and sticky jam.

"The nice thing about crumpets," Lira continued, "is that they can keep, unlike Pip's spectacular rolls, which are best eaten when they're hot and soft."

"Not that we've ever had a problem finishing anything Pip bakes."

Lira tapped a finger on her chin. "That is true, but just imagine being able to keep a tin of crumpets in the kitchen on the off chance you forget to eat one night."

Sass snorted a laugh at this. It seemed like they were so busy that she forgot to eat most nights. "Sold. Let's make crumpets."

Lira reached for an earthenware mixing bowl and made quick work of scooping flour and several other dry ingredients into it. Just as she added the water and mixed it all with a wooden spoon, there was a yelp from outside the doors.

Sass stiffened. Had Florin found her already?

Lira snatched up one of her old rogue's daggers that had been given a second life as kitchen knives and hurried to the swinging doors, mouthing for Sass to stay behind her. Sass didn't argue, as the yelp had devolved into the shuffling and scuffling of boots.

When Lira pushed open the doors and rushed out, she almost instantly lowered her blade. "Hells and cinders! What are you doing?"

Nine

SASS DUCKED AROUND LIRA, gaping as she saw who was making all the racket. It wasn't Florin or the dwarf search party. But it was a dwarf. Well, a dwarf and a Hellkin.

"Vaskel, let him go!" Lira's hands were squarely on her hips as she eyed her former crew mate grappling with Thrain.

Vaskel jerked up, which gave Thrain a chance to slip from the Hellkin's headlock. "But he was sneaking around the tavern, and I'm pretty sure I saw him skulking around last night."

"I wasn't skulking." Thrain's face was red as he brushed his hair off his face and tugged his tunic back into place. "I came down to see if there was breakfast to be had." He sniffed the air, which carried a hint of the spices bubbling on the stove. "It smells good."

"That's the chai," Lira said, quirking her lips when the dwarf's grin faded.

"What do you mean you came down?" Vaskel flicked his gaze to the stairs that led to the rooms over the tavern, which had only ever been occupied by the former tavernkeep, Durn, and then Lira and Sass. Then he seemed to notice that the dwarf wore nothing but a long tunic over linen breeches. "What's going on? Are we letting out rooms now?"

Sass cleared her throat. "Not exactly. Thrain is a friend of mine from home."

Vaskel's fiery expression inched toward embarrassment, and his pointed tail ceased slashing behind him. "Well, why didn't you say you were a friend of Sass?"

Thrain rubbed the back of his neck as he peered at the tall, crimson-skinned creature. "You didn't give me much time for introductions."

Vaskel pivoted to Sass and pinned her with a stern look. "Why didn't you tell me you had a visitor? Is this why you were so jumpy last night?"

Sass swallowed hard as she felt Lira's eyes on her. She owed Vaskel the same honesty she'd finally given Lira. "Yes and no. I didn't know it was Thrain who'd tracked me down."

Lira gestured to the kitchen with the point of her knife. "Why don't I work on breakfast while you bring Vaskel up to speed?"

Sass nodded, her nerves jangling even though she shouldn't be nervous. She'd already told Lira, who was the one she'd kept secrets from the longest. Telling the Hellkin, who no doubt had a bevy of his own closely held secrets, should be easy. Then why did her heart race as she led Vaskel and Thrain into the great room?

Instead of taking up his usual post behind the bar, Vaskel took a seat at the end of one of the long tables. Sass sat across from him, and Thrain hesitated for a moment before choosing the spot next to her.

"So this fellow is your friend, but you were afraid he was someone else?" Vaskel jerked his head toward Thrain. "Someone you wouldn't be sitting calmly next to right about now?"

Sass rubbed her hands down the front of her apron. "Aye, that's the gist of it. I told Lira I left the Ice Lands because I didn't want to be a miner, which was true, but the whole truth is that I ran away from an arranged marriage."

This made Vaskel's dark brows lift. "You're a runaway bride?"

"She's a bride who ran away from a royal wedding," Thrain added, which gained him a dirty look from Sass.

"A royal wedding?" Vaskel swept a hand through his black hair, his fingers bumping along the ridges of his scarlet horns. "Are you telling me you're a princess, Sass?"

"That she is," Thrain answered before Sass could.

"Thank you, Thrain," she said through gritted teeth, pinning him with a scorching look. "Why don't you let me tell it?"

Thrain lifted his hands as if in supplication. "Fine by me, lass, although it seems you've had plenty of time to tell folks before now."

Sass dearly wished she had Lira's newfound elf power to blast energy from her hands, but her angry glare seemed to do the trick, and Thrain crossed his arms and pressed his lips together.

"It's true, I've kept my past a secret," Sass told Vaskel when she turned her attention back to him, "but it was only because I left all that behind me. I came to Wayside for a fresh start. Not for folks to treat me differently because my family rules beneath the mountains."

Vaskel nodded slowly. "We all have a past and things in it we'd like to forget. You don't need to explain your reasons to me."

Sass wondered exactly what secrets the Hellkin was keeping to himself, but she suspected they were much more scandalous than hers.

"You should know that my past is no longer in my past," Sass continued. "Thrain came here to warn me that my former fiancée has been searching for me with an armed party."

"A former fiancée who stabbed another dwarf for calling her princess," Thrain added, holding up a finger. "When she was four years old."

Vaskel face went slack and he slid a worried glance to Sass. "It isn't dwarf custom to put a runaway bride to death, is it?"

"Grognick's beard!" Thrain said, rearing back. "Dwarves might be formidable warriors, but we aren't brutes."

Vaskel didn't look convinced. The story about Florin probably hadn't helped.

"Florin isn't coming to kill me. I took something when I left." Sass shook her head, regretting her impulsive decision not for the first time. "It was an engagement present—an amulet crafted by Florin's clan."

Vaskel twirled the tip of his short beard with two fingers. "That's a long way to travel for a piece of jewelry."

"It's not just for the jewelry," Lira said as she emerged from the kitchen with a tray in her hand. "Her jilted ex wants Sass back."

Vaskel leaned back as Lira slid the tray onto the table in front of them. Rounds of pale, pockmarked bread filled a plate, and a generous scoop of butter clung to the lip. A pewter pot of jam sat off to the side with a spoon balanced across the lip.

"Your dwarven flatbread has a few holes in it," Thrain told Lira as he eyed the offering.

Sass elbowed him, but Lira was already laughing.

"This isn't dwarven flatbread. These are crumpets, and they're supposed to have holes."

Sass breathed in the rich scent of the steam rising from the plate.

"Go on," Lira said. "But make sure you put butter and jam on them."

Vaskel didn't hesitate to pick up one round, slathering first butter then jam before he bit into it.

Thrain picked up a crumpet but took his time sniffing and eyeing it. "I thought that flying weasel was called Crumpet."

"Flutterstoat." Lira flashed Thrain a tolerant smile. "And he's named after crumpets because he's so good at baking."

This made the dwarf's bushy brows pop high. "I've always heard that the Ageless Lands were peculiar..."

Sass scowled at him. "Just eat, you grump."

Thrain frowned, but then shoved the entire crumpet in his mouth.

"I didn't think I could like anything more than your scones," Vaskel mumbled around the mouthful of crumpet, "but I could eat a hundred of these."

Sass took her time smoothing butter over the pockmarked surface of her crumpet, letting the butter melt into the holes before coating it with sticky jam. Lira watched as she took her first bite, grinning when Sass moaned and let her eyelids flutter shut.

They didn't have the sweet punch of Pip's lemon rolls, but there was something seductive about their savory flavor. Like Vaskel had said, they made you want to eat a hundred of them.

"How long have you known about the dwarf search party coming for Sass?" Vaskel asked Lira as he wiped the crumpet crumbs from his mouth and flicked them from his beard.

"Since last night."

Vaskel folded his arms over his chest. "Then if I know you at all, you've been doing more than working on new recipes."

Lira's grin quirked into a mischievous smirk. "You know me too well, Vask."

The door of the tavern swung open, and Thrain leapt to his feet, fumbling for a weapon when he spotted the figure silhouetted in the doorway. "Hells and cinders!"

Ten

KORL PAUSED in the tavern's entrance, his eyes wide at the dwarf struggling to brandish his axe.

"Relax." Sass rested a hand on Thrain's arm. "That's just Lira's fiancé, Korl."

Thrain lowered himself onto the bench. "Lots of curious folks seem to walk in here."

"Well, it is a tavern." Sass brushed crumpet crumbs from her lace-up bodice and then glanced at Lira. "Do I need to tell my whole story to Korl now?"

Lira shook her head. "I saved you the trouble, but in my defense, I had to tell him. It seemed too suspicious that I had been searching for all kinds of spells and charms last night."

"I won't lie." Korl's deep voice was a rumble as he walked up to Lira and coiled an arm around her waist. "It was more than unsettling to see her looking up half a dozen ways to make someone vanish."

Vaskel's grin matched the wicked glint in his eyes. "Now we're talking. Did you find anything good?"

"I don't know," Lira said with a sigh. "I'm not a mage, so I don't know how any of my gran's spells work. And knowing that not all of them turned out the way she intended, I'm afraid to try one and turn Sass into a newt."

Sass almost choked on a mouthful of crumpet. She thought of the bookwyrms that lived in the apothecary's back room, tiny creatures that looked like baby dragons morphed with hummingbirds. Those had resulted from a spell gone wrong by Lira's gran.

"I'll bet going back home isn't sounding so bad about now," Thrain whispered to her.

"Maybe we should loop in Iris," Vaskel suggested. "She was your gran's best friend, and they ran together for years. She must have more insight into some of the spells."

"Before we think about all the ways to fight Florin with magic, we should talk about the easiest solution." Sass looked from Lira to Korl to Vaskel, finally letting her gaze come to rest on Thrain. "I need to consider moving on."

As Lira opened her mouth to protest, Sass held up her hands to stop her. "It's the obvious answer. I escaped in the first place by running. Maybe I should run again."

Thrain grunted. "You want to spend the rest of your days on the run? You know Florin won't give up. Especially if you take the amulet with you."

"What if I don't? What if I leave that here or give it to you? I know Florin is threatening retribution unless I return, but who's to say searching for me won't get old? If the Trollbanes have their amulet, there's a chance they'll give up their claim, especially if it means they won't have to tramp through the marshes near Port Frey or cross the Riddle Vales."

Thrain stroked his beard. "Perhaps."

Lira shook her head, and a few strands of hair slipped from her makeshift bun. "I still don't like this plan. Not if it means you have to leave."

Sass let loose a breath. She despised the thought of leaving too, but she couldn't put her friends at risk.

"That must be some amulet," Korl said in a low voice.

Lira tipped her head back to meet his eyes. "What?"

"If dwarves would give up the chance of battle, that must be an impressive jewel."

Lira returned her gaze to Sass. "Korl makes a good point. I want to see an amulet that's worth crossing the Known Lands to retrieve." She patted Sass's shoulder. "I'm dying to know what's so special about this amulet, especially if the dwarf clan is known for their metalwork."

Sass shrugged. It was a fair request, although she hadn't laid eyes on the thing since she'd jammed it under the swayback mattress. She'd almost forgotten about it entirely, which she knew was her way of trying to forget about what she'd left and the possibility that one day it would catch up with her.

"I have nothing to hide," she said as she stood, "anymore, that is."

Sass left her friends and hurried up to the room that she and Lira had shared until the half-elf had moved in with Korl. Despite her friend's absence, Sass hadn't changed the room. It still had two beds and a nightstand between them, with Lira's old bed neatly covered with the vibrantly floral bedspread that matched her own.

As happy as she was for Lira and Korl, there were nights that she missed whispering in the dark with her friend or climbing out the window to sit on the roof and talk over the day's events. Before meeting Lira, Sass had never sat on a rooftop in her entire life. Now, even with Lira living in the village, Sass would sometimes climb out onto the thatched roof to think.

Today, she didn't glance at the window as she plunged her arm under the mattress. Her fingers closed over the velvet bag, and she experienced both a small thrill and a pang of sadness that the amulet was still there. There was no pretending that none of this was happening when she held the evidence of her past misdeeds in her hand.

Sass closed her bedroom door behind her and walked briskly down the stairs again, avoiding the one creaky step out of habit. She crossed the great room to her friends and pushed the tray of crumpets to one side.

"I haven't laid eyes on this since I arrived," she explained as she opened the dove gray, drawstring pouch, shook the amulet into her hand, and then laid it on the table. The silver of the chain glittered, but it was the massive blue-green stone surrounded by metallic swirls and points that made everyone suck in their breath.

"What kind of stone is that?" Lira whispered as she leaned closer.

"The kind you cross a continent to find," Vaskel growled, his voice carrying a warning that was impossible to miss.

Sass hadn't worn the amulet since she'd fled the Ice Lands, but she touched her neck at the memory of how the jeweled sunburst had felt cool and menacing pressed to her skin. It reminded her exactly why she had run and why she would never go back.

Eleven

"THAT EXPLAINS why your ex is so eager to reclaim the amulet," Lira said in a hushed voice, as she tentatively touched the stone that seemed to glow from within.

Thrain let out a gravelly laugh. "To be fair, the Trollbane clan is known for crafting jewelry like this. It's beautiful, but not extraordinary for them."

The group murmured appreciative sounds as they leaned in closer to the necklace, which seemed out of place on the rustic wooden table.

Lira gingerly touched the amulet. "Florin's female, right?"

Sass nodded. "The strongest alliances in the Ice Lands are forged through the daughters. I'm the eldest and only daughter of my clan, and Florin is the eldest in hers. That's why our families were so eager for the match."

"So the dwarf who's been hunting you down is a princess." Lira sat at the end of the bench next to Thrain. "That explains the excellent taste in jewelry."

Sass exchanged an amused glance with Thrain. "I'd never call Florin a princess to her face."

"Nor would I," her friend said, as he shook his head and crumbs rained from his beard. "Not if I wanted to keep my head."

Korl rested his hand on the hilt of his broadsword. "She sounds dangerous."

Sass didn't want to lie to her friends. Not anymore. "She is. Florin has always gotten what she wants, so she isn't a gracious loser. Not that I believe she ever truly wanted me, but she's also the type to only desire what she thinks is unattainable."

"So by jilting her, you made yourself even more of a prize?" Vaskel asked. "I would congratulate anyone else for such a clever strategy."

"If you ask me," Thrain said, "Florin is looking for an excuse to take retribution. She's always been bloodthirsty, even for a Trollbane."

"Clearly, if she blinded her own sister." Lira shuddered, picked up a cooled crumpet, and tore off a bite with her fingers. "Which brings us back to where we were. If Florin is itching for a fight, Sass running won't make a bit of difference."

"She blinded her sister?" Vaskel hissed to Thrain, who nodded with wide eyes.

Sass tried to ignore Vaskel's horrified expression. "But we know that her catching up to me means I either go back with her or risk putting all my friends and family in danger."

Lira popped the bit of crumpet in her mouth and made a face.

"Definitely better with butter and jam." She swallowed. "We can't be sure that returning the amulet and negotiating will fail, especially if I can figure out some spells in my gran's book."

"You've got a spell in your book to make dwarves more agreeable?" Vaskel asked, which got him a scowl from Thrain and a roll of the eyes from Sass.

Lira ignored the Tielfing's question and squinted at the amulet. "Are we sure this isn't magical?"

"Aside from the stone being a valuable one that only comes from the Trollbane's mountain?" Sass shook her head. "Dwarves are masters at metalworking, not enchantments."

"What are we looking at?"

Everyone jumped as Val poked her head into the group and peered at the amulet.

Sass pressed a hand to her heart. "You nearly scared the life out of me."

Val swiveled her head to Korl. "You said to meet you at The Tusk & Tail before work, so here I am. I didn't know I'd be crashing a secret meeting to look at a pretty necklace."

"It's a bit more than a pretty necklace," Thrain said.

Val tilted her head at the dwarf and gave him a quick once-over. "I don't believe we've met."

Thrain stood and proffered his hand. "Thrain Rockborn. Sass's friend."

Val's expression brightened. "From the Ice Lands?"

"The very place." Thrain squared his shoulders and puffed out his chest, although he was still wearing nothing but a tunic and linen breeches.

"Any friend of Sass's is welcome here." Val cast her an affectionate smile and a slow wink, neither of which were missed by Thrain.

Sass's cheeks heated as she avoided her friend's eyes and flicked a grin at the blonde guard, then she scooped up the amulet and dropped it into the velvet bag. "Val's right. It's time to get to work.

I wanted to dust out the curtains before we opened." She shoved the pouch into her pocket and cleared her throat, making shooing motions at Vaskel. "Don't you have work to do behind the bar?"

He grumbled as he rose, snatching a final crumpet from the plate and heading toward the long bar with a swish of his tail.

Sass felt Val's eyes on her, but she couldn't bring herself to meet them. Not when she hadn't been forthright about herself.

It isn't like you're a couple, she reminded herself. You're just friends.

Somehow, that was small comfort. She'd have to find a time to talk to Val and explain things, but the time wasn't now.

"See you later?" she asked, her gaze sliding from Korl to Val and her smile uncertain.

Val grinned at her. "I haven't forgotten your knitting lesson."

Sass cobbled together a smile, but her stomach tightened at the thought of what she'd need to confess first.

Lira shattered the brittle moment by shoving the plate of remaining crumpets between Sass and Val. "Take a crumpet for the road."

Val and Korl both took one, which gave Sass the chance to turn away and head for the windows and the curtains that she wanted to shake out.

"Wait up," Thrain called out to Korl and Val. "You're guards, right? From Castle Greyhelm? You mind if I walk with you and ask you a few questions?"

Sass had to stop herself from telling her friend not to bother the pair, but she didn't want to be Thrain's keeper.

"Fine by me." Val patted the dwarf on the back as he fell in step with them. "What do you want to know?"

Sass noticed Thrain cut her a furtive glance. "We don't have castles in the Ice Lands. At least, not ones above ground. I'd love a tour."

"We could give you one now," Korl said.

Now Sass did turn to Thrain. "What are you—?"

"Nothing to worry yourself over," he said, waving off her concern.

"We'll take good care of him," Val called to Sass as she munched on her crumpet.

Sass bit back the protests that were on the tip of her tongue, turning her attention back to the curtains. Thrain was up to something, she could feel it in her bones.

"You mind if I ask you what the deal is with the fancy necklace?" Val asked Thrain as they reached the door and Korl held it open.

"Amulet," Thrain corrected before Sass could stop him. "It was a gift from Sass's fiancée."

Sass froze, all thoughts of what Thrain might be up to fleeing her mind, as she held her breath.

"Fiancée?" The confusion in the woman's voice was unmistakable.

"Well, former fiancée, I suppose. Sass ran out on the wedding and didn't stop running until she ended up here."

Sass cringed, unable to look over her shoulder at Val. She closed her eyes and waited for more questions from the guard. But none came.

When she opened her eyes, the woman was gone.

Twelve

SASS TUCKED the amulet firmly back under her mattress where it couldn't cause any more trouble, but she lingered in her room. She couldn't bear to go back downstairs and face all the questions, all the curious looks. Not yet, at least. Instead, she clambered out her bedroom window and onto the roof, the rough thatch beneath her palms damp with the morning's dew, though the midday sun was doing its best to burn it away.

The first time she'd found Lira sitting on the roof, she'd been baffled, but now she understood it. From her perch, she could see the whole of the village spread before her. Whitewashed buildings pressed together as if for warmth, smoke twirled lazily from chimneys, and the chatter of daily life drifted up to her. Voices called out, cart wheels creaked along the dirt road, and horses snuffled and whinnied.

Sass caught the whiff of Pip's bakery on the breeze, her stomach responding with the barest rumble, though it was more memory than hunger. She'd eaten her fill of Lira's crumpets, but there was something about the smell of baking bread that made her mouth water.

Across the stream, the rhythmic splash of the waterwheel beside the blacksmith and wheelwright shop melded with the clang of hammer on anvil. Sass was all too familiar with the sound of striking metal. Those sounds had echoed beneath the mountains in the Ice Lands, but here she didn't shiver from the cold or squint through darkness.

Here, the sounds felt warm. They felt like belonging.

The clip-clop of horses' hooves on the dirt road drew her attention to the main thoroughfare, where a merchant's wagon ambled toward the market square. The driver bellowed a greeting to someone Sass couldn't see, and the easy familiarity of it made her heart squeeze.

She wrenched her knees to her chest and circled her arms around them, her dark plait falling over one shoulder. The Ice Lands had never felt like home, not really. It had been the place she was born, the place where her family's expectations had weighed on her like stone.

But Sass had wanted a different life.

She'd wanted to feel sunlight on her face and breathe air that didn't smell of rock dust and forge fires. She'd wanted to meet people who didn't know her family name, who didn't have expectations about what she should be based on her lineage, who would like her just for her.

She'd found that in Wayside. She'd found a place where she

could make a difference and found people who knew nothing about her past. People who'd become her family. People who'd become home.

And now she might lose it all.

The thought of the amulet twisted her stomach into a hard ball of dread. It wasn't just a piece of jewelry. It was a link to her past, a chain that could drag her back to the Ice Lands whether or not she wanted to go.

She pressed her face against her knees, breathing in the scent of her own wool skirt and the lingering smell of the tavern's hearth smoke that clung to her clothes. Would she have to run again? Would she have to pack her few belongings in the dead of night and slip away before dawn, leaving nothing but a cold bed and unanswered questions? The thought of Lira coming to the tavern to find her gone made her throat burn with unshed tears.

Or worse—would she have to return to the Ice Lands? If the political situation was as tenuous as Thrain said, if her refusing to return could somehow bring retribution onto her family. . .

"You know," said a familiar voice from behind her, "you're sitting in my spot."

Sass didn't turn around, but she felt her lips curve in the first genuine smile she'd managed in a while. "Your spot?"

The thatch rustled as Lira climbed out and settled herself beside Sass, close enough that their shoulders touched. "I was the one who first christened this roof as a thinking spot. If I remember correctly, you thought I was mad to sit on the roof."

"That was back when the roof was so rotten I almost lost a leg in it."

Lira bumped her shoulder against Sass's. "But I caught you before you took the shortcut to the first floor."

"Aye, you did. I'm grateful to you for that, and to Korl and Val for fixing the roof so sitting out here doesn't risk life or limb."

They sat in comfortable silence for a few moments before Lira wrapped her arm around Sass's shoulder. "We're going to figure it out. All right?"

Sass leaned into the embrace, drawing strength from Lira's certainty even as her own world felt like it was splintering around the edges. "What if you can't? What if there's no way to figure it out?"

"You're talking to a woman in possession of a spell book she doesn't know how to use. I'll practice the spells until I find one that can keep you safe, even if it means I have to turn everyone in Wayside into newts."

"I hope you'd only turn some people into newts," Sass managed, wiping at her eyes with the back of her hand.

"I wish Silas still came around. I would have liked to see him as a newt."

Sass snorted a laugh at the memory of the curmudgeon who'd once been a regular. "Vaskel would make a particularly handsome newt."

"I won't tell him you said that. It would only go to his already inflated head."

The pair laughed together before they lapsed into silence again, but it was an easy quiet, one softened by shared laughter and the simple comfort of not being alone with her fears.

"Well, I'd better get back to the kitchen," Lira said suddenly, straightening. "I need to start the cinnamon scones."

"I'll be right behind you."

"And Sass?" Lira's tone made her turn to face her fully. "Don't worry about Val. She'll understand."

Sass felt heat bloom across her cheeks like she'd stuck her face too close to a forge. "I'm not worried. We're just—"

"I know, I know. You're just friends. She's only teaching you to knit." Lira winked. "And Korl was just bringing me a new stove because he wanted to eat more scones."

Sass shot her a look. "That's completely different."

"Is it?" Lira was already moving toward the window, preparing to climb back inside, but she looked back over her shoulder with a grin that was pure mischief. "Is it really?"

And with that, she disappeared through the window, leaving Sass alone on the roof with her scorched cheeks and new worries about how she was going to explain all her secrets to the guard.

Thirteen

SASS HESITATED as the doors to the kitchen swung shut behind her. She was used to seeing Lira at work at the large wooden table surrounded by bowls and ingredients, but somehow the ingredients scattered around the woman looked wrong.

Instead of cinnamon sticks and butter, there were wee burlap bags that Sass didn't recognize and scents that reminded her of Iris's apothecary instead of a bakery.

"Why do I have the feeling you're not working on cinnamon scones?"

Lira glanced up, her wrinkled brow smoothing. "Oh, good, it's just you."

Sass took a step closer, noticing that Crumpet was standing next to the heavy spell book that was propped up on a sack of sugar. The pages were opened to a spread that looked suspiciously like a spell and not a recipe for muffins or crumpets.

"I thought you were going to start on the scones." Sass clocked a couple of black-glass bottles she knew had come from Iris's shelves.

"I was," Lira said, "but then I realized that baking can wait. I need to try one of these spells."

Crumpet eyed the bowl, wrinkling his tiny nose at what it contained already.

"Do you?" Sass had every faith in her friend as a baker, but Lira had never attempted one of her gran's spells. Considering that her gran had been a trained mage and had still made magical mistakes, Sass feared that this might not be the best plan.

"I'm starting small," Lira reassured her as she narrowed her eyes at the pages of the book. "It's a temporary vanishing powder, and it only requires a handful of ingredients and a few incantations. I should be able to pull it off. I'm good at following recipes, after all."

"Is magic that easy?" Sass asked, hoping that Lira's attempts at a vanishing powder didn't make the entire tavern disappear.

Lira shrugged. "Why shouldn't it be? This book has all the spells written out. If I follow the steps, I can't go wrong."

"I thought you said that your gran's baking recipes were loose on the amounts and required some testing to get right."

Lira peered up and nibbled her lower lip. "You're right. I did say that." She shook her head and returned her gaze to the spell. "But this is different. The measurements are much more exact for her spells. See?" She pointed to the page. "One spoonful of burdock root mixed with an equal amount of bone dust."

Sass watched nervously as Lira scooped a spoonful from two

different burlap bags and poured the powders into her mixing bowl. "Do I need to ask where you got these?"

"Iris doesn't know why I wanted them, but she knows I've been curious about trying my gran's spells."

Sass made a mental note to talk to the apothecary later about giving Lira magical ingredients. Especially since Iris knew well that the spells from the mage's book hadn't always worked as they should have.

"Now I stir it with a raven's feather," Lira said, picking up a blue-black feather and using the pointed tip to mix the ingredients.

"I thought we agreed that a vanishing spell wouldn't be all that much help," Sass said, as Lira motioned for Crumpet to turn the page of the book.

"This is just for practice," Lira grinned at her as Crumpet fluttered from one side of the sizable leather book to the other to flip the page. "Once I've mastered the easy spells, I can move on to something that can do some real damage."

Sass bit back a groan, suspecting that an untrained rogue playing mage could do a decent amount of damage even with easy spells.

Lira turned back to the book, squinting at the spidery script on the yellowed parchment. "Now I add a cup of sugar and a pinch of salt."

"Why don't I ask Iris to help?" Sass hitched a thumb behind her. "She ran with your gran for ages before they both retired. Maybe she has some insight into the spells."

Lira added the sugar and salt as she shook her head. "No need. I'm almost done. I only need to mix in the water and oil and then blend everything until it forms a sticky dough...wait, this doesn't sound right."

Sass took a step back.

Lira straightened, frowning. "This isn't the rest of the instructions to make the vanishing powder." She bent forward and eyed the corners of the pages, then slid a withering glance to the flutter-stoat. "Crumpet, why are these pages stuck together?"

The enchanted creature let out a flurry of indignant squawks as he stamped on tiny feet to the edge of the table and then took flight across the room and out the window.

Lira sighed as she pried apart two of the thick parchment pages. "It isn't Crumpet's fault. These pages are old and stuck together because the book was closed for so long. Most of the spells are in the back, but it looks like my gran added the occasional recipe between the spells."

Sass blinked at the bowl and then at Lira. "Are you telling me you almost made vanishing cookies?"

Lira gave Sass an apologetic look. "I guess I shouldn't be experimenting with spells I don't understand. Sorry, Sass. I really thought my gran's magic might be the answer."

Sass marched over, picked up the bowl, and promptly walked to the window and tipped the contents out of it. "Promise me you'll never try to make a potion or craft a spell again." When Lira opened her mouth to protest, Sass added, "without supervision by a trained mage."

Lira fluttered a hand at the window where her botched powder had been tossed. "That wouldn't have been so bad."

"Until we tried to make Florin vanish by hurling cookies at her."

Lira put a hand over her mouth. "Or we served them to our patrons, and parts of them started disappearing."

Sass shuddered as she thunked the earthenware mixing bowl back on the table. "No more freewheeling magic. I have enough to worry about without thinking that you might be accidentally whipping up a batch of truth serum scones."

Lira's eyes brightened for a beat at that thought, then she schooled her face, nodding solemnly. "I promise. No more attempts at magic." She furtively stowed the burlap bags of questionable ingredients. "The only scones I'll make today will be cinnamon ones."

Sass's shoulders relaxed, and she rested a hand on Lira's arm. "Thanks for trying, though."

Lira patted Sass's hand. "Don't worry. This might not have worked, but we'll figure something out."

Sass returned her friend's smile but didn't respond as she left the kitchen for the great room. She hoped rather than believed that Lira was right.

Fourteen

THE TAVERN'S din washed over Sass in waves: the clink of pewter mugs, the scrape of chairs across worn floorboards, the rumble of conversation punctuated by bursts of laughter. The evening rush had settled into a comfortable rhythm, and the tavern was alive with the glow of flickering lanterns and the rich aroma of roasted meat encased in buttery crust. Sass moved between the crowded tables with practiced ease, her tray laden with foaming tankards of ale and steaming meat pies.

Yet even as she smiled and traded jokes with the regulars, her gaze kept drifting to the heavy oak door. Each time it swung open, her heart lurched. Part of her watched for Val's tall silhouette, but another part braced for a band of armed dwarves to pour through the doorway.

"Another round for table seven," Vaskel called from behind the bar. His crimson horns gleamed in the lamplight as he pulled pints and slid them across the polished wood toward the end of the bar, where they miraculously came to a stop with only the smallest amount of foam cresting the lips.

Sass nodded and collected the drinks, weaving her way through the crowd toward the corner where Tinpin and Pip continued their animated debate. The halfling baker leaned forward conspiratorially. "Wait until you taste what I'm preparing for the Harvest Festival. Something special, something that will make even the most stubborn gnome admit that halfling baking is superior."

Sass plunked down their drinks with a slight smile, intrigued despite her distraction. "Planning something spectacular for the festival, Pip?"

The halfling baker's grin widened. "Let's just say I've been experimenting with some new recipes."

"And you?" She asked Tin. "Any special decor planned?"

The gnome rubbed his small hands together. "Yes, indeed. I understand the village hasn't held a Harvest Festival in years, so I'm going to make sure it's memorable. Very memorable, indeed."

"I look forward to it." Her gaze swept the room, noting that Val's chair by the fire remained empty, and she excused herself with a distracted nod, moving on to the next table where Thrain held court with a group of fascinated listeners.

He'd been less than forthcoming when he'd returned from his tour of the castle, only saying that Sass didn't need to worry. Knowing the dwarf the way she did, she was sure he was up to something. He also hadn't been able to tell her if Val had seemed upset. Not that Sass expected Thrain to be as sensitive to the guard's emotions as she was.

What was not surprising was the crowd gathered around her old friend. He'd always been skilled at weaving a tale. Whether it was entirely true was another matter.

"There we were, fifty feet below the surface in the crystal caves, when boom." Thrain slammed his palm onto the table. "An ice troll comes crashing through the cavern wall like it was made of parchment!"

The villagers gaped as they hung onto Thrain's every word. Words that weren't exactly accurate, Sass thought as she paused at the edge of the group, recognizing the tale. It was one of the childhood adventures they'd shared, though her memories were a touch different.

"The beast was enormous—easily twice the size of any troll you'd find in these southern lands. Its breath could freeze a dwarf solid from twenty paces!" Thrain's eyes found Sass in the crowd, and he gave her a conspiratorial wink. "Course, it didn't freeze me."

"That's because you were running too fast," Sass said, setting down a fresh ale at his elbow. "Although your screams might have also frightened it. I hear tell that trolls are afraid of banshees."

The table erupted in laughter, and Thrain clutched his chest in mock indignation. "Screaming? I was merely alerting you to danger."

"Loudly and repeatedly as you raced ahead of me," Sass added.

"Aye, but you have to admit," Thrain continued, raising his tankard in a toast, "we alerted the rest of the mountain to the danger."

Sass shook her head at him but couldn't suppress her own laughter. For all his exaggerations and dramatics, Thrain had been her closest friend, her childhood partner in countless adventures. As an only child, he'd been the closest thing she'd had to a brother. The thought of what she'd put him through when she fled made her stomach twist with guilt.

She made her way to the bar, grateful that Iris and Cali sat nursing their drinks with their heads together as they talked. At least with these two, she knew they weren't sharing exaggerated stories. At least, not ones in which they played a starring role.

"I'm telling you, Cali, you have to give it a chance," Iris said with a wave of her hand that jingled her bangles. "The heroine is a sea witch who falls in love with a common merman. The romance is absolutely swoon-worthy, and the underwater palace descriptions are gorgeous."

Cali's dark, pointed ears twitched. "Mermaid romance, Iris? Really?"

"Don't knock it until you've tried it." Iris pushed the red leather book across the bar. "Besides, you said you were looking for something different to read."

"Only because I've read all the pirate romances you own."

Sass bit back a sigh. Here were two more friends who would need to know the truth about her past. The thought of seeing disappointment or, worse, fear in their eyes made her chest tighten. How many people would she lose when word spread that she wasn't just Sass the dwarf turned tavernkeep, but a runaway princess with dangerous enemies?

She slipped behind the bar to collect more drinks, trying to push the dark thoughts away. The familiar routine of serving guests usually soothed her, but tonight even the simplest tasks felt heavy.

"You're worrying so loudly I can hear you from here." Vaskel stood next to her, his head facing forward, but his piercing blue eyes cutting to her. The pointed tip of his tail quivered, a sure sign that he was picking up on her distress.

Sass straightened and dragged the back of her hand across her forehead. "I'm fine, Vaskel. Just a long day."

The Hellkin studied her with an intensity that made her want to squirm. "Listen, Sass. I know you're worried about unwelcome visitors. But you should know that nobody's taking you anywhere on my watch. You're part of my crew now, and I never let a crew mate down."

The sharp edge of protectiveness in his voice caught her off guard. She'd known Vaskel liked her well enough, but he'd been Lira's friend and crew mate. They were the ones who'd run together, the ones who shared a past. Until that moment, she hadn't known that Vaskel considered her part of his circle.

"Thanks, Vask," she said quietly. "That means more than you know."

But even as she spoke, she knew it wasn't only the possibility of Florin's arrival that had her stomach in knots. It was the empty chair by the hearth where Val usually sat, the absence that seemed to taunt her.

Korl had stopped by earlier and tried to make excuses for Val, saying that she'd had a long day on watch. But Sass knew better. She could see it in the way the orc's eyes wouldn't quite meet hers, in the slight hesitation before he spoke. Val was avoiding her, and Sass knew why.

Vaskel cocked his head at her and stepped closer, lowering his voice. "It's more than the dwarf hunting party closing in on you, isn't it?"

Sass wrenched her gaze from the chairs nestled by the fire, but she wasn't quick enough.

"Ah." The edges of Vaskel's mouth quirked as he let out a breath. "You're afraid your secret might impact your knitting lessons."

She snatched the rag that was tucked into her waistband and swatted him with it, but it was the loud thunk of pewter on wood that made them both glance up. Cali had dropped her ale, which had sloshed onto the bar, and her eyes were wide.

Orc's blood! How had Sass not remembered that the Pantheri had enhanced hearing?

"Did you say dwarf hunting party?" Cali asked before cringing. "I swear I wasn't trying to eavesdrop, but..." she gestured to her ears, "Pantheri hearing, you know."

Sass's face warmed as Iris shot a look first at Cali and then at her. "It's all right, Cali. Actually, I was going to tell you and Iris. Both of you deserve to know the truth."

Iris had yet to blink. "The truth about what, pet?"

Sass took a deep breath, glancing once more at the empty chair. "About who I really am, why I'm here, and why I might be putting all of you in danger by staying."

Sass was encouraged when neither Cali nor Iris gasped in horror once she'd unspooled her story to them. It wasn't lost on her that Cali's eyes narrowed, and when she slipped away without a proper goodbye, Sass suspected that her secret might have bothered the Pantheri more than she'd let on.

"She'll come around, love," Iris said quietly, as she slipped off her stool later in the evening.

"Thanks, Iris," she said, and her thanks was for more than the reassurance about Cali. Then again, Iris had kept secrets from Lira when she'd first arrived, so she understood that the truth wasn't always easy to share.

As the night wound down, Sass reminded herself that Cali and Iris weren't the only ones who deserved the truth from her. She needed to tell Val.

But first, she'd have to find her.

Fifteen

WHEN THE LAST of the evening's patrons had finally teetered out the door and into the night, a comfortable quiet blanketed the tavern. Sass moved through the empty great room, collecting abandoned tankards and wiping down tables that still bore the sticky rings of ale and the crumb trails of quickly devoured pies. The fireplace had burned down to glowing embers, and wax candles had melted into misshapen nubs and pooled into their brass holders.

She slid chairs and benches under tables with brisk movements, but her mind wasn't on the familiar routine. Every few moments, her gaze would drift toward the door, as if willing it to open and reveal Val. Sass told herself she was being ridiculous to miss the guard's presence—they were friends, nothing more—but the hollow feeling in her chest told another story.

Clangs and clattering came from the kitchen, a good reminder that Lira was still cleaning up. Sass was hooking the last errant tankard on her pinky finger when her friend emerged through the swinging doors, carrying a cloth-wrapped bundle that smelled distinctly of spice.

"Here," Lira said, extending the bundle toward Sass. "Take this with you."

Sass clunked the dirty tankards onto the bar and eyed her friend and the bundle. "Take what where?"

"Apple cider cake." Lira jutted the wrapped cake toward Sass again. "And as for where, well... Vaskel might have mentioned that you needed to find Val."

Heat crawled up Sass's neck. "He told you?"

"Only that you wanted to explain everything to her, which I get. You are good friends, after all." There was no tone of mockery in her voice. "And if I know Val, she's where she feels most at home, and that means Korl's dads. I thought that if you were going there, you should take this." She cut her gaze to the bundle. "It's their favorite."

"You made me a bribe?" Even as Sass raised a brow, she had to admit this wasn't Lira's worst idea. It was loads better than her vanishing spell that almost became biscuits.

"If you ask me, a slice of cake and a sprinkle of kindness can solve any problem."

Sass eyed the cake. "And you didn't do anything funny to it?"

Lira's jaw dropped then she jerked one shoulder. "I guess that's fair, but this is regular cake. No magic. I did promise, you know."

Sass finally took the cake from Lira, the warmth of it seeping through the cloth and into her fingers. "I suppose baking solved a lot of problems when we were trying to attract folks back to the tavern. Didn't you also use an apple cider cake as a thank you after Korl made you an oven?"

Lira's cheeks flushed pink, but she laughed. "I might have, which is how I know it works. No magic needed."

Sass lifted the wrapped cake to her nose, inhaling the rich scents of cinnamon and tart apple cider that wafted from the cloth. "If this works, I'll owe you one."

Her friend squeezed her shoulder gently. "That's what friends do. Now go on, before you lose your nerve and the cake loses its heat."

Sass gave a determined nod as she left her apron on the bar and strode from the tavern. The door of The Tusk & Tail closed behind her with a soft click, and she took a beat to breathe in the cool air. Even though she'd left the Ice Lands and didn't miss the cold, she also wasn't sad that cooler weather was coming. It was more reason to pull a chair up around a fire and sip hot drinks, which Sass counted among her favorite things to do.

The gravel crunched under her boots as she made her way along the familiar path; the stream gurgling on one side and horses' hooves shuffling in the distance on the other. As she approached the stone bridge that spanned the stream, Sass could smell the lingering traces of heated metal and wood smoke from the day's work at the blacksmith's forge.

The combined blacksmith and wheelwright workshops stood on the far side of the bridge, and smoke still drifted from the forge's chimney, suggesting that Vorto and Klaff had been working late into the evening. The house attached to the workshops spilled golden light from its windows, and Sass could see movement through them as she hurried across the bridge.

She paused when she reached the door, her heart knocking against her ribs. The cake in her arms was leaden, and she couldn't seem to raise an arm to knock. What if Val was angry at her? Or worse, what if she'd misread the situation entirely and Val didn't care?

One foot was poised to spin her around, but she gritted her teeth and rapped one knuckle on the door before she could talk herself out of it. When there was nothing but silence inside, her heart plummeted.

"Hells and cinders," she muttered as she looked back at the bridge and wondered how fast her short legs could take her back over it. "This was a mistake."

Sixteen

BEFORE SHE COULD PUT her running to the test, the door swung open to reveal Klaff's dusky green, weathered face. The orc's eyes widened in surprise, then crinkled with genuine pleasure.

"Sass!" he boomed, his voice almost knocking her back a step. "What brings you out so late? And what's that delicious smell?"

"Apple cider cake," she managed, holding up the bundle. "Lira made it and... I brought it."

Her nonsensical explanation did not dissuade the orc. Sass guessed she needed little excuse when she came bearing a cake.

"Apple cider cake!" Vorto's voice carried to them from inside the house, followed by the scrape of a chair being pushed back. "Did someone say apple cider cake?"

Klaff chuckled and stepped aside, gesturing for her to come in. "You'd better get in here before my husband tramples us both in his eagerness."

The interior of the orcs' home was warm and welcoming, with thick wooden beams overhead and a massive iron table that dominated the main room. The orc-sized furniture made Sass feel like a child again, but the feeling wasn't unpleasant. It was cozy in the way that only truly lived-in spaces could be.

"Sass!" Vorto emerged from what she assumed was the kitchen, wiping his hands on a dish towel the size of a blanket. His face lit up at the sight of the cake. "And apple cider cake? Lira's apple cider cake? I don't know what we did this time to deserve it, but far be it from me to question good fortune."

Sass couldn't help but smile at the orc's enthusiasm, some of her nervousness beginning to fade. But then she caught sight of the figure sitting at the far end of the table, and her heart did that peculiar little skip it always did when Val was near.

The guard looked up as Sass entered, her blue eyes reflecting the lamplight. She managed a wary smile as her large hands fidgeted with what looked like an unevenly knitted section of scarf.

"I'll just put this on the table," Sass said, her voice sounding higher-pitched than intended. She unwrapped the cake, revealing a golden-brown surface that was crackled and sugary.

"Beautiful!" Vorto declared, already moving toward a cabinet to retrieve plates and a knife. "Absolute perfection."

His husband peered over his shoulder, nodding approvingly. "Lira's gotten as good as her gran, and that's saying something."

Within moments, the cake was hacked into generous slabs and distributed around the table on platter-sized plates. Sass sat across from Val, acutely aware of every movement the other woman made. The orcs insisted everyone try the cake immediately, their enthusiasm brooking no argument. Sass knew from Lira that Klaff and Vorto did not believe in saving food for later or in savoring baked goods over many days.

Orcs lived in the moment, enjoying things fully and not worrying about the future, and Sass couldn't argue with their life philosophy.

It took two hands for her to maneuver the giant fork so she could take a bite, but when she did, Sass was rewarded with the perfect blend of warming spices and sweet apples. At any other time, Sass would have savored every morsel. Tonight, however, the nervous flutter in her stomach overshadowed her love of cake.

"Lira really has outdone herself," Val said, which Sass realized was the first time the guard had spoken since she'd arrived.

Vorto was already reaching for a second slice when Klaff cleared his throat meaningfully. "I believe *we* should go to bed. We have an early day tomorrow."

"Early day?" Vorto looked confused for a moment, then caught sight of his husband's pointed expression. "Oh! Yes, very early day. Extremely early. Should probably go to bed right now, in fact."

He was still chewing his cake as Klaff practically hauled him toward the stairs, the larger orc calling out goodnights over his shoulder while his husband chewed and waved.

And then they were gone, leaving Sass and Val alone at the table with the remains of the cake and the weight of unspoken words.

Sass took a breath and launched into the apology she'd been rehearsing. "Val, I owe you an explanation. About what you heard this morning, about—"

"You don't owe me anything," Val interrupted, her voice quiet but firm. "Your past isn't my business."

Sass leaned forward. "But it is because I like to think we're friends, and friends should be honest with each other."

Val's expression softened, and she let her enormous fork clatter to the empty plate. "All right. I'm listening."

Sass gathered her courage, her fingers nervously working the edge of her napkin. "I had a fiancée. Florin Trollbane. But it was an arranged marriage, negotiated by our families when I was barely old enough to hold an axe without tipping over. I never loved her, Val. I barely even knew her."

She tracked Val's expressions, searching for any sign of judgment or disappointment. Instead, she saw understanding and then the briefest glimmer of relief.

"That's why you ran away?" Val asked.

"That's why I ran away," Sass said, all the old reasons making her spine straighten. "I couldn't marry someone I didn't love, couldn't spend my life living someone else's idea of what I should be. So I took back my life, even if it meant leaving everything I'd ever known."

Val was quiet for a long moment, her blue eyes holding Sass's with an intensity that made the dwarf want to squirm. Finally, she spoke. "I'm glad you ran away."

Breath hitched in Sass's chest. "You are?"

"If you hadn't, you never would have come to Wayside. And Wayside is better with you in it." Val's cheeks flushed slightly, but she held Sass's gaze. "I'm better with you in it."

The words hung between them, and Sass was afraid to speak, afraid to breathe, in case she broke the fragile feeling of hope that fluttered in her chest.

"There's something else you should know," Sass finally said, forcing herself to continue despite the way Val's admission had scrambled her thoughts. "Thrain—the dwarf who came to the tavern—he warned me that Florin and her search party are looking for me. They could arrive in Wayside any day now. Florin has threatened retribution against my clan unless I return and marry her."

Val straightened immediately, her gaze sharpening in the space of a heartbeat. "Then we'll be ready for them."

"We?"

"Did you think I'd let them take you without a fight?" Val's voice was as sharp and hard as a sword's blade. "This is your home now, Sass. No one will take you from it."

Even though they were talking about battle, Sass's mouth curved into a smile. Before she'd ended up in Wayside, she'd spent so long alone that having someone stand beside her was still an odd sensation.

"Thanks, Val."

Val reached across the table and hacked off two more slices of cake. "Now, let's eat more of this excellent cake before Vorto and Klaff sneak back down and finish it. I've never known a cake to last a full day in this house."

Sass accepted the slice with a smile. "Even though Korl doesn't live here anymore?"

Val snorted a laugh. "He's not the one who claims to sleepwalk and devours anything sweet that's left in the kitchen."

Sass tipped her head as if to look through the ceiling to the second floor. "Klaff?"

Val shook her head and whispered, "Vorto, but don't tell him I told you."

Sass mimed buttoning her mouth and pretended to mumble promises through sealed lips. A bark of laughter burst from Val, and she slapped a hand over her mouth as she rocked back in her chair.

Sitting across from Val and attempting to laugh quietly as they ate cake, Sass let her fears drift away into the night, replaced by the tender glow of possibility.

THE MORNING SUN unfurled ribbons of golden light across the village of Wayside as Sass made her way down the dirt road from The Tusk & Tail. Her steps felt lighter than they had in days, buoyed by the memory of last night's conversation with Val. She wasn't sure if it was the delicious cake or the company that had chased away her fears, but she suspected it was a bit of both.

Maybe Lira was right about baked goods being like magic. She would swear on the long wall that Pip's sweet rolls cast a spell over anyone who ate one.

As she reached the village, it was in the throes of rousing from sleep. Shop doors stood ajar, curtains were open, and brooms swished across paving stones. From the stables came the gentle nickering of horses and the jingle of harnesses. Birds cooed in building eaves, and somewhere in the distance, an owl released a sleepy hoot. There were no sounds of marching dwarf feet or the striking of axe blades.

Sass checked over her shoulder only twice during her walk, and both times it was more from habit than genuine worry. The conversation with Val had done more than clear the air between them. It had reminded Sass that she wasn't facing her troubles alone. The knowledge that she had friends willing to stand beside her made even the threat of Florin's arrival seem less over-whelming.

She'd left Thrain snoring loudly enough to rattle the windows of his room above the tavern. Since Thrain had been swaying on his feet and mumbling about ice trolls the size of mountains by the time he'd stumbled to bed the night before, she was confident he wouldn't wake before noon, which gave her plenty of time for her morning errands.

The scent hit her halfway down the main road — the kind of intoxicating aroma that could lead a person by the nose, and Sass found herself drawn inexorably toward Pip's bakery. The bakery itself was a welcoming sight, with its weathered wooden facade and cheerful yellow shutters. The baskets behind the counter boasted piles of split-top loaves and round, flour-dusted boules.

As Sass approached, she spied Pip through the open doorway. His wiry hair stood up in all directions, liberally dusted with flour. More flour coated his forest-green waistcoat and the burlap apron tied around his comfortable middle, and what looked suspiciously like honey glaze slicked down one oven-warmed cheek.

"Morning, Sass!" Lira's voice called from inside the bakery.

Sass almost yelped. She'd been so focused on the bread and the baker that she hadn't noticed her friend.

"Perfect timing," the redhead said, unaware that she'd startled Sass. "You're just in time to watch Cali surrender to temptation again."

Sass stepped through the doorway, immediately enveloped by the bakery's warmth and the blend of sweet and savory scents that made her slightly dizzy with hunger. Lira and Cali stood to one side of the counter, the Pantheri's gray striped tail twitching.

Sass was pleased to see the Pantheri, but she was also aware that her friend might still be hurt about the secret she'd kept. Judging from how she'd left the tavern so quickly after Sass had told her, the dwarf knew she had more fences to mend.

She closed the distance between her and Cali. "I know you're upset about—"

Cali shook her head. "I'm not. I mean, I was, but then I thought of all the secrets I've kept. Running with a crew doesn't exactly lend itself to full disclosure, especially when you're pulling off heists that aren't quite legal."

Lira shot her a look, clearly not thrilled that the Pantheri was discussing their dodgy past. Sass didn't know all the details of their time running together or how the Pantheri had become such a skilled archer, and she'd never pressed her about it.

"But I didn't hide my past because it was criminal," Sass said, keeping her voice low as Pip bustled behind the counter.

"No, but you had your reasons." Cali put a clawed hand on the dwarf's arm. "I understand running from your past and being afraid it will catch up to you. I think we've all wanted to pretend our past didn't exist at some point or another. At least now that you've told us, we can have your back."

Sass hitched a smile, grateful for her friend's kindness and understanding. "Thanks, Cal."

Cali curled an arm around Sass's shoulders and her tail around her leg, pivoting toward the bakery baskets brimming with loaves and golden buns. "Speaking of temptation, does anyone resist it when they smell Pip's pastries?"

"I can't think why they would," Lira said.

Cali's golden eyes focused on the glass dome covering a towering stack of what appeared to be lemon sweet rolls. "And with my extra-sensitive sense of smell? Forget it."

"She's been standing here breathing deeply," Lira told Sass with a grin. "I think she's trying to absorb the flavor through her nose."

Sass laughed, happy to talk about the simple pleasures in life like pastries. "I've seen no point in resisting, especially when Pip weaves his halfling baking magic like he does."

"Halfling baking magic?" Pip's head popped up from behind the counter, his large eyes twinkling. "Bless the stars! I've always said that the strongest magic isn't cast with wands or spells; it's baked in the oven."

He bustled around the counter almost dancing on his toes, his flour-dusted hands fluttering enthusiastically as he spoke. "I've been experimenting with a new sweet roll flavor for the Harvest Festival. This morning's batch is made with pumpkin and cinnamon, with just a touch of nutmeg and cloves."

"Pumpkin sweet rolls?" Sass felt the possibility of a light breakfast crumble like week-old biscuits. "Pip, you're going to be the death of me."

"Or the salvation of you," the halfling replied with a wink. "Nothing starts a day better than something sweet. Here, try one while they're still fresh from the oven."

He lifted the glass dome with a flourish, releasing a cloud of aromatic steam that made all three women sigh in unison, although Cali's sigh was more of a purr. The sweet rolls were golden-orange and glossy with glaze, the scent of spices mingling with the decadent aroma of pumpkin and butter.

Sass couldn't resist biting into hers immediately, barely waiting for Pip to hand it over. The roll was still warm, the gooey glaze covering her mouth as her teeth sank into the dough.

"Sweet simmering cauldrons," she breathed. "Pip, this is incredible."

Pip rubbed his hands together. "Better than the lemon ones?"

Lira's euphoric expression slipped from her face. "You aren't going to make us pick, are you?"

"That's like choosing a favorite member of your crew," Cali murmured as she swallowed and swiped her tongue to clean her sticky lips.

"Me, of course," Lira said, grinning at Cali, who nudged her and nodded.

The interior door that connected the bakery to the cheese shop swung open, and Fenni appeared with his usual impeccable timing. Unlike his brother, the cheesemonger was pristine as always, not a hair out of place or a smudge on his three-piece houndstooth suit. He took in the scene with an amused smile.

"Let me guess," he said, straightening his jacket with a two-handed tug. "You tried the treats Pip's been working on all night."

"All night?" Sass raised an eyebrow at the baker, who had the grace to look slightly sheepish.

"Well, not all night," Pip protested, though the flour in his hair and the slightly manic gleam in his eyes suggested otherwise. "Just since about one this morning. I had an inspiration, you see, and when inspiration strikes, you must follow it!"

"He does this," Fenni explained with the long-suffering tone of someone who'd dealt with his brother's creative obsessions for decades. "Gets an idea and can't rest until he's perfected it. I came down this morning to find him surrounded by mixing bowls and muttering about the perfect spice blend. I told you to get some sleep, didn't I Pip?"

"That you did," Pip muttered.

"This only proves that the festival is going to be magnificent," Lira said, taking another appreciative bite of her sweet roll. "The whole village is buzzing with excitement."

"It's wonderful to see everyone so enthusiastic," Fenni agreed, his face brightening. "We haven't had a proper autumnal celebration in Wayside for far too long."

As more early customers trickled in, drawn by the irresistible aromas and the promise of Pip's genius baking, the halfling hurried behind his counter again. Lira, Cali and Sass stepped aside to let Pip serve the villagers while they licked fingers and took final bites of the pumpkin sweet rolls.

Sass knew everyone who was lining up to buy bread. Wayside was a small village, after all. Everyone but one, she thought, as she watched a petite, well-dressed figure slip through the door. The man was clearly not a local. His clothes were too fine, his boots too polished, and the feather-plumed hat perched jauntily on his head was not the sort of thing you saw in Wayside.

Sass tracked him, taking a step closer to listen when he reached the counter.

"I'll take six of your largest loaves," the stranger said, producing a leather purse that clinked promisingly. "And perhaps some of these sticky buns. We've heard excellent things about your baking."

Sass felt a chill run down her spine at the word *we*.

"Cali," Sass said quietly, moving closer to her friend. "Is anyone new staying at the inn?"

The Pantheri's ears flicked toward the stranger, then back to Sass. "No," she said softly. "Just Vaskel and me, and we've been there for weeks now. Why?"

Sass watched as the stranger completed his purchase, accepting the wrapped loaves and sweet rolls with efficient politeness. It was entirely possible that a merchant was passing through or a nobleman had sent his servant in to purchase bread during a long journey.

"No reason," she said, but her eyes never left the man as he headed for the door. "Just curious."

The stranger paused at the threshold, his gaze sweeping the bakery one final time before he stepped out into the morning sunlight. Through the window, Sass watched him walk down the main road at an unhurried pace. There was no nobleman's carriage or merchant wagon in sight.

At the edge of the village, where the road gave way to forest, the man turned left instead of continuing toward the main trade routes. The path he chose led into the deep woods that surrounded Wayside, the kind of place where travelers might make a hidden camp if they didn't want to be seen.

Sass felt her stomach clench with a familiar mixture of dread and determination. A well-dressed stranger buying provisions for a group, then disappearing into the forest? The only reason Sass didn't allow fear to overtake her was the undeniable fact that the stranger had not been a dwarf.

Even so, somewhere in the woods, there was someone—many someones, if the quantity of bread was any sign—who wished to remain hidden.

Eighteen

"SASS?" Lira's voice broke through her trance. "Are you all right?"

Sass blinked and turned to find her friends watching her with worried expressions. Cali's ears were flattened, while Lira's dark eyes searched her face for signs of distress.

"Of course I'm all right," Sass said with a laugh that sounded forced even to her own ears. "Just wondering where that fellow's headed. He was awfully well-dressed to be tramping through the woods."

"Maybe he's camping," Cali suggested, though her tone carried its own note of uncertainty. "Some travelers prefer the woods to paying for a room at the inn."

"Aye, probably," Sass agreed quickly, eager to change the subject before her friends could read too much into her worry.

"He wasn't a dwarf," Lira said quietly, which told Sass that she hadn't been the only one to register his presence.

But Lira was right. He hadn't been a dwarf, which meant the chances were high he was no threat to her.

"You want me to follow him?" Cali asked.

Sass shook her head. Now wasn't the time to fall victim to paranoia. "He was just a fellow buying bread. Not our concern."

Lira studied her for another moment, then seemed to accept the explanation. "Well, Cali and I were planning to pop in and visit Iris at the apothecary. Want to join us?"

The offer was exactly the distraction Sass needed. "I'd love to. It's been too long since I've been in her shop."

They made their way past Fenni's storefront and then the haberdasher. Sass spotted Tin inside surrounded by bolts of fabric and gave him a wave. The morning was ambling along, and more villagers were emerging to tend to their daily business. The normalcy of it all should have been comforting, but Sass scanned every face, looking for more strangers.

The apothecary perched at the end of the row of shops, its darkened windows tucked beneath the black-and-white-striped fabric awning. Sass paused at the threshold, remembering her first visit to this place months ago when she'd been new to Wayside.

Then, the shop had appeared curious and mysterious. The shelves lined with black glass bottles had been like nothing she'd seen before, their curling paper labels promising everything from bone powder to belladonna, and the mingled scents of a hundred different oils and potions had been a confusing cacophony that had made her nose twitch.

But now, knowing Iris as she did, the shop felt familiar and welcoming. The same dark wood shelves still held the same mysterious bottles, the same combination of scents still hung in the air like incense, but it all seemed cozy rather than ominous. It was the difference between entering a stranger's domain and stepping into a friend's sanctuary.

The bell above the door chimed softly as they entered, and Iris looked up from behind the counter where she'd been grinding something with her mortar and pestle. Her face brightened immediately at the sight of them.

"Well, this is a lovely surprise!" she exclaimed, setting down her work and coming around the counter to greet them.

Sass had always admired Iris's distinctive style. Today she wore a flowing patchwork skirt in shades of deep purple and forest green that swished and jingled with each step thanks to the tiny bells sewn along the hem. Her dark hair, generously streaked with silver, was piled high on her head in a deliberately messy arrangement that somehow looked perfectly elegant, with escaped curls framing her face. Bangles clinked on her wrists as she moved, and her colorful shawl clung valiantly to one shoulder.

"Come to the back, loves," Iris said, gesturing toward the heavy curtain that separated the front of the shop from her private domain. "I was just about to put the kettle on."

They followed her through the curtain into the book-lined room that served as Iris's private sitting area. The transformation from the front shop to this cozy retreat never failed to amaze Sass. Where the front was all dark mystery, the back room felt like an overstuffed library crossed with a messy parlor.

Bookshelves stretched from floor to ceiling, packed snugly with ancient-looking tomes bound in cracked leather. A round table sat in the center of the room, its surface cluttered with open books, empty teacups, and plates that held nothing but crumbs.

The moment they entered, a flutter of wings overhead announced Iris's bookwyrms. The tiny creatures emerged from their hiding places among the shelves, their iridescent wings catching the light as they darted through the air like miniature dragons morphed with hummingbirds.

Sass knew the story of how these creatures came to be—the result of one of Lira's gran's magical experiments gone delightfully awry. Instead of whatever the elder mage had been trying to create, she'd ended up with creatures whose primary purpose was eating dust without damaging the books they cleaned.

"Tea?" Iris offered, already bustling toward an alcove tucked behind the room where she kept her tea brewing. "I've got a lovely summer berry blend that's perfect for the morning."

"That sounds wonderful," Cali said, settling into one of the large, lumpy chairs with a grateful sigh.

As Iris poured steaming tea into delicate floral cups, she glanced at Sass with a thoughtful expression. "You know, pet, I've been thinking about your personal problem."

Lira pressed her lips together to keep from laughing. "Maybe we shouldn't call it that. It makes it sound like Sass has some sort of rash."

"Florin is like a rash," Sass muttered, accepting her teacup with a rueful smile. "Irritating and persistent."

Iris nodded as she settled into her own chair. "I've been researching some protective measures. Poultices that could ward off 'negative influences.' Herbs that might provide some protection or at least muddy the waters for anyone trying to track you."

"That's thoughtful of you," Sass said, touched by the apothecary's concern. "Though I'm not sure how much herbs can do against a determined dwarf with a grudge and an armed search party."

"Don't underestimate the power of the right combination of plants," Iris said with a mysterious smile. "Though I have to admit, I wish Lira's grandmother were still with us. She would have been able to craft an obscuring spell that would make you nearly impossible to find."

Lira and Sass exchanged a look.

"I've found some of those spells in her book," Lira said, her gaze not meeting Iris's. "But I've decided not to try them without more training."

"Not try them again," Sass muttered into her teacup.

Iris's eyes went wide with alarm, and she set down her teacup with a sharp clink. "Lira, love, you mustn't attempt untrained magic! The consequences of a spell gone wrong can be..." She gestured vaguely at the bookwyrms fluttering overhead. "Well, these little fellows are an example of magic going sideways. Your grandmother was lucky that her failed experiment created something harmless and helpful. Not all magical mishaps are so benevolent."

Cali cleared her throat softly and gave Lira a pointed look. "Remember what happened when Malek got in over his head with magic?"

The room fell silent at the mention of their former companion. Sass knew all about Malek, the mage who had been part of Lira and Cali's adventuring crew before dark magic had corrupted him beyond redemption. The memory of his transformation and ultimate fate cast a shadow over the cozy room.

Lira drained the rest of her tea in one gulp and set the cup down with finality. "We should probably head back to the tavern. I've got scones to bake." She smiled at Iris, who was wringing her hands. "You don't need to worry about me trying magic. I'm far too busy with the tavern to do much else."

As they headed for the curtained doorway, Iris caught Sass's arm gently. "Don't worry too much, dear. I'll keep thinking about ways to keep you safe." She darted a glance at her stuffed shelves. "There are more options than you might realize."

Before Sass could respond, Iris slipped something into her pocket with the practiced skill of someone who had once been a rogue herself. The bundle felt soft and crinkled slightly, smelling of dried herbs and something floral that Sass couldn't immediately identify.

"What's this?" Sass asked, touching her pocket.

"Just a little something for luck," Iris said with a wink. "Lavender for peace, rosemary for protection, and a few other things Lira's gran taught me about. It can't hurt to have a bit of extra fortune on your side."

Sass felt a smile tug at her lips despite her worries. "I've been pretty lucky so far finding Wayside, Lira, and all of you, but I'll take all the help I can get."

"That's the spirit, pet," Iris gave her arm one last reassuring squeeze. "And remember, you're not facing this alone. The support of true friends carries more power than any enchantment."

As Sass followed Lira and Cali from the back room, she touched the wee bundle in her pocket again. She wasn't entirely sure she believed in the protective power of herbs, but there was something undeniably comforting about carrying a token of luck made for her by a friend.

Then, a chill slipped unbidden down her spine. Freeing herself from Florin was going to take more than luck.

Nineteen

THE AFTERNOON CHAI and scone service at The Tusk &
Tail was winding down as Sass made her final rounds, gathering
empty mugs and crumb-scattered plates. The late afternoon light
filtered through the tavern's windows and illuminated dancing
dust motes that Sass suspected were mostly sugar and cinnamon.

Sass paused when she noticed that Korl and Val remained in
their usual chairs by the hearth. The sight of Val sent a flutter
through her stomach, made even more pronounced when the

guard caught her eye and gave her a sly wink that sent a flush of heat slinking up her neck.

She still wasn't entirely sure where she stood with Val, but the fact that the woman was here meant she could breathe easier. She'd hated the thought of Val being upset with her, and clearing the air meant she could face whatever might come for her with all her friends by her side.

Lira emerged from the kitchen with Crumpet perched on her shoulder. The flutterstoat stretched his white wings as he chittered softly, apparently pleased to be out of the steamy kitchen now that the day's baking was complete. The creature was so adorable, with dark markings around his eyes that made him look like he was a tiny bandit, that Sass couldn't imagine any of their patrons having an issue with him, but Lira had made a good point that not everyone was open-minded about enchantments. The last thing any of them needed was unwanted attention on the tavern and the village, especially since Crumpet wasn't the only enchanted creature in Wayside.

"Just us left then?" Lira asked, looking around the nearly empty tavern as she wiped her hands on the front of her apron.

"Just us," Sass confirmed, settling the last of the mugs onto the bar. "And our favorite guards, of course."

Lira immediately crossed the tavern and perched on Korl's lap, which made Sass's heart twist with a mixture of happiness for her friend and longing for the same love Lira had found with the orc. Some might say they were an unusual pairing—a half-elf former rogue and a strong, silent orc guardsman—but they comple-mented each other perfectly. And Lira made a point not to mention any of her law-breaking adventures when Korl was within earshot.

Vaskel stepped from behind the bar where he'd been cleaning glasses, walking with Sass to join the others at the hearth. His tail slashed behind him, which meant that there was something on his mind, something that worried him. "Lira mentioned there was a stranger in the village this morning."

Korl and Val immediately straightened, their relaxed demeanor shifting in an instant.

"What stranger?" Val asked, her gaze darting to Sass.

Korl leveled a look at Lira. "You did not mention this."

Lira shrugged. "I've been busy. It's not like we've seen each other since this morning." She nudged him. "You were still tinkering in the shop when I left."

Korl cleared his throat. "I got distracted fixing a contraption Tin brought me." Then he frowned. "But that doesn't mean I don't want to know if there are threats to the village. I am still a guard."

"I know, I know." Lira patted his chest. "But it's not like the stranger was a threat. He wasn't even a dwarf." She glanced at Sass. "Sass didn't seem worried, so I didn't want to make a big deal about it."

Everyone looked at Sass as if asking if this was true.

She flipped her braid off her shoulder. "He wasn't a dwarf, but I'd be lying if I said I hadn't been thinking about him."

She described the well-dressed man she'd seen at Pip's bakery and the fact that he'd purchased more bread and pastries than one person could eat. Most importantly, she told them about watching him leave the village and detour into the woods.

"It just struck me as odd," she concluded. "Why would a traveler buy that much bread and then head into the forest unless he was returning to a group camping there?"

Vaskel's crimson brow bunched, but he rocked back on the heels of his boots. "It isn't unusual for groups to camp nearby."

"No, it's not," Cali said as she entered the tavern. "I was just coming to tell you all that I can hear sounds from outside the village. Not only is someone camping in the forest, I'm positive it's several someones."

Val leaned forward. "What kind of sounds? Does it sound like a hunting party? Even if the man from the village wasn't a dwarf, he could have been an envoy for them."

Sass scrunched her nose at this. A dwarf hunting party would never have an envoy who wasn't a dwarf. That went double for Florin, who believed that dwarves were innately superior to all other species.

Cali's ears flicked as she considered the question. "That's the strange part. I would swear I'm hearing lute music."

"Not singing?" Sass asked, the tightness in her stomach loosening. Dwarves might belt out a traditional mining chant or drinking song, but lute music was decidedly not part of their repertoire.

"Definitely instrumental."

Korl was already rising to his feet, forcing Lira to scramble off his lap with an undignified squeak. "We need to check this out. I don't like the idea of strangers living in the woods, even if they enjoy the lute."

"I want to come with you," Sass said.

Before Korl could voice what was clearly going to be a protest, Val spoke up. "We should let her come. Nothing cures fear better than seeing the proof for yourself."

A throaty growl from the back of the tavern made them all turn. "Then I'm coming too."

Thrain descended the stairs with the slightly rumpled appearance of someone who had finally awakened from a deep sleep. His dark hair was sticking up at odd angles, and even his beard looked rumpled.

"It's about time you woke up," Sass said as she assessed her friend. "I was beginning to think you planned to sleep until next week."

"Dwarf tales and good ale make for a powerful combination." Thrain stroked a hand down his scraggly beard. "But I'm awake now, and if there's trouble brewing, you'll want a dwarf who knows how to handle it."

Lira pointed a stern finger at Vaskel. "You have to stay here with me. I can't manage the kitchen and the bar, and I need to prepare for the dinner service."

Vaskel met Korl's eyes across the room, and some silent communication passed between them. "I'll keep things safe here at the tavern while you all go investigate, but be careful out there."

Cali's whiskers twitched as she patted the quiver slung across her back. "I have my bow and arrows, just in case this turns out to be more than a peaceful camping party."

As the group prepared for their expedition into the woods, Val turned to Sass with a carefully neutral expression. "What are the chances we're about to meet your fiancée?"

Sass's gut clenched at the thought, a cold knot of dread settling just below her ribs. The possibility had been lurking at the back of her mind all day, but reason won out. "I can't imagine Florin allowing lute music."

But even as she spoke the words, she couldn't shake the feeling that something was off. The timing was too coincidental. What were the odds that Thrain would arrive to warn her about Florin's search party closing in and then a stranger—one who was hiding in the woods with a group—would appear in the village?

Sass untied her apron and handed it to Lira. "I'll be back soon."

Lira accepted the apron with a weak smile. "You'd better be. The tavern couldn't run without you."

The words cheered Sass's heart despite her jangling nerves. She looked around the great room one more time. The Tusk & Tail represented everything she'd hoped to find when she fled the Ice Lands—independence, friendship, purpose, and a place where she could be simply Sass rather than Princess Sarsaparilla Thornshield.

Whatever they found in the forest, she was determined to fight for all of it.

Twenty

SASS'S FEET crunched on the carpet of leaves as they wound through towering oaks whose high branches filtered the fading sunlight into dappled patterns on the forest floor.

Korl and Val took point with their swords sheathed, but their heads swiveling as they scanned for signs of danger. Cali flanked them to one side, walking backward with an arrow already notched in her bow, and Thrain tromped beside Sass, his battle axe gripped tightly in his calloused hands. Part of Sass wished she'd brought a weapon. For a dwarf, there was something reassuring about having iron in hand when facing the unknown.

Sass could almost hear her mum's voice reminding her about being prepared. "A dwarf with a sharp axe finds a door where others only encounter walls."

Her mum's words had been why she'd left the Ice Lands with several daggers and the amulet, and now they rang in her ears. As they traipsed farther into the woods, Sass's mind drifted to the last time she'd walked through the forest.

Even though it had been many months ago, she remembered that night with startling clarity. The weariness from her journey had been bone-deep, making every step an effort, and gnawing hunger had become her constant companion.

The forest had seemed endless then, dark and menacing as she'd pushed through undergrowth that snagged at her clothing and stumbled over roots that threatened to send her sprawling. Cold rain had soaked through her traveling cloak to chill her to the core, and wind had whipped her sodden hair against her cheeks. Lightning had licked the sky, and thunder had rumbled like the war drums of the Deep Guard echoing through the mountain halls.

When she'd finally staggered from the tree line and seen the lights of Wayside flickering through the sheeting rain, she'd nearly wept with relief. Even The Tusk & Tail, neglected and crumbling, had seemed like a refuge.

She could still remember the pungent odor of rancid ale and general neglect that had greeted her when she'd pushed through the tavern's heavy door. The great room had been dimly lit by a few guttering candles, the tables were sticky with grime, and cobwebs had dripped from the wooden beams overhead. It seemed almost miraculous now that the ramshackle tavern she'd taken shelter in had become home.

The sound of Thrain's gruff voice snapped her back to the

present. "That doesn't sound like dwarves," he muttered, his grip loosening on his axe as the lute music grew louder.

Sass tilted her head, listening to the strumming that drifted through the trees. "Florin wouldn't be making so much noise anyway. She's more subtle than that and more strategic. If she were out here, we'd never know until she wanted us to."

Not only was the music coming from a stringed instrument, the precise notes spoke of a trained musician rather than dwarves trying to pass the time around a campfire. As they drew closer to the source of the sound, even Cali lowered her bow slightly, her gray ears pricked forward with curiosity rather than alarm.

They crested a small rise and looked down into a natural clearing where the forest opened to reveal a sight that made Sass's eyes widen in amazement. Several elaborate tents circled a central fire pit, but these were nothing like the utilitarian shelters mercenaries or even traders would choose.

Constructed from sumptuous, silky fabrics in opulent shades of sapphire blue, emerald green, and deep crimson, each tent was edged with gold fringe, and each towering tent pole boasted a gilded finial. The largest tent, positioned at the center of the clearing, was particularly magnificent, its fabric like liquid gold flowing down from the many tall poles. And did it have a skylight and an attached turret?

"Definitely not dwarves," Thrain huffed, lowering his axe.

"Then who?" Val asked, echoing the question that was on all their minds.

Korl simply grunted and led them down into the clearing. As they approached the encampment, Sass spied a lute player perched on a tufted ottoman beside the fire, his fingers dancing over the strings. A willowy woman with pointed ears tended to something in a glittering copper pot, but even from a distance, Sass could tell this wasn't typical campfire fare. The aromas drifting toward them were complex and sophisticated. This was no rustic stew.

The elves milling around the tents and fire wore fabrics so luxurious that Tinpin the haberdasher would have swooned at the sight. Not only did they look fit to be presented at court, but they also drank from delicate glass goblets rather than dented metal cups that were the hallmark of most travelers.

Who were these elves, and why were they camping near Wayside of all places? And was that a lavender-plumed ostrich adorned with a bejeweled lead and tethered to a gilded pole?

The lute player noticed their approach first, his fingers gradually slowing the melody until the music died away entirely. Then the ostrich swung its beak in their direction, eyes narrowing as if it wanted to charge. Sass had never been intimidated by a bird, but she'd also never been appraised by one with so much regal disdain.

The sudden silence seemed to draw the attention of everyone in the camp, and Sass felt a moment of awkwardness as the elegantly dressed people turned to stare at their small, motley group. For the first time in ages, Sass felt both underdressed and out of place.

Before anyone could speak, the ostrich shrieked and then turned away with what could only be described as a dismissive sniff. A tall figure emerged from the tent next to the ostrich, and his gaze landed on them.

As a dwarf, she'd learned not to trust elves, but she couldn't help but be fascinated by this one. It was impossible to tell his age, but he wore his silver hair primly tied back. Sparkling rings adorned every finger, and his robes were both voluminous and sleek.

His face lit up with what appeared to be genuine delight as he absentmindedly patted the ostrich on the head. "Don't pay any attention to my battle ostrich. Glen takes a while to warm up to strangers."

Glen? Sass exchanged a glance with Val, who looked more amused than anything.

"Battle ostrich?" mouthed Val.

The elf clapped his hands together as he glided toward them, unaware or uninterested in the confused looks their group was exchanging. "Welcome, friends! I've been hoping you'd come!"

Twenty-One

THE RELIEF that this wasn't Florin's hunting party warred with a completely new set of questions. Why had an elf set up camp near Wayside, and why in the hells would he be hoping they'd come? Even more perplexing, why had he brought a battle ostrich?

Val, ever practical and direct, stepped forward slightly and braced her hands on her hips. "Who are you, and why are you hiding out in the woods like...like bandits?"

The elf's radiant smile flickered for just a moment, and he pressed a dramatically bejeweled hand to his chest as if Val had slapped him across the face with a glove. "Hiding? My dear woman, we are most certainly not hiding, and bandits do not travel in such magnificent style."

He had a point there. Sass had never seen any type of bandits or thieving party exude quite so much style—or travel with an ostrich and lute player.

He gestured grandly at the silk tents around them. "I am Erindil of Lananore, and this is my traveling party. We are the farthest thing from bandits you could imagine."

Korl grunted. "That doesn't explain why you're here."

Erindil's smile brightened again, as if Korl had asked exactly the right question. "Ah, but of course you're curious! Please, come sit with me." He waved them forward, and his silk robes rustled like autumn leaves. "Allow me to offer you some mulled wine—my own personal blend. I never travel without it."

The elf settled himself gracefully onto what could only be described as a throne in miniature—a high-backed chair upholstered in emerald velvet and trimmed with gold cord. The piece of furniture looked like it belonged in a palace rather than a forest clearing, yet here it sat as if it had sprouted from the earth itself.

As if there had been an unspoken signal, the other members of the traveling party resumed their activities. The lute player's fingers found his strings again, the elf near the fire continued stirring something in the ornate copper pot, and the others sipped their wine as if they were guests at an elegant reception. Even Glen resumed looking bored.

Sass gave her head a small shake as she followed the elf onto the colorful, woven rugs scattered over the patchy moss and crumpled leaves of the forest floor. Around the elf's chair, there were ottomans in rich brocade and padded benches covered in brushed velvet, each perfectly suited to willowy elves.

Korl approached one ottoman with obvious suspicion, then attempted to fold his massive frame onto the delicate furniture. Sass pressed her lips together to stifle a laugh as his knees practically reached his ears. Val didn't even attempt to sit, and neither did Cali, whose bow remained unsheathed with an arrow notched but pointed safely toward the ground.

If Erindil was bothered by Cali's wariness, he gave no sign of it. He summoned his attendants to offer goblets of wine, which Sass accepted before staring into the ruby-red liquid. She held the goblet close to her nose and sniffed carefully, trying to detect any hint of something sinister beneath the spiced wine.

Thrain, apparently having no such concerns, downed his entire goblet in three enthusiastic gulps and immediately held it out for a refill. "That's the finest mulled wine I've had since the winter feast in the Ice Lands."

Erindil beamed at the praise. "I add a touch of honey from the royal apiaries of Lananore, and just a whisper of moonflower essence. It's quite impossible to replicate unless one has access to very specific ingredients."

Korl waved off the offered goblet entirely, his expression growing more stern by the moment. "How do you know who we are, and why are you really here?"

The elf's eyes sparkled with what looked suspiciously like amusement. "I know all of you." His attention lingered on Val, then Cali, and finally settled on Sass with an intensity that made her skin prickle. Finally, he slid his gaze to Thrain. "Well, almost all of you. The dwarf gentleman is new to me."

Korl's scowl deepened, creating furrows across his broad forehead. "How do you know us? Have you been watching the village?"

Erindil chuckled. "Watching? Oh, my dear fellow, you make it sound so sinister. I prefer to think of it as merely taking an interest. Besides, this isn't my first visit to your charming little village."

The words sent a chill down Sass's spine that had nothing to do with the quickly sinking sun, the cool breeze, and lengthening shadows.

Erindil leaned forward slightly, his voice dropping to a conspiratorial hush as he stared at Sass. "The first time I came to Wayside, I acquired a tavern for you and Lira."

Twenty-Two

IF SASS HAD THOUGHT she couldn't be more surprised by the elf and his elaborate campsite, she'd been spectacularly wrong. Only when he cocked his head at her in amusement did she realize she was gaping at Erindil with her mouth dangling open.

Korl attempted to stand quickly, but his massive frame had been so awkwardly perched on the low ottoman that he rolled sideways off the furniture, catching himself before his face met the carpeted floor. Val helped Korl get to his feet, as Thrain's grip on his battle axe slackened so much that the weapon nearly slipped from his fingers. Even Cali's ears lay flat, and the fur on the back of her neck stood on end.

When Sass finally spoke, the words came out as little more than a strangled whisper. "You're the one who bought the tavern for us?"

She and Lira had wondered about their mysterious benefactor, the anonymous elf who had purchased The Tusk & Tail and quietly transferred ownership to them. She'd never imagined that the answer would be sitting on a velvet chair in a forest clearing drinking mulled wine.

Then another possibility struck her like a hammer blow. Her eyes widened as she peered at Erindil. "Are you Lira's father?"

The effect of her words on the elf was immediate. Erindil's crystal goblet froze halfway to his lips, his eyes flying wide. For a moment, he looked as if he might keel over. Then he started laughing.

"A father? Me?" His laugh was both musical and slightly manic. "No, no, my dear. I am most certainly not Lira's father." He paused, seeming to gather himself before putting his goblet on the low table beside his chair, steepling his fingers, and gazing over them. "But I am her uncle."

Everyone in their group went silent, and Korl stiffened. Even the lute player paused, as if sensing the import of the moment.

Lira's uncle? Sass hadn't known that Lira had an uncle, and she suspected Lira didn't know either.

Cali was the first to recover her voice, her ears pricking forward as she fixed Erindil with narrowed gold eyes. "This is a conversation that Lira should be a part of."

Sass recognized the protective tone of someone who had known Lira for years and considered her family.

Erindil nodded gravely, his expression solemn for the first time since they'd arrived. "I agree completely," he said, his voice losing some of its theatrical lilt. "In fact, I've been trying to work up the nerve to approach her without completely upending her life."

Korl crossed his arms over his chest. "Why would you upend her life?"

Erindil reached for his goblet again, taking a longer sip of the mulled wine as if he needed the fortification. When he set it down, his hands were steadier, but his slender face remained pinched.

"Lira's father—my brother—left Lananore long ago." He sighed. "He was never one to stay in one place for long, preferring the freedom of exploration to the responsibilities of court life. But he returned for brief visits over the years, and during one of those visits, he mentioned having a daughter who was half human." The elf's gaze grew distant, as if he were looking back over years. "Since my brother never lingered anywhere for long, I made it my business to learn about this niece I'd never met. It took me quite some time to track her down, but when I finally did..." He gestured vaguely in the direction of Wayside. "She seemed happily ensconced at The Tusk & Tail, working alongside a dwarf companion to rebuild it from near ruin. It seemed only fair to ensure that both of you received ownership of the tavern, since I'd observed you working together to restore it."

Sass was pleased to hear about what she and Lira had accomplished, but another question quickly overshadowed it. "Then why come back?"

Erindil's smile flickered as the creature Sass had seen in the village approached with a tray of Pip's sweet rolls. The elf plucked one and held it up. "Aside from a fondness for halfling pastries?"

The man walked the tray of pastries around their group, but Thrain was the only one who took a sweet roll. Even Erindil set his pastry down untouched, his rings catching the firelight as his hands fidgeted with the silk tassels of his robes.

"I never planned to return," he admitted, his voice growing quieter. "Why stir up old family wounds for Lira when she seemed content with her life here? But recent events in Lananore have forced my hand."

He paused, seeming to gather his thoughts before continuing

with obvious reluctance. "We recently celebrated the ascension of a new Lord of Lananore—a position that comes with considerable ceremony and tradition. All members of the family are expected to attend, regardless of how far they might have wandered or how long they'd been away."

Korl's frown deepened as a growl rumbled in his chest. "What does that have to do with Lira? The elves didn't expect her to attend, did they?"

Erindil's shoulders sagged, and he looked suddenly smaller. "Because Lira's grandfather is the new Lord of Lananore. I can think of very few reasons her father—my brother—would miss such an important family occasion."

Sass tried to make sense of what the elf had said. She knew little of elf customs, but she knew they held their ceremonies in high regard and their royalty in even higher esteem.

"I still don't understand how this connects to Lira," Sass said, glancing at her friends in case they understood something she didn't. "As far as I know, she's never laid eyes on her father."

Erindil nodded. "She might not know him, but that doesn't mean he doesn't know her. Or that he hasn't kept track of her. I came here to find out if Lira's father also visited Wayside and to see if I could track him from here."

Korl fisted his hands at his side. "And what did you learn?"

Erindil reached for his goblet with shaky hands. "He has been to Wayside—many times. But so far, I have not discovered where he went when he last left. I fear something might have befallen him."

Korl's scowl summed up how Sass felt. She thought of Lira learning not only that she had family she'd never known about, but that the father she'd never known was missing. The part of Sass that loved Lira fiercely and wanted to protect her from any more pain wished desperately that they'd stumbled upon a camp of warring dwarves instead.

Twenty-Three

SASS PUSHED through the swinging doors into the kitchen, as Lira yanked another baking sheet from the oven with more force than was necessary. The metal clanged against the counter as she set it down with obvious irritation.

They had told her about Erindil as soon as they'd returned from the forest, expecting perhaps excitement or curiosity about this mysterious uncle who had been watching over her from afar. Instead, Lira's reaction had been anything but pleased.

"Is this still about your uncle?" Sass asked as she glanced at

Crumpet, who was not taking Lira's agitation in stride. The flutterstoat darted frantically from the copper pots hanging overhead to his perch on the windowsill, then back to the worktable.

"I don't have time for some long-lost uncle," Lira muttered, using her hands to toss the golden crescents from the baking sheet to a serving tray. "The Harvest Festival is in two days, I've got a tavern full of hungry customers, there might be a band of dwarves closing in on you, and now I'm supposed to drop everything because some uncle I've never met pops out of the woods? And even worse, that a father I've never met is missing?"

Sass dodged around her friend's agitated movements, nudging the hand pies into place on the tray. "Everything will be fine, Lira. You've been working on your recipe for the festival, and that's well in hand. There's no sign of dwarves, as of yet. And I know you don't want to hear about him, but Erindil seems nice enough. There are certainly worse uncles to have."

Despite her obvious frustration, Lira glanced up with a raised eyebrow. "Worse how?"

Sass couldn't help but snort out a laugh at the memory that surfaced. "One of my uncles lost an eye wrestling an ice badger when he was drunk on fermented mountain ale. He kept his own eyeball in a jar of spirits by his bed and used to take it out during family dinners to show us young ones. Said it was a 'teaching moment'."

"Did it teach you not to drink?"

"Of course not, but it taught us not to wrestle ice badgers."

Lira's mouth twitched in what might have been the beginning of a smile. But the moment passed quickly, and she returned to aggressively stirring the meat filling that simmered on the stove. "I'd take Uncle GlassEye over one who hides in the woods watching me like some kind of woodland stalker."

Sass leaned in to inhale the savory steam rising from the savory pies. Thank goodness Lira's mood hadn't affected her baking. "I'll take these out to the dining room," Sass said, recognizing that her friend needed space to work through her feelings and she didn't want to be in the line of fire when Lira started waving her spoon and meat filling started flying.

She pushed through the swinging doors and into the great room, pausing for a beat to take in the bustling scene that was such a change from the first night her feet had darkened the threshold. Conversation was a merry hum, interspersed with the thunking of mugs and the scraping of chairs. Vaskel stood at his post behind the bar, pulling pints and flashing wicked grins to the ladies gathered around.

Sass made her way to the chairs by the fire where Korl and Val sat, turning sideways to squeeze through a group of farmers at one table and a band of ogre mercenaries crowding the other.

"Hand pies, fresh from the oven," Sass announced, offering the tray to her friends.

Val looked up from her knitting. "So Lira calmed down?"

Korl grunted and plucked a golden-brown crescent from the tray. "Just because she's baking doesn't mean she's calm."

The orc knew his fiancée well. Although Lira baked to calm herself, it didn't always work. At least not right away.

"Is that why you're out here and not in there?" Val teased him.

He grunted again but didn't answer. The orc was wiser than anyone gave him credit for.

Val took one of the proffered hand pies and grinned at her friend. "Korl knows better than to try to calm down a female."

Korl shot Val a look. "Learned it the hard way."

"And he means hard," Val said. "I might have thrown a few things at him back in the day."

A particularly loud clatter echoed from the kitchen, drawing a few glances before curious patrons returned to their eating and drinking.

"So definitely *not* calmed down," Val mumbled around a bite of meat pie.

"Better check on her." Sass hurried back toward the kitchen

and imagined what chaos she might find. She pushed through the swinging doors just in time to see Lira squatting on the floor beside a fallen baking sheet, half-moon shaped pastries scattered across the floor like bones rolled for chance.

Sass rushed to her friend's side. "Let me help."

Together, they knelt on the crumb-dusted kitchen floor, carefully gathering the hand pies that had escaped the confines of the baking sheet. The pastries were still blazingly hot, and Sass could feel the heat searing her fingertips as she helped collect them, but she didn't complain. The pain seemed minor compared to the defeated slump of Lira's shoulders.

When they had retrieved the last of the scattered pastries, Lira finally looked up, and Sass could see that the anger had burned itself out, leaving behind something more vulnerable and raw.

"Thanks, Sass." Lira's voice barely rose above a whisper. "I know it's ridiculous that I would care this much about a family I never knew, but..." She trailed off, seeming to struggle with how to say what she was feeling.

Sass waited patiently, recognizing that her friend needed to find the words in her own time.

"In a way, I'm still grieving losing my gran," Lira continued, her voice thick. "She was the only family I ever knew, and I thought I'd made peace with that. But now there's this uncle I didn't know existed, and a father who's apparently been wandering the Known Lands for ages and knew about me, but now he's missing and might be..." She sucked in a jerky breath. "I don't know if I can handle grieving someone I've never even met."

Sass's heart clenched at the pain in her friend's voice. Even though her parents weren't dead, she understood loss and grieving for something that was never really yours. She'd been quietly grieving the loss of a future in her homeland since she'd run from it. Sass reached out without hesitation, pulling Lira into a fierce hug.

Lira melted into the embrace, her shoulders softening as she allowed herself to accept the comfort. The unlikely friends stayed like that for several long breaths, surrounded by the coziness of the kitchen and the muffled chaos of the tavern beyond the doors. Soon Sass felt Crumpet's tiny paws as he landed on her shoulder and wrapped his wings around both their heads.

"Thanks, Crump," Lira said through a watery laugh. She pulled back and smiled at both Sass and the flutterstoat balanced on the dwarf's shoulder. "I feel better already."

Before Sass could ask her if she wanted to take a longer break, Iris burst through the kitchen doors, her colorful skirts swirling around her ankles and her silver-streaked curly hair an untamed halo around her head.

"I came as quickly as I could," she announced breathlessly, putting one hand to her waist as if she had a stitch in her side. "What's this I hear about an elf uncle in the woods?"

Twenty-Four

VASKEL SLID a glass of whiskey across the polished bar to Iris and then followed it up with one of his most charming winks—the kind Lira claimed had gotten him into trouble with merchant wives and noble daughters across the Known Lands.

Sass rolled her eyes as she stood beside him, polishing the last of the evening's tankards she'd gathered from the tables. "You realize that flattery won't make the cleaning go any faster, don't you?"

"But it makes the work more pleasant," Vaskel replied with

another grin, his tail swishing behind him as he wiped down the bar's surface.

The dinner rush had finally died down, leaving The Tusk & Tail in that comfortable state of post-service calm that Sass had grown to treasure. The great room still held the lingering aromas of roasted meat and buttery pastry, mixed with the earthy scent of smoldering peat and the sweet tang of ale.

Cali perched on the barstool next to Iris, her golden eyes watchful and her ears twitching at the occasional creak of settling timber, the distant howl of a dire wolf, the soft shuffle of Korl adjusting his position in his chair by the hearth.

Lira emerged from the kitchen, her apron untied and hanging loose around her waist. Her expression had shifted from simmering anger to something approaching calm. "I'm ready to talk."

Cali immediately straightened. "I told Iris about Erindil. I didn't know if it was a secret, but I thought Iris should—"

Lira waved off the apology before Cali could finish. "It's fine. I'm glad Iris knows. I would have told her myself, anyway." She settled onto a barstool next to the apothecary, her green eyes seeking her grandmother's oldest friend. "In fact, I'm hoping she can fill in some of the blanks that Erindil left."

Iris shook her head slowly, her silver-streaked curls quivering. "I can't believe he arrived with an entire traveling party. Although I suppose I shouldn't be surprised. The elves of Lananore were never known for their subtlety."

Lira's eyes narrowed, and Sass could practically see her friend's mind working to piece things together. "What exactly do you know about Erindil? About my father? About any of my elf family?"

Iris took a sip from her glass and sighed deeply, her gaze dropping to study the amber liquid inside.

"Your gran told me that your father wasn't just any elf from Lananore," Iris said finally. "He was from one of the ruling families. Elvish royalty." She took another drink, as if gathering her thoughts or choosing her words before continuing. "Not that it mattered to your gran. Or you. Elves aren't known for welcoming half-bloods into the fold."

Lira flinched at this. Without a word, Korl rose from his chair by the fire and made his way over to them. He stood behind Lira's stool and wrapped one massive arm around her waist from behind, as if offering himself as a buffer for what was to come.

Val followed her friend, slipping onto the barstool next to Cali. When she caught Sass's eye and offered one of her wide smiles, heat prickled Sass's cheeks, and she had to focus intently on the glass she was polishing to avoid dropping it.

"Is that all you know?" Lira asked as she leaned into Korl.

Iris met her gaze squarely, nibbling her lower lip. "I only know what your gran told me, love. And she didn't speak of your father often—or your mother. Too painful."

Iris set down her whiskey and leaned forward. "Your mother was as beautiful as you are, and twice as headstrong. When she met a charming young elf—well, young for their kind—who wove tales of distant lands and elvish magic, she was absolutely smitten. Your gran tried to warn her about elves and how their long lives made them take risks and forget that others didn't have the luxury of immortality." The lines around Iris's eyes deepened. "But young love rarely listens to wisdom, does it? And as quickly as he'd romanced her, sweeping her off her feet with promises and pretty words, he moved on to whatever new adventure called to him next."

Sass gripped the glass she'd been polishing so tightly that her knuckles had gone white, her heart aching for Lira.

"Did he ever know about me?" Lira asked, her voice cracking.

Iris didn't meet her eyes as she nodded, and Sass felt her stomach drop.

"He visited you and your gran once, when you were small." Iris's soft voice fought to be heard over the crackling of the dying fire. "Maybe three or four years old. He wanted to take you back to Lananore, so you could be raised there."

Sass noticed Korl's arm tighten protectively around Lira's waist.

"Obviously, your gran refused," Iris continued, her voice holding unmistakable approval for Elia's choice. "She told him you belonged here, with her, where you'd be loved for who you were rather than judged for what you weren't."

No one spoke or even moved, their group seeming to hold its collective breath as Lira closed her eyes and squeezed them until a single tear escaped from one corner and slipped down her cheek.

"That sounds like Gran," Lira finally whispered.

Iris managed a wavering smile. "And that's all I know, love. As far as your gran ever told me, he never came back. She raised you the way she thought best, and I'd say she did a fine job of it." Then Iris reached for Lira's hand. "I know you have reason to be angry at your gran for all her secrets, but she only ever wanted to protect you. You were a child, and she didn't want you to be hurt."

Lira nodded. "I know she wanted to protect me, and I don't blame her for that. But..."

"You can't live much of a life without getting hurt," Sass said, as if finishing Lira's thought. "A battle axe without nicks has never swung true."

Lira met her eyes and nodded. "I had to go out and get hurt to learn what I needed to learn about life."

Iris released a breath. "But you could only go out into the world as bravely as you did because you'd been raised with love, your gran's unconditional love. Someone believed in you, which meant that you believed in yourself. I don't know if you would have turned out so strong and confident if you'd been surrounded by elves who considered you less than them."

Lira blinked quickly as if banishing tears from her eyes. "You're right. Gran was there for me, and she will always be my family. That doesn't mean I don't want to fill in the blanks about the rest of it." She gave a single nod of her head. "I'll meet with Erindil. I owe him thanks for the tavern, if nothing else. But there's nothing I can tell him that will help find my father. I was too young to remember his visit, and Gran never spoke of him to me."

"I'll go with you to speak to Erindil." Korl's voice was a velvet rumble he whispered in her ear.

She smiled up at him. "Or he can come here. He bought this tavern, after all." She slid her gaze to Sass again. "Besides, I have a favor to ask him."

Sass tilted her head at Lira, familiar with the scheming look on her face. "Aside from the gift of a tavern?"

"Erindil is an elf, right? And elves have powers, correct?"

Everyone nodded, glancing at each other.

"Then maybe my long-lost uncle can use his powers to keep that dwarf search party from finding Sass."

Twenty-Five

"I KNOW I said I wanted to meet him, but how am I supposed to coordinate a meeting with Erindil and finish our preparations for the Harvest Festival?" Lira asked Sass as they made their way down the dirt road toward the village the next morning.

"Maybe you'll meet him at the festival," Sass suggested as they reached the stone bridge. "Erindil mentioned an interest in the celebration. You could do two things at once. One swing of the pickaxe mines the gold *and* creates the tunnel."

Lira gave her a side-eye glance. "Did your mum say that?"

Sass quirked her lips. "That one was from my gran. No one could swing a pickaxe like she could."

Lira shook her head. "I think our grans were very different."

Sass laughed, glad for a distraction from her own gnawing worry. She tried not to think that somewhere out there, possibly getting closer with each passing hour, were Florin and her hunting party. If she didn't love her friends and Wayside so dearly, she would have run already.

A smile tugged at her mouth as they turned the corner and she took in her beloved adopted village. As she knew it would, Wayside was transforming into something magical for the upcoming festival.

Orange and gold pennants fluttered like sun-burnished leaves across the main road, their vibrant colors catching the morning sunlight and casting dancing shadows across the well-worn path. Sass knew it was the skilled handiwork of the village haberdasher.

Perched on the top rungs of ladders, Korl and Val were coordinating their movements to attach more colorful streamers across the fabric awnings that shaded the shop windows. When Val glanced down and caught sight of them, offering a cheerful wave, Sass's face flamed and she waved back perhaps a bit too enthusiastically.

Lira gave her an amused look that suggested she was about to say something when a familiar figure came rushing toward them with arms waving.

"Perfect timing! Perfect, perfect!" Tinpin called out, practically bouncing on his toes as he approached. It was his habit to repeat himself, and even moreso when he was excited. Streamers of green and russet fabric draped around his neck like colorful scarves, and amber and brown fabric pom-poms dangled from his arms like gaudy baubles. "As head of the decor committee, I simply must have your opinions on our look! I simply must!"

Sass glanced at Lira, who leaned close enough to whisper, "He's the only member of the committee. He created it himself."

Both Sass and Lira assured the gnome haberdasher that the decorations looked absolutely splendid and were perfect for a festival to celebrate the end of the summer and the harkening of autumn. His beaming smile and enthusiastic hand-rubbing suggested that they'd said precisely the right things.

"Excellent, excellent! I knew my instincts were spot on about the warmer palette. I just knew it." He absently fluffed one of the fabric pom-poms. "Now, if you'll excuse me, I must oversee the installation of the remaining streamers. The symmetry is crucial. Absolutely crucial."

He bustled off, leaving Sass and Lira shaking their heads as they continued through the bustling village.

Near the cheese shop, they spotted Fenni setting up a wooden table outside his establishment. The finely dressed halfling was stacking wheels of cheese as if he was crafting an elaborate wedding cake with bunches of fresh herbs adorning the tiers like flowers.

"Are you partnering with the beekeeper again for special cheese and honey pairings?" Sass called out, remembering the successful collaboration from Night Faires.

Fenni's face lit up at the question. "Indeed, I am! She's created a special whipped pumpkin honey butter that pairs beautifully with one of my new Elmshire farm cheeses. The sweetness of the pumpkin and honey complements the sharp, nutty flavor of the aged cheese perfectly."

Lira's eyes brightened, and she touched a hand to her stomach. "Save some for us to try."

"Consider it done," Fenni assured them with a courtly bow. "And what culinary delights are you preparing for the festival? I heard rumors you've been experimenting with something special."

"It's a surprise," Lira said with a mysterious smile.

Fenni nodded knowingly and gestured toward his brother's bakery, where the windows were opaque with steam. "Just like Pip. He's been working all night on his festival creation. I haven't seen him this excited about a new recipe since he came up with his lemon sweet rolls."

"Something other than the pumpkin sweet rolls?" Lira asked.

Fenni rolled his eyes dramatically. "That's what he says, but he'll say only that."

Sass's stomach rumbled audibly as the most delectable aromas seeped from the bakery—yeast and sugar, cinnamon and vanilla, and something she couldn't place but that made her mouth water instantly. She made a mental note to visit Pip first thing when the festival officially started.

Lira nudged Sass, drawing her gaze to a familiar figure setting up luminaries along the road. Durn, the former barkeep and owner of The Tusk & Tail, was working alongside a petite gnome with lavender hair, the village chandler and his new wife, Penny.

"More evidence that you're indispensable to the village," Lira said under her breath as they waved at the couple that Sass had worked her matchmaking skills on.

Durn waved back with a grin wider than Sass had ever seen him wear during his days behind the tavern bar. The transformation was remarkable. Once he'd been surly and defeated, gnarled and bent by grief. Now he practically glowed with happiness and purpose as he helped Penny set out her beautiful, hand-cut luminaries for the festival.

"It's amazing how love can transform a person, isn't it?" Lira observed. No doubt the woman was also thinking about how her own life had changed when she found love with the shy orc guardsman.

But Sass was only half-listening to her friend's musings. A flash of something all too familiar caught her attention from the corner of her eye—the back of a squat figure ducking down a narrow alley just beyond the potter's workshop.

She could have sworn she'd left Thrain sleeping soundly in his room above the tavern, snoring loudly enough to wake the dead.

So what was he doing sneaking around the village like he had something to hide?

As her mind began racing through unpleasant possibilities, Sass felt her chest tighten with a cold knot of dread. Either her best friend from home was keeping secrets from her—which would be completely unlike the dwarf she'd known since childhood—or that figure hadn't been Thrain at all.

One thing she knew for certain was that she'd just spotted a dwarf. Could Florin's advance scouts have found her already? Was her former fiancée's hunting party closer than she'd dared to imagine?

Lost in her roiling thoughts, Sass didn't notice the hand reach for her arm from behind until it was too late.

Twenty-Six

THE SCREAM WAS ALREADY FORMING in Sass's throat when she recognized the familiar interior of the apothecary shop. She breathed in bergamot and lavender as the cool hush enveloped her and the heavy door swung shut behind her and Lira.

Sass spun around to see the apothecary and then pressed a hand to her chest, trying to slow her galloping heart. "Sweet simmering cauldrons, Iris! You nearly scared the life out of me."

Iris glanced behind them at the shop's darkened windows, muttering apologies under her breath. "I didn't mean to frighten you, pet, but I didn't want to draw attention by calling out in the street."

Lira looked like she was working to calm her own racing heart, her green eyes still wide from the shock of being suddenly yanked from the idyllic festival preparations. "Then maybe next time you shouldn't abduct people from the sidewalk."

Iris laughed the accusation away with a dismissive flap of her hand, the bangles on her wrist chiming. "Oh, love, if I were kidnapping you, you'd never have seen me coming." She gestured for them to follow her toward the back room. "Now come along, both of you. We have important matters to discuss."

They hesitated at the threshold, exchanging uncertain glances, when Cali's distinctive feline face appeared through the gap in the heavy curtain that separated the front shop from Iris's private domain.

"Hurry," the Pantheri urged. "You're going to want to see this."

Sass and Lira exchanged another wary look but followed Iris through the curtain.

Overhead, the bookwyrms fluttered in lazy circles, and the air smelled less of potions and more of chamomile and book dust, with just a hint of the almond cookies that Iris nibbled while she read.

"Why are you and Cali being so secretive?" Lira asked, sinking into one of the overstuffed chairs tucked in the corner of the room. "Is this about what you're planning for the Harvest Festival?"

Iris chuckled as she moved to retrieve the kettle, her turquoise skirt swishing. "Well, even though I rarely set out wares for the Night Faires, I am planning to have a table for the Harvest Festival. Folks always want healing tinctures and warming draughts once the nights grow longer and the shadows deepen." She paused in her tea pouring to fix them with a significant look. "But that's not why I pulled you in here."

"Then is this about Lira's uncle?" Sass asked, eyeing Cali's self-satisfied grin.

Iris shook her head. "No, although I admit I'm intensely curious to learn more about this mysterious Erindil." Her expression grew more serious as she turned to face them fully, bringing the kettle with her and spilling tea in the saucer of one of the flowery teacups. "No, this is about protecting Sass."

Sass opened her mouth in surprise. She'd been touched when Iris had given her some herbs for luck, but she'd thought that would be the extent of it.

Lira sat forward in her chair. "Korl and Val are on high alert, and so is Vaskel. Between the three of them, no one's getting to Sass without being stopped." She nodded toward Cali. "And no one can shoot as straight as our archer here."

Cali preened at the compliment, twirling one side of her whiskers with obvious pleasure. "I have excellent aim."

Iris nodded briskly as she handed out teacups. "All of that is well and good, and I'm glad to know we have such capable defenders. But that assumes we'll see the dwarves coming." She turned to fix Sass with an intense stare. "You said this Florin is skilled in battle and always gets what she wants, correct?"

Sass nodded reluctantly, her stomach twisting at the memory of her former fiancée. Florin Trollbane had always been like a force of nature—beautiful, terrible, and utterly relentless in pursuit of whatever she desired. The thought of that focused determination being turned toward hunting her made Sass feel slightly queasy.

"Then we can't assume she'll play fair or announce her arrival with trumpets and banners." Iris brought her own teacup to her lips and blew on the steaming contents. "Someone that determined and resourceful will likely try stealth and surprise rather than a direct assault."

Sass wasn't sure she agreed. Dwarves rarely bothered with stealth. But Iris was right that Florin was more strategic than your average dwarf.

Iris took a sip of tea, winced from the heat of it, and put the cup and saucer down on a stack of books. She moved to one of the many shelves that lined the room, her fingers searching among the various leather-bound tomes until she pulled out a battered one. She flipped it open and retrieved something wedged between the brittle pages, and when she turned back to them, she was holding a small silver ring.

"This might help even the score," she said, extending the ring toward Sass.

They all leaned closer to examine the delicate piece of jewelry. It was clearly masterly crafted and engraved with intricate patterns that seemed to catch the light, but it appeared to be just a ring.

"This is from the days when I ran with Lira's gran and worked as a rogue," Iris explained. "An elf gave it to me after my quick thinking saved him from a band of trolls who'd been terrorizing the passes in the Riddle Vales. Nasty creatures, trolls." She grimaced. "Absolutely no sense of personal hygiene."

"What does it do?" Lira asked, reaching out to touch the ring with one careful finger.

Iris handed it directly to Sass, who was surprised by how warm the metal felt against her skin. "Put it on, love. It's sized for slender elf fingers, but it might fit your pinky finger."

Sass ignored the slight on her pudgy hands and slid the ring over her smallest finger, only jamming it a bit to get it over the knuckle. The metal seemed to adjust itself to her finger, and the warmth that radiated from it was oddly comforting.

"This ring was forged by a renowned crafter in Lananore using a special metal imbued with powers I honestly don't understand," Iris explained, retrieving her teacup and taking another sip. "All I know for certain is that it will prickle noticeably when hostile intent is directed at the wearer. Think of it as an early warning system against dwarf search parties."

Lira clinked her cup back onto its saucer. "Why have you never told me about this before? How did I not know you had a magic ring all this time?"

Iris's cheeks flushed pink, and she kept her eyes on her tea. "It's not exactly magic, love. It can't ward away danger or help you eliminate it. It's more like enhanced intuition. And it will only warn you if the threat is yours. So if someone else is threatened, the ring won't prickle even if you're standing next to them." She released a sigh. "And to be completely honest, I thought I'd lost it years ago."

Lira's eyes widened even further. "You misplaced an enchanted ring?"

"It's tiny." Iris's voice took on a defensive tone. "I'd put it away for safekeeping when magic items became unfashionable and dangerous to own. The problem was that I outsmarted myself and hid it so well that I couldn't remember where I'd put it."

Sass and Lira both glanced around the back room, which was in a constant state of what could charitably be called a delightful muddle.

"I turned this place upside down searching for it when you first arrived and were worried about Rygor," Iris continued. "Spent weeks going through every shelf and every hiding place imaginable. Finally found it a few days ago tucked inside a book that I hadn't opened in ages, which was why it was such a good hiding spot, of course."

Sass honestly couldn't see how anyone could tell if the place had been searched or not. It looked like a whirlwind had blown through it on the best of days.

"The point is that I found it, and now Sass can be alerted to danger before it arrives," Iris said firmly and drained the last of her tea.

Lira examined the ring on Sass's finger. "I have to admit, that makes me feel considerably better about everything. I was worried that the merriment of the Harvest Festival would provide perfect cover for a dwarf search party."

Cali crossed her arms over her chest with satisfaction. "Well, now we're ready to defend Sass, plus we have a magical early warning system. I'd say we're as prepared as we can be."

Sass looked down at the ring, which felt comfortable on her

finger but showed no signs of the prickling sensation Iris had described. Maybe she'd been wrong about the figure she'd thought she'd seen earlier. Maybe her nerves were just getting the better of her, and that hadn't been a dwarf at all. If Florin really was nearby, surely the ring would have reacted by now.

For the first time in days, Sass released an easy breath. Her finger wasn't pricking, but a spark of hope fluttered to life in her chest.

Twenty-Seven

SASS STOOD before the small mirror that hung on the wall of her room above The Tusk & Tail, tugging nervously at the neckline of her new dress. The burgundy velvet felt impossibly luxurious against her skin, so different from the practical wool and linen garments she'd worn her entire life. In the Ice Lands, fashion was linked closely to survival. Dwarf garments were layers upon layers of heavy wool, leather, and fur designed to keep the bitter mountain cold from seeping into your bones.

This dress was the opposite of all that. Where her dwarf

clothing had covered every inch of skin, this gown featured a low neckline and a skirt gathered high on one side, revealing far more leg than she'd ever shown.

"Sweet simmering cauldrons," she muttered to her reflection.

When Tinpin had insisted on designing the dress for her, she'd trusted his expertise. The gnome haberdasher had an eye for fashion, but seeing herself in the finished product, she wondered if Tin had gotten a bit carried away.

"The burgundy will complement your brown hair and skin beautifully, absolutely beautifully," Tin had said during the fitting, his nimble fingers adjusting the drape of the skirt. "And this cut will make your legs look longer. Much longer. We vertically challenged folk need to use all the tricks of the trade, don't we?" He'd winked at her conspiratorially, his pointed ears twitching as he'd tucked and pinned.

At the time, his enthusiasm had been infectious. Now, staring at herself in the mirror, Sass felt like a child playing dress-up. She'd spent most of her life trying to blend into the background and not look like a princess.

She ran her hands over the fabric. "So much for that plan."

Her gaze snagged on the silver ring circling her pinky finger, and she spun it with the pad of her thumb, grateful that it remained warm but showed no signs of the prickling sensation Iris had described. The lack of warning gave her hope that perhaps Florin really was still far away, that maybe she'd have this one perfect evening before her past came crashing back into her carefully constructed new life.

Her plan for her one perfect evening was simple. She was going to find Val and finally tell her how she really felt. No more hiding behind knitting lessons.

The problem was that despite Lira's confidence, Sass still wasn't entirely convinced that Val saw her as anything more than a good friend. The guard was kind to everyone, charming and amiable with all the tavern's regulars. What if the smiles and winks that made Sass's knees weak were just Val's way?

She shook her head and scowled at herself in the mirror. Life was too short and too uncertain to waste time being afraid. If finding her heart's home in Wayside had taught her anything, it was that happiness was something you had to work for, something you had to be brave enough to reach for even when you weren't sure you deserved it.

A soft knock on the door interrupted her thoughts, and she expected to see Thrain's bearded face appear. Her dwarf friend had been strangely absent all day, although he had never been one for rousing early.

Instead, Lira peeked around the door, her eyes immediately widening as she took in Sass's appearance. She stepped fully into the room and closed the door behind her. "Sass, you look absolutely stunning."

"Go on with you. You don't think it's too much?" Sass asked, smoothing her hands over the rich fabric and trying to ignore her hot cheeks.

"Are you kidding?" Lira moved to sit on what had once been her own bed, the floral coverlet making it look like she was cocooned inside a giant yellow rose. "You look like a queen. A very sexy, very confident queen who's about to sweep a certain guard off her feet."

If it were possible for Sass's cheeks to flame hotter, they did. She sat down beside her friend, the skirt pooling around her.

"I sometimes miss sharing a room with you," Lira said softly, reaching over to take Sass's hand. "Even though I absolutely adore Korl and love having our own space, there was something special about those early days when we were just two lost souls trying to figure it all out together."

Sass linked her fingers with Lira's. "I miss it too, but I couldn't be happier that you found your person. Korl adores you, and watching you two together makes me believe that there's someone perfect for everyone out there."

Lira's eyes glistened. "And Val won't be able to resist you in that dress. Trust me, no one could look at you right now and want to be just friends."

Sass laughed despite her nerves. "I didn't get this dress just for Val."

Lira's brows lifted. "Didn't you?"

Sass groaned. "Ugh. How do you know me so well?"

The woman twitched one shoulder. "I'd do the same thing."

Sass gave her friend a small shove with her shoulder. "Korl wouldn't think you were any less beautiful if you wore a flour sack."

Lira laughed. "Just promise me you won't be so busy with Val that you forget to help at our table. With so many ladies wearing their best dresses, I can't rely on Vaskel not to wander off if he spots a pretty face in the crowd."

The sound of music drifting in through the open window made both women turn. The Harvest Festival was beginning, and somewhere below them, the village was coming alive.

"You can count on me," Sass promised, standing and smoothing down her skirt one final time.

Lira opened the door, and they both stopped, mouths falling open as Thrain stood just outside.

"What...?" Sass started to ask before the words died on her lips.

"That haberdasher," Thrain grumbled, looking down at the head-to-toe orange outfit that encased his stocky frame. "He insisted I needed a special outfit for the occasion, said my clothes were giving mountain grunge."

Mountain grunge? Lira mouthed to Sass as she clearly attempted to suppress a laugh.

"You let Tin dress you?" Sass couldn't take her eyes off the dwarf. Or maybe it was the orange ascot she couldn't stop staring at.

Thrain grunted. "He made it sound like everyone would dress for the occasion, and this outfit would make me look splendid. "

Lira stepped forward and looped an arm through his. "Well, I think you do look splendid. The haberdasher was right, of course. Folks are dressing for the occasion." She jerked a thumb at Sass. "Just look at your friend."

Thrain mumbled something about Sass not looking like a walking pumpkin, but Lira had spun him around and was steering him toward the stairs, giving Sass an amused look over her shoulder.

Sass shook her head and followed, her shoulders shaking. She brushed the ring again. No prickling. Maybe this was going to be her night after all.

Twenty-Eight

"YOU'RE sure you don't mind?" Sass asked Vaskel and Lira, who were busy arranging the tavern's display table underneath the swinging wooden Tusk & Tail sign. Steam rose from the copper pot of chai that Vaskel was ladling into ceramic mugs, while Lira's apple crumble bars sat in neat rows on wooden boards, their bumpy tops burnished brown.

"I promise it will be a quick spin around the village to see what everyone's displaying," she added. "For Thrain's sake."

Lira waved a hand at her, more focused on her display than on Sass. "Go, so you can hurry back!"

Thrain nudged her with his elbow as they walked away. "You just want to get some of whatever that halfling baker is selling."

Sass laughed, feeling lighter than she had in days. "You know me too well. There's no point pretending I have any willpower when it comes to Pip's creations."

The golden sunset painted Wayside in balmy stripes of amber as Sass and Thrain made their way from The Tusk & Tail toward the heart of the village. The usual sounds of a work day ending— the clink of hammer on anvil from the blacksmith, the creak of wagon wheels over dirt, the calls of merchants hawking their remaining wares at the market—had been replaced by music drifting on the evening breeze, the bright laughter of children, and the eager chatter of villagers.

Wayside didn't just sound different; it smelled different too. Sass was accustomed to the scent of yeast billowing from Pip's bakery, but now that mingled with sugar so pungent she was surprised she couldn't see frothy clouds of it bobbing overhead.

As they walked, Sass twirled the enchanted ring with her thumb. The metal remained warm, giving no sign of prickling. For the first time since Thrain had arrived with news of Florin's search party, Sass felt like she could actually enjoy herself.

She waved at Vorto and Klaff, who were setting up a horseshoe toss game outside their workshop. Children were already milling about and eyeing the whistles that the orcs had crafted to look like ears of corn.

"Wouldn't mind trying my hand at that later," Thrain said, even though Sass didn't let them stop. Not yet. Not until they'd eaten.

They'd barely made it to the shops when Pip spotted them and began waving enthusiastically from behind his festival table. The baker was practically bouncing with excitement, his dough-smudged apron tied tight around his middle as he gestured for them to come over.

"Bless the stars!" he cried. "I hoped you'd visit before I got too busy. I have a new creation you must try."

Sass needed no more convincing than that. She recognized the baskets of pumpkin cinnamon sweet rolls he'd been perfecting, the golden glaze as shiny as glass. But the tray next to them held something new. The brown, bumpy cookies didn't look as decadent as his rolls, but they smelled divine.

Sass leaned down and breathed in the sweet aroma surrounding them. "Hells and cinders, they smell good!"

Pip's eyes twinkled with pride as he leaned forward conspiratorially. "Brown butter pumpkin cookies with a dash of oats," he whispered, cupping his hand around his mouth as if sharing heavily guarded secrets. "They taste even better than they smell."

Sass felt her enthusiasm falter slightly at the mention of oats. In the Ice Lands, oats were not prized for cooking. Beside her, Thrain wrinkled his large nose.

"Oats?" Thrain's question carried the tone of someone who'd just been offered gruel for dinner.

"Trust me," Pip said. "Just try one. I guarantee you'll change your mind about oats forever."

Despite their reservations, they each accepted a cookie from Pip's outstretched hands. The moment Sass bit into hers, she couldn't suppress the moan of pure pleasure that escaped her lips. It was crispy on the outside with a tender, chewy center that melted on her tongue. She didn't even mind the oats. Hells, she was so busy savoring the buttery sweetness, she'd forgotten all about them.

Thrain's expression of skepticism melted into one of blissful surrender as he chewed. "Grognick's beard," he mumbled through his mouthful, "this is incredible. How do you make oats taste like this?"

"Elmshire secrets." Pip puffed out his chest with pride.

"Though I will say that browning the butter makes all the difference."

Sass immediately purchased a bag of the cookies to share with Lira and Vaskel, but she and Thrain had almost devoured their pumpkin sweet rolls before they walked away.

They continued their stroll through the festival, waving to Fenni who was deep in animated conversation with the sprite beekeeper at their shared table. The tiny, winged woman kept fluttering her gossamer wings and levitating above the cheese and honey display, which was probably why the halfling had one hand on her foot.

Durn nodded at Sass as he stood beside his wife outside their chandler shop, their table filled with candles carved to look like apples and pumpkins. Even the potter, who rarely emerged from his store, had set up a large basin for apple bobbing with a line curving past the tinker shop that was now Korl's.

Even though she knew the orc was not planning on having a display, Sass couldn't help glancing at the darkened storefront, hoping to see Val inside with Korl. But neither guard was there, and Sass looked toward the market stalls hoping to glimpse the blonde head above the rest of the crowd.

One good thing about Val—she was usually easy to spot. But Sass didn't see her anywhere.

Tinpin had positioned himself strategically near the village center, handing out streamers on wooden sticks in brilliant shades of orange and gold for children to wave. He'd donned a vest of emerald velvet over a shirt of burnished copper, with a cravat that seemed to shift color from amber to rust in the changing light.

"Thrain!" Tin called out as they passed. "You look splendid, absolutely splendid."

Thrain grunted, unable to respond with a mouth full of sticky sweet roll, but Sass gave the haberdasher a thumbs up.

"You can't tell him you feel like a walking pumpkin," Sass said from one side of her mouth. "He'll be devastated."

"How do you think the walking pumpkin feels?" Thrain muttered in response but threw a wave to Tin.

They passed Iris's table, where the apothecary was selling healing herb bundles and warming draughts for the coming winter. Several ladies were gathered around her, but she caught sight of Sass over their heads and winked, her gaze dropping to the ring on Sass's finger. Sass waved back with her ring hand, feeling a rush of gratitude that Iris had found the ring and given it to her.

Near the stone monument in the village center, Cali had set up an archery demonstration, shooting arrows with deadly precision at apples perched on wooden stakes. A small crowd had gathered to watch the Pantheri's impressive skills, gasping and applauding with each perfect shot.

Sass paused to admire her friend's ability to split an apple clean in half from thirty paces. While she watched, Thrain wandered over to an unfamiliar gnome woman with curly golden hair who was selling bottles from the back of an enclosed wagon. Wayside's festivals were beginning to draw traveling vendors, which was surely a good sign.

When the dwarf wandered back and offered Sass a sip of the apple brandy, she declined with a shake of her head. "I want to keep my wits about me tonight."

What she really meant was that she hadn't spotted Val yet and wanted to be fully present when she finally worked up the courage to tell the woman how she felt.

"We'd better head back and help Lira," she said when she glimpsed Vaskel at Iris's table. She wasn't sure if he was there for the healing remedies or the apothecary herself, but she wouldn't put it past the Hellkin to multitask.

The festival was reaching full swing now, with more people arriving from neighboring villages and the music growing louder and more festive.

"I understand why you don't want to leave Wayside," Thrain said quietly as they walked back toward The Tusk & Tail and munched on Pip's addictive cookies. "This place has become your home in a way that the Ice Lands never was, hasn't it?"

Sass's chest tightened at the wistful tone in her friend's voice. It was true, but she hated to remind Thrain that she wouldn't be returning with him. She was saved from finding the right words by their arrival back at Lira's table.

Sass held out the bag of cookies. "Pip's latest creation. They have oats in them, but don't let that fool you. They're delicious."

But Lira wasn't looking at the cookies. Her attention was fixed on the bottle of apple brandy that Thrain was casually sipping from, and her wide eyes held something that looked suspiciously like alarm.

Vaskel had wandered back, although he carried no wares from the apothecary, and the Hellkin's gaze sharpened when he spotted the bottle in Thrain's hand.

"Where did you get that?" Vaskel asked, his voice a velvet rasp that made the hairs on the back of Sass's neck stand at attention.

Twenty-Nine

THRAIN WENT STILL mid-gulp as Lira and Vaskel goggled at the apple brandy in his hand. After a few moments of undignified coughing and spluttering, he finally swallowed the mouthful and jerked a thumb behind him toward the village center.

"Gnome lady was selling them by the village square." His voice was hoarse from coughing. "Out of the back of a traveling wagon."

Lira and Vaskel exchanged a speaking look, and Sass nervously twisted the ring around her little finger. Why were they so interested in a gnome selling home-brewed brandy?

Lira shook her head. "It can't be."

Without a word of explanation, Vaskel reached over and plucked the bottle from Thrain's grasp, ignoring the dwarf's blustery protests. The Hellkin brought the bottle to his nose and inhaled deeply.

Sass wondered that the brandy vapors didn't singe his eyebrows since she could smell the home-brewed booze from where she stood, but Vaskel only grinned.

He handed the bottle back to a still-spluttering Thrain and turned to Lira. "Who else could it be?"

Sass glanced down at her ring, searching for any sign of prickling. The silver band remained quiet against her skin, which meant either there wasn't any threat or the ring didn't work.

"Watch the table for a bit," Lira said to Sass, already grabbing Vaskel's sleeve and pulling him with her.

Then they were off, hurrying toward the village center and presumably the brandy merchant. Sass stared after them for a moment before her own curiosity got the better of her.

"Take over for me," she said to Thrain as she backed away. "Two bits for an apple crumble bar, half a bit for chai!"

Thrain stood at the table looking bewildered by the sudden abandonment. "What? But where...?"

She didn't linger to hear the rest of his question or answer it, her shorter legs working overtime to catch up to Lira and Vaskel. By the time she reached her friends, they were almost to the stone monument and had slowed to scan the festival crowd.

Cali, who'd been demonstrating her archery skills to a group of clapping children, stopped mid-draw when the trio rushed past her. "What's going on?"

Vaskel threw two words over his shoulder without slowing down: "Apple brandy."

The effect on Cali was immediate. Her ears flattened, her whiskers twitched, and for a moment she simply stared after them.

Then she was moving, abandoning her demonstration to jog after them, with her bow still clutched in one hand.

They finally came to a halt in front of a plump gnome woman with curly hair and a pink cap whose long point sagged to one side. She sat on the back step of an enclosed wooden cart that must have once been brightly painted, as Sass could make out the sun-faded shapes of formerly red apples on the sides. Bottles of amber liquid were neatly arranged on a small table abutting the wagon, and the gnome had an open one tucked close to her hip.

She eyed their group, then broke into a bright smile. Without turning around, the gnome called over her shoulder and through the wagon's slightly open door.

"Rog! Your friends are here!"

There was a moment of quiet and then rattling from inside the wagon. A gnome with a spectacular blue beard that matched his equally blue hair poked his head out the wooden door. His frown was laden with suspicion until he spotted who was waiting for him.

"There you are!" He stepped fully from the cart with short arms spread wide. "I knew I'd find you!"

Lira, Vaskel, and Cali stood frozen for several beats, mouths open as if they weren't sure if they could believe their own eyes. Sass wasn't sure who the gnome was to them, but their expressions told her they were both shocked and relieved.

"Aren't you going to greet your old crew mate?" Rog asked with obvious amusement, bounding down the steps of the wagon and walking toward them on the balls of his feet in a way that reminded Sass of Pip when he was excited about a new recipe.

Lira was the first to break from the spell, rushing forward and bending down so she could throw her arms around the gnome with such enthusiasm that she nearly knocked him over. Cali joined the embrace a moment later, her tail curling around Lira and the gnome.

When they both finally pulled back, wiping at their eyes, Vaskel strode forward and yanked Rog into a fierce hug that he finished with a brusque thump on the gnome's back.

"Glad to see you're still breathing," Vaskel said gruffly. "Wasn't sure I'd ever see you again after everything went to hells. You know I've been looking for you, right?"

"I heard you were looking." Rog's smile faded, and his face clouded. "I also got word about Pirrin, so I figured it was time to find what was left of my crew before we were next." He glanced meaningfully at the lady gnome behind the table. "Figured it was also time you met my better half."

All eyes turned to the female gnome, who wore a knowing smile that suggested she'd heard many stories about her husband's crew.

"This is my wife, Rosie," Rog said, his voice carrying such obvious pride and affection that it made Sass's heart squeeze. "The most talented distiller in three kingdoms and the love of my life."

Lira stepped forward and took the woman's hand. "Rosie! Rog talked about nothing but you when we were running together. Well," she added with a grin, "you and your apple brandy."

Vaskel chuckled. "We always knew when it was time for a break when Rog's brandy stash ran low."

"It wasn't only the brandy I missed." Rog slipped an arm around his wife's waist and pulled her close. "I can't get enough of my Rosie or her apple brandy. I'm lucky she ever agreed to marry me."

Rosie laughed and swatted playfully at her husband's arm. "Flatterer. As if I could have resisted that blue beard of yours forever."

As Lira asked Rog to catch them up on what he'd been doing and how he'd tracked them down, Sass wondered just how many long-lost companions were going to end up in Wayside. At this rate, the village would need to charge admission to what was clearly becoming the most popular reunion destination in the Known Lands.

Not that Sass minded the arrival of long-lost friends and family. She gave her ring another absentminded twist. As long as that didn't include former fiancées with a penchant for bloodshed.

Thirty

SASS'S FEET throbbed something fierce, and she shifted her weight from foot to foot as the Harvest Festival wound down. She and Lira had sold every apple crumble bar from their table, and they'd regretfully consumed all of Pip's magnificent brown butter pumpkin cookies.

The festival atmosphere had mellowed, and the music had shifted from lively dance tunes to slower melodies that seemed to encourage quiet conversations and fond farewells. Rog and Rosie had repositioned their painted wagon outside The Tusk & Tail earlier, setting up their apple brandy display alongside Sass and Lira's table. The arrangement had been a stroke of genius because the apple brandy paired perfectly with the apple crumble bars, and the constant stream of customers had kept everyone busy.

For the past hour, Vaskel, Thrain, and Rog had been passing a bottle of Rosie's finest apple brandy between the three of them, their voices growing increasingly animated as they exchanged stories. After winning one of Vorto and Klaff's iron whistles at the horseshoe toss, Thrain had regaled everyone with tales of life beneath the mountains in the Ice Lands while Vaskel and Rog countered with increasingly embellished accounts of their adventuring days, each tale growing more outrageous with every swig of brandy.

"And then the forest troll—easily the size of a small tree— charged just as Lira was trying to pick the lock on the treasure chest and Pirrin was defending her back," Rog stroked his blue beard as he leaned forward. "But did our ranger panic? Not a bit! He fought off the troll, and Lira got us the treasure."

Lira rolled her eyes and leaned closer to Sass. "They're exaggerating. The troll was barely bigger than a sapling, and the treasure was pixie gold, which meant it was worthless."

Rosie caught the comment and winked at them both. "Rog never met a tall tale he couldn't make taller. By the time he's done telling it, that troll will be big enough to level kingdoms."

Cali had returned to her archery demonstration after the reunion, but she'd promised to help Iris pack up her table of healing remedies once the festival was over. True to her suspicions, the apothecary had done a brisk business peddling tonics and draughts for the coming darker months.

Despite staying busy and meeting the last member of Lira's crew, Sass was very aware that she hadn't laid eyes on Val the entire night. She'd been trying not to feel disappointed, but the absence was weighing on her like pockets filled with rune stones. All her careful planning, the beautiful dress, and the courage she'd mustered felt wasted.

It was Lira who finally voiced what Sass had been thinking. "I'm starting to worry about Korl. He wasn't planning to have a table set up for his tinker work, but I'd hoped he would come help me with ours. He said that he and Val had something to do before I left for the tavern earlier, but I didn't expect him to miss the entire festival."

Sass sighed. "Once a guardsman, always a guardsman, I suppose. Duty before festivals."

Rosie, who'd been listening while she counted the evening's coins, cocked her head. "Maybe it has something to do with the dwarves we passed on our way to Wayside. The ones that were staying well off the main road and trying very hard not to attract attention."

Rog nodded vigorously, his cap bobbing. "I'm used to spotting folks who are trying to hide, and these dwarves were trying their best not to be noticed. As much as any dwarf can be subtle." He cut an apologetic look at Thrain. "No offense intended."

Their small group swiveled their gazes to the gnome couple at the casual way they'd mentioned dwarves lurking near Wayside.

"Dwarves?" Sass asked, her voice coming out as more of a squeak than she'd intended. "You're absolutely sure it was dwarves?"

Rog chuckled and tipped his head toward Thrain with obvious amusement. "As sure as I know he's a dwarf. Beards like that don't grow on halflings, after all."

Lira shot Sass a concerned look, and as if summoned by their growing alarm, Sass's ring prickled ever so faintly against her finger. The sensation was barely more than a whisper of warning, but it was there. She pressed her thumb against the silver band as her heart seized.

Before Sass could tell Lira or Vaskel, Korl and Val strode up to them. They were fully decked out in their guard armor, and nothing about their demeanor matched the lighthearted atmosphere of the rest of the village.

"Where have you been?" Lira asked Korl, an edge creeping into her voice that Sass rarely heard. "I thought something had happened to you."

Korl cleared his throat, but it was Val who stepped forward to answer. Even though Korl had come out of his shell a bit since finding Lira, speaking for the both of them was a habit Val hadn't completely broken.

"We wanted to go see Erindil again. Korl thought it would be better to arrange a proper time for him to meet you rather than leaving it to chance."

Korl nodded earnestly. "I didn't think you'd want to be surprised by a relative you've never met appearing in the middle of the festival."

Lira's pinched expression softened. "That was very thoughtful of you. I was worried about exactly that scenario." She glanced around at the last villagers meandering along the road. "Since I haven't seen any mysterious elves wandering around tonight, I assume he agreed to wait to meet me properly?"

Korl and Val exchanged one of those loaded looks that made Sass's stomach drop. The ring on her finger prickled more intensely, as if responding to the look itself.

Korl frowned as he spoke. "He wasn't there."

"The entire campsite was empty, and it looked like they'd left in a hurry," Val added.

Lira's face fell. "He left without meeting me? But why would he go to all the trouble of buying me a tavern, returning to talk to me, and then leaving before we could even meet?"

Korl stepped forward and took her hand in his massive ones, his voice gentle but firm. "Val and I did a thorough search of the area. We don't think Erindil packed up and left voluntarily."

Val shook her head grimly. "The way they left the campsite, I'd say they were chased off. Hastily abandoned meals, scattered belongings, lavender feathers floating in the air. Ernidil was way too priss...I mean proper, to leave like that."

Korl glanced furtively at Sass. "And based on the tracks we found, there's strong evidence that dwarves are the reason they left."

Thrain jumped to his feet with such haste that he nearly knocked over the bottle of apple brandy, while Vaskel's entire body went rigid. Fear made Sass go cold all over, and she had to lean heavily on the table to keep from falling as her knees threatened to give out. The ring was prickling insistently now, and she wanted to rip the hot metal off her finger.

Rog produced a wicked-looking dagger from seemingly nowhere and let out a gravelly chuckle. "I don't know what this is all about, but it sounds like I got here just in time for our crew to take care of business again."

Thirty-One

SASS PUSHED through the kitchen doors with an empty basket, grateful that the festival was over. Despite the unexpected arrival of Rog and Rosie, the event had been a success for everyone. All the apple crumble bars had been sold, every drop of spicy chai had been consumed, and the villagers had enjoyed playing games and celebrating the end of the warm season and the coming of cooler weather. Even Sass, who'd fled frigid lands, was eagerly anticipating the cozier season with its roaring fires, hot apple cider, and more pumpkin delicacies baked by Pip.

In the corner of the counter, Crumpet stirred from his makeshift bed of Lira's softest dishcloths. The flutterstoat lifted his head sleepily, his whiskers twitching. Instead of chittering at the intrusion, he simply curled into a tighter ball, tucking his white tail around himself like a fluffy stole and drifting back to sleep.

"Sorry, Crump," Lira whispered as she entered behind Sass and set another empty basket on the wooden worktable. "Didn't mean to wake you."

Sass almost laughed at the tender way Lira addressed the magical creature, but the sound caught in her throat as she gazed at Crumpet. Was she jealous of his peaceful sleep and simple existence?

"We can leave all the clean-up until tomorrow," Lira said as she turned to leave the kitchen and then paused, glancing back at Sass. "You okay?"

"Why wouldn't I be? I only have a band of dwarves searching for me so they can force me to return home."

"We won't let that happen," Lira said firmly as she wrapped Sass in a tight hug. "I promise you that."

Sass felt some of the tension leave her shoulders, but she couldn't silence the voice of doubt that had been her constant companion since Thrain's arrival. "You don't know Florin," she said, her words muffled against Lira's shoulder. "You don't know what she's capable of when someone crosses her."

Lira pulled back, keeping her hands on Sass's shoulders and holding her at arm's length. "Florin hasn't dealt with my crew before," she said, and there was steel in her voice that reminded Sass that her friend had once been a rogue who'd roamed The Known Lands and operated on the dangerous fringes of society. "The crew I ran with is my family. Now you're part of that, and no one messes with our family."

The happiness that fizzed through Sass's chest at those words was almost overwhelming, but before she could respond, Lira's fierce expression morphed into a grin that transformed her entire face. "Besides, you've got lots of bodyguards tonight. Even a band of dwarves won't be able to get through all of us."

Sass blinked. "What do you mean?"

Lira's grin widened, and she looked like a Pantheri who'd lapped up all the cream. "Korl and Val are insisting on staying at The Tusk & Tail tonight. Vaskel and Cali too. The whole lot of them are determined to keep watch." She reached up and tucked a wayward curl behind Sass's ear with gentle fingers. "And I'm going to share our room with you again, if you'll have me."

Sass opened her mouth to protest, to say that it wasn't necessary, that she couldn't ask her friends to put themselves at risk for her troubles. But all she could manage was to swallow hard against the unexpected surge of emotion and nod mutely.

The kitchen doors swung open, and Thrain shouldered his way into the room carrying a tray laden with empty chai mugs, their ceramic lips bearing the traces of spiced tea. He set the tray down on the worktable with a clunk. "We're going to need a few more blankets for everyone bedding down in the great room tonight."

Then he strode from the kitchen as briskly as he'd entered, and Sass followed the dwarf back through the swinging doors and into the tavern's great room. What she saw made her stop short and press a hand to her heart, though for the first time since Korl and Val had returned, the magical ring on her finger was quiet.

The great room looked more like a campsite than a tavern. Blankets and cushions sprawled around the hearth, while Vaskel pushed tables aside and pulled benches closer to the fire. Korl's broad shoulders were bunched under his leather armor as he fed chunks of peat into the flames while Val stoked the fire with an iron poker, sending sparks dancing up the chimney.

"Hells and cinders," Sass murmured, watching as her friends settled themselves around the hearth as if they were taking up posts.

Lira came up behind Sass and put a hand on her shoulder.

"Well, if we're going to be up late keeping watch, we're going to need something to drink." She pivoted on one heel and headed back toward the kitchen. "I'll put on the chai."

As Lira disappeared into the kitchen again, Val spotted Sass and abandoned her fire-tending to join her.

"Thank you for staying, but it wasn't…" Sass's words tumbled from her in a messy jumble. She cleared her throat and tried again. "I mean, you don't have to, but—" She paused, swallowing against the thickness in her voice. "But I'm glad you're staying."

Val's response was a slow wink that sent an entirely different warmth curling through Sass's chest. "We do have a knitting lesson to make up."

The tingle in Sass's chest spread outward, radiating through her entire body like she'd taken a long swig of Lira's spiced chai. For the moment, she didn't care if she still wasn't sure about Val's feelings. It was enough that she was here, that they all had stayed to keep her safe.

For a moment, Sass allowed herself simply to stand next to Val and absorb the scene. She breathed in the aroma of peat smoke, watched Thrain offer his advice to Korl on proper fire construction, and smiled at Cali curling up in one of the oversized chairs, her bow propped to one side and within easy reach.

Even the ring that had been a prickling reminder of danger seemed subdued inside the tavern, its magical warning reduced to barely more than a whisper against her skin. Whether it was because the immediate threat was not so dire, or because so much protection surrounded her, she couldn't say. What mattered was that for the first time since Thrain had arrived with his warnings, Sass felt something approaching peace.

Thirty-Two

THE FIRE HAD BURNED down to glowing embers, empty chai mugs scattered the tables and floor, and the air still held the lingering aroma of the crumpets that Lira had whipped up to dispel late-night hunger.

Cali had moved to one of the smaller tables near the hearth, her arms folded beneath her head as a makeshift pillow and her tail curled around her as she dozed fitfully, occasionally twitching an ear or whisker.

At a long table closer to the fire, Vaskel, Thrain, and Korl were focused on a collection of carved stone tiles etched with ancient dwarven runes. The tiles were sorted into neat piles, and each player had a small collection arranged before them on the worn wooden surface.

Thrain dragged his hand down his beard as he contemplated his tiles. "The key to the game is understanding that each clan rune tells part of a story. You don't just match them—you build legends." He selected a tile inscribed with what looked like a hammer crossed with flames and placed it deliberately on the table. "Forge Set. Three consecutive from the Ironforge clan."

Vaskel leaned forward, his burgundy vest unlaced and his black hair falling forward. "There's no way you just drew exactly what you needed." He gestured dramatically at Thrain's tiles. "Are you sure you've explained all the rules to us?"

"I hope you're not suggesting I'm cheating." Thrain's eyes glinted sharply as he slid three Honor Stones into his pile.

Korl grunted and pulled a tile from Vaskel's row. "You discarded the North Mountain tile I needed for my Direction Set, so I'm playing the grudge marker."

"The grudge marker?" Vaskel sputtered, his cheeks becoming a deeper shade of crimson. "What is that?"

Thrain rocked back and clapped his hands. "And I'll take that marker and double my Mine Lore."

Sass looked up from where she's been trying to sleep in front of the dying fire but had really been listening to the conversation, a small smile playing at her lips. For one of the few times since she'd met the Hellkin, he looked truly like a demon as he seethed and scowled.

"He's not cheating, Vaskel. That's how good Thrain is at Rune Stones. It seems like he must be using trickery, but he's good at reading the patterns and knows all the dwarf legends."

Vaskel muttered something about the truth of dwarf legends as he selected a tile bearing the image of a wave. The kitchen doors swung open and Lira emerged carrying a steaming copper pot of fresh chai.

"How's the game?" Lira asked as she moved between the scattered chairs and the tables, refilling mugs and sending steam curling to the rafters.

Vaskel pushed back from the table, accidentally scattering several of his Clan Runes. "Nonsensical."

"What's nonsensical?" Rog's voice seemed to precede him as the gnome entered the tavern and crossed the great room.

"Thrain's teaching him how to play Rune Stones," Sass said.

"It's not going well." Cali lifted her head long enough for a satisfied grin to stretch across her face before settling back down.

Rog chuckled. "Vask has never liked to lose."

"Which is why our crew rarely did," the Hellkin said under his breath.

Lira rested the chai pot on the nearest table, her own smile shifting into something more serious. "Is Rosie okay outside?"

Rog's expression softened at the mention of his wife. "She's fast asleep in the cart, bless her. The journey and festival wore her out more than she'll admit." He gestured toward where he'd stationed his wagon outside the front door. "I've been keeping watch, but it's all quiet. Not a dwarf in sight, aside from the ones in here."

The casual mention of the threat that hung over her made Sass's stomach clench. As much as she was touched by her friends staying in the tavern with her and even the gnomes keeping watch outside, the presence of so many people edged toward suffocating rather than comforting.

Sass pushed herself up from her chair, her legs stiff from sitting for so long. "I'm going to get some air," she murmured, though she wasn't sure if anyone heard her over the newly ignited debate over the dwarf rune game.

She slipped toward the exit, the heavy wooden door opening

with a soft creak, and stepped out into the night. Danger might lurk somewhere in the darkness beyond Wayside, but for a moment, Sass allowed herself to breathe freely, thinking that no one had noticed her departure.

But she was wrong.

SASS STOOD OUTSIDE THE TAVERN, blinking at the deep indigo that was fading to a paler shade along the horizon, where the first whisper of dawn was teasing the far corners of the Known Lands. Hints of pink seeped over the treetops, and birdsong was quickly replacing the chirp of crickets. The air smelled of grass, wild honeysuckle, and the smoke of the village chimneys, and Sass sucked it in greedily.

She realized with a start that they'd been awake all night. Morning was approaching, and she was still safe. There was no sign of Florin or her retinue, no armed dwarves demanding her return to a life she'd fled. For now at least, she was exactly where she wanted to be.

The door behind her creaked, and Sass turned, expecting to see Lira. Instead, she looked up at Val silhouetted against the yellow light spilling from inside the tavern.

A smile tugged at the corners of Sass's mouth, and she felt some of the tension leave her shoulders. "Did you come to remind me we still have a knitting lesson to make up?"

Val let the door shut behind her and joined Sass in looking toward the horizon, where the sun would soon soak the sky in flames of morning light.

"I'm not here for the knitting, Sass," Val said quietly. "Even when I've been teaching you to knit, it hasn't been about the knitting. I hope you know that."

Sass opened her mouth, then closed it again, all the air snatched from her lungs. "I didn't know until now," she finally admitted, "but I'd hoped it wasn't just about the knitting. Especially since I'm really not very good at it."

Val's laugh was low and throaty, rippling through the quiet. "You really aren't, are you?"

Sass couldn't help but join in the laughter, even as she attempted mild protests about her improving skills and how the needles were trickier than they looked.

When their laughter faded, a comfortable silence settled over them, and Sass sank into it like snuggling under a thick blanket.

"I know you've got a lot going on right now," Val said without turning to face Sass, "and a lot to figure out. But whenever you're ready, I'll be here."

Even though she'd grown up deep in mountain halls surrounded by dwarves who believed that louder was better and bold moves were the only ones worth taking, it was enough for her to know simply that Val was there and she cared. After a lifetime of being told what she should want and who she should be, Val's gentle understanding was like gold.

Without giving herself time to question herself, Sass turned toward Val and placed her hand on the tall woman's stomach, feeling the quilted leather of her vest beneath her palm. It was warm from Val's body heat, and Sass's open hand rose and fell with the steady rhythm of the woman's breathing.

"One thing I don't need time to figure out," Sass said, peering into Val's eyes, "is how I feel about you."

Val's breath hitched. "Oh, well, that's nice to hear." She exhaled a heavy breath and cut her gaze to the ground. "I know I do the talking for Korl, or at least I used to, but I'm better at doing things than saying things. Give me a sword to swing or even knitting needles to work, and I'm good. It's trying to find the right words to say so I don't mess things up that's the hard part."

Sass didn't think that Val could ever say something to mess things up with her, but the guard's sudden shyness was sweet. Suddenly, Sass didn't feel so nervous knowing that someone as strong and capable—and tall—as Val wasn't always sure of herself.

Acting on pure instinct, Sass gripped the edge of Val's vest and yanked her down while propelling herself up on her toes. Their lips bumped together awkwardly at first, but then Val steadied herself and curled a hand around the back of Sass's head.

Sass didn't know what she'd expected, but she'd never imagined that the tough guard would have such soft lips. Her head swam as she sank into the kiss, her lips moving slowly at first and then more urgently. When Val slackened her grip on Sass's head and broke the kiss, Sass dropped back on flat feet and stared up at Val, stunned.

"I'd say you're pretty good at things like this," she said, even as she brought one finger to her tingling lips.

Before Val could respond or Sass could pull her into another kiss as she desperately wanted to do, a rustling in the bushes made them both go still. Sass couldn't tell how close it was, but she knew it wasn't an animal creeping through underbrush. The unnatural sound was more like the whisper of fabric against fabric followed by a footstep in the dry grass.

Val crouched into a battle stance, her hand going to the hilt of the sword that hung at her side, and Sass tensed, her thumb touching the ring on her finger. The metal should have been prickling, but it wasn't.

Orc's blood, had she put too much faith in a magic ring that didn't work?

Thirty-Four

"WE HAVE A VISITOR," Sass announced as she stepped into the tavern again, the peat-laced warmth a sudden change from the cool morning air outside.

Val joined her and slid Sass a sidelong grin. "Actually, a few visitors."

They stepped aside to allow Erindil to sweep into the great room in a swish of sheer, midnight-blue robes and a cloud of exotic spices. His attendants hurried in after him, each wearing equally ornate sleeping clothes and as out of place in the rustic tavern as peacocks parading through a chicken coop. Speaking of peacocks, was Erindil's diaphanous robe edged in peacock feathers?

Lira, who had been lifting a mug of chai to her lips, almost dropped it in surprise. Only Cali's quick reflexes saved the ceramic vessel from shattering on the floor as the Pantheri roused herself from sleep, reached across the table, and snatched the mug from Lira's suddenly slack fingers.

"I'm so sorry to intrude." Erindil lifted one elegant hand to flick a strand of silver hair from his face, the gesture somehow both casual and theatrical. "But I bring news."

The tavern fell into a stunned silence broken only by the soft crackle of the dying embers in the hearth and the thunk of a pewter mug as Rog nearly dropped his ale and stared slack-jawed at the newcomers streaming through the door. At least Erindil had been convinced to leave Glen tethered outside the tavern.

The traveling lute player seemed to be the only one undeterred by the charged atmosphere. He quickly found a chair tucked in a corner and began tuning his instrument. The gentle plinking of strings snapped Korl from his shock.

The orc rose from his chair and moved toward Lira, putting a hand on her shoulder. If he'd been planning to explain who the visitor was, Lira beat him to it.

She stood, lifting her chin so she looked nearly as regal as her uncle. "I know who this is."

Erindil's face brightened at this. "Lira, my dear." He flattened a bejeweled hand to his heart. "I would know you anywhere." Then he sank into a courtly bow. "I am Erindil, your uncle."

Sass watched her friend carefully, wondering how Lira would react to the relative she'd never met but who clearly knew her. It wasn't every day you met an elf wearing a nightgown trimmed in peacock feathers, much less one related to you.

But Lira managed a smile, though Sass could see the tightness around her eyes that suggested she was struggling with complicated emotions. "We heard you left your campsite."

Erindil bustled forward and took Lira's hands in both of his. "We were forced to leave unless we wished to be overrun by the dwarves." He shuddered, his long nose wrinkling. "If there's one thing I can't abide, it's a band of dwarves." Then his gaze flicked to Thrain and to Sass. "No offense intended, my dears."

In this one instance, Sass found herself in the unusual position of agreeing with the elf. "None taken."

Thrain, however, didn't appear as forgiving. His lips had disappeared in a tight line somewhere within his beard, and his eyes were slits.

"I'm glad you and your friends are okay," Lira said after a few moments of uncomfortable silence.

The friends in question were wasting no time making themselves comfortable in the tavern, filling the tables and even bellying up to the bar. Vaskel took his post behind it, and Sass wasn't sure if he was there to offer drinks or make sure the finely dressed guests didn't help themselves.

Erindil's grip on Lira's hands tightened, and his eyes shone. "Can you ever forgive me? This isn't the first time I've been to Wayside, nor the first time I've seen you."

Lira nodded slowly. "I know you bought the tavern for Sass and me. Thank you."

The elf fluttered one hand dismissively, though his smile remained genial. "The least I could do, my dear. The very least."

Lira slid Sass a look, but Sass didn't think it was her call to make. She shrugged, and Lira scrunched her lips to one side. Or maybe Lira wanted her to make the call.

"We don't have room to put everyone up at the tavern," Sass said before Lira had to, "but there's chai if you and your traveling party are thirsty."

Erindil pivoted to her and beamed. "You serve chai? How absolutely delightful!"

For an immortal being who clearly had the means to surround himself with opulence, Erindil was easily impressed.

Lira stood and smoothed her hands down the front of her apron. "I'll get a fresh pot of chai started."

"My cook can help," Erindil said, as the woman they'd seen cooking at their campsite followed Lira to the kitchen.

The rest of the new guests continued to make themselves at home, rearranging benches and chairs and even settling on the blankets spread in front of the hearth. Cali was begrudgingly making room while Thrain was grumbling under his breath about there being "too many bloody elves for his liking," though he kept his voice low enough that hopefully not everyone heard him.

Val cleared her throat above the din. "Erindil has more information."

The elf snapped his fingers as if he'd completely forgotten the urgent nature of his visit. "Of course!" He graced Val with a beneficent smile. "Thank you for reminding me, my dear. We didn't come only hoping for the warm welcome we've received."

He lowered himself into one of the ladder-back chairs, flinching slightly when he touched down on hard wood. "Like I mentioned earlier, we left our campsite because my sentries spotted a dwarf party headed our way. Normally, a bunch of mountain-dwellers wouldn't bother me." He gave Sass another glance. "Again, no offense, dear."

Sass shot Thrain a quelling look to keep him from throttling the elf.

Erindil interlaced his long fingers and settled them over one knee. "But these dwarves seemed unusually well-armed and spoiling for a fight."

Rog nodded grimly from where he sat, now flanked and over-shadowed by Erindil's attendants. "Rosie and I saw the same dwarves on our way here. We steered well clear of them. They looked like they meant business, and not the pleasant kind."

Korl folded his arms across his chest armor. "Do you know where they are now?"

Erindil sniffed delicately. "In my campsite, naturally. It was beautifully cleared and leveled, with lovely acoustics for evening entertainment. Not that the brutes would care about such refinements."

"No offense taken," Sass said quickly, before Erindil could add his usual disclaimer.

"Speak for yourself, lass," Thrain growled.

Val rested a hand on Sass's shoulder. "That's what Korl and I suspected. At least we're now certain about where they are."

Sass nodded, the weight of Val's hand grounding her. The fear still lay coiled in her chest like a sleeping serpent, but she had a new sense of certainty.

She knew exactly where Florin was now. She knew where she could find her former fiancée and make a deal that would protect everyone she loved.

Thirty-Five

SASS YAWNED SO WIDELY that her jaw made a small popping sound as she sat perched on her usual stool in the tavern's kitchen, her feet dangling above the bottom rung. The morning light filtering through the windows was soft, but it did nothing to ease her bone-deep weariness after being up all night.

She rubbed her eyes with the backs of her hands. "I don't suppose you secretly held back any of those apple crumble bars from the Harvest Festival? Right now I'd trade a battle axe for something sweet."

Lira looked equally bleary-eyed as she moved around the kitchen. Her messy bun was secured with what appeared to be a wooden cooking spoon, and the purple beneath her eyes spoke of too little sleep and too much worry.

"I wish I'd had the forethought to hide some away, but no."

Sass glanced at Crumpet, who was grooming himself fastidiously in his bed of dishrags, looking remarkably refreshed and alert. "At least someone got some sleep. He's bright-eyed and bushy-tailed, the lucky wee beastie."

Crumpet paused in his grooming to fix them both with what Sass could have sworn was a smug look before returning to cleaning his whiskers with tiny pink paws.

"The crumpets should be out of the oven in a few minutes," Lira continued, moving to check the copper sauce pot simmering on the stove. "In the meantime, can I interest you in more chai?"

The rich aroma of cardamom and cinnamon wafted through the kitchen and tangled with the savory scent of the baking crumpets.

Sass took a tentative sip of her chai, letting the spiced warmth roll across her tongue and down her throat. Despite her initial hesitation about the milky drink, she'd grown fond of it. "I might need a bucket of this to keep my eyes open."

Lira turned from the stove to give her friend a concerned look. "Why don't you go take a nap? Now that it's daytime, the chance of a dwarf gang sneaking into Wayside is much less of a threat. Even Florin wouldn't be bold enough to attack a village in broad daylight."

She moved to the oven and pulled out a pan filled with perfectly golden crumpets, their surfaces dotted with the characteristic holes that would soak up butter and jam like tiny, delicious sponges. The yeasty scent that rose from them was intoxicating and made Sass's mouth water despite her exhaustion.

"Besides," Lira continued as she carefully transferred the crumpets to a woven basket, "Korl went to his dads' to ask them to alert us to anyone coming over the bridge, and Rog is sleeping in his wagon while Rosie keeps watch. We're well-protected."

Lira set aside a crumpet on a small plate, tearing off a corner for the flutterstoat, who chittered his appreciation and flew down to claim his portion. "Would you mind taking this basket out to anyone who's still awake in the great room? I need to start on the next batch. But be sure to take one for yourself."

Sass slid off her stool, grateful for something to do that didn't require deep thinking. The basket was warm in her hands, and she could feel the heat seeping through the woven bottom as she pushed through the swinging doors into the great room.

As Lira had guessed, not everyone in the rest of the tavern was awake. Thrain was folded over one of the smaller tables, his arms pillowing his head as soft snores rumbled from his chest. His beard fanned across the wooden surface, and one of his hands still loosely gripped an empty chai mug.

Cali had claimed one of the overstuffed chairs near the hearth, her slender form curled into an impossibly compact ball. Her tail encircled her, and her ears twitched occasionally as if she were chasing dream foes. Sass thought there was something deeply reassuring about watching her friends sleep safely.

Vaskel hadn't succumbed to sleep, though, and he still stood behind the long wooden bar even though most of the guests from Erindil's party had drifted off to sleep or to talk quietly elsewhere. Sass suspected his alertness had less to do with Hellkin stamina and more to do with the fact that Iris perched on one of the bar stools facing him.

The apothecary's cheeks were flushed a delicate pink that complemented her dark curls, and Sass wondered when she'd arrived and how long she and Vaskel had been deep in conversation. She reminded herself that not everyone was immune to the Hellkin's considerable charms like she and Lira were. In fact, she suspected that most folks relished his sultry smiles and potent attention.

"Crumpets, anyone?" she offered, approaching the pair with the basket.

Both Vaskel and Iris looked up, and Sass didn't miss the way Iris's hand moved to smooth her hair self-consciously.

"Oh, wonderful," Iris said, accepting one of the toasted crumpets. "I was just about to pop into the kitchen and check on Lira."

Vaskel took a crumpet and eyed it with devilish desire before taking a ravenous bite.

"How are you holding up, pet?" Iris asked. "Anything from the ring?"

Sass touched the back of the silver band with the pad of her thumb. "Aye, a bit, but it hasn't prickled since Erindil showed up."

Iris tapped her chin. "Curious. It is elven-made. I wonder if his presence dilutes its power." She gave her head a shake. "Speaking of the elf, where is he? I was hoping to meet Lira's uncle."

Sass gestured vaguely toward the back of the tavern. "Erindil agreed to set up his camp behind the building. He said something about not wanting to impose on our 'rustic accommodations' any more than absolutely necessary."

As if on cue, the faint sound of lute music drifted through one of the open tavern windows.

"Does that lute player ever sleep?" Vaskel grumbled.

Sass laughed and continued her walk across the great room, glancing back at Vaskel and Iris, who had already returned to their intense conversation. Not finding anyone else who looked alert or hungry, she dropped the basket of crumpets on the nearest table and eyed the door.

Sass had been turning the problem over in her mind all night, and she'd reached a conclusion that felt both terrifying and inevitable. She was sure she could make a deal with Florin that would protect Wayside and everyone she cared about. It would certainly mean returning the amulet and possibly returning to the Ice Lands, but if it kept her friends safe, it would be worth it.

The key was to approach Florin first, not wait for the dwarf princess to come stalking through the village with her armed guards. If Sass could present herself voluntarily, perhaps she could negotiate from a position of relative strength.

She moved quietly toward the front door, careful not to disturb Thrain's snoring or wake Cali. She took her time opening the heavy door as slowly as possible so it wouldn't creak, holding her breath as, for once, it moved on silent hinges. She stepped outside and allowed herself a relieved release of breath. Then she almost walked straight into Val.

The blonde guard must have been standing watch outside the tavern door because it had only taken one step for her to block Sass's path. A slow grin spread across Val's face. "I thought you might try to do something brave and foolish. That's why I've been waiting out here."

Sass opened her mouth to argue, to insist that she was just getting some fresh air, but the words died in her throat. She didn't want to lie to Val. She couldn't.

Then Val stepped closer and brushed one finger along Sass's jawline. "I'm here to be brave and foolish with you."

<h1 style="text-align:center">Thirty-Six</h1>

SASS BLINKED AT Val in disbelief. Maybe lack of sleep had made her delusional. "You're what?"

"I'm coming with you." Val widened her stance as if daring Sass to pass. "You're going to do something incredibly foolhardy, right?" When Sass didn't answer, Val nodded. "Well, I'm coming too."

Sass huffed out an exasperated breath. "Fine." She folded her arms over her chest in a gesture that was equal parts defensive and defeated. "I was planning to sneak to the dwarf campsite and try to negotiate with Florin."

Val raised one eyebrow but didn't look particularly surprised by this revelation. "I figured as much. You got a look in your eyes last night when Erindil mentioned that the dwarves took his campsite. Like you were going to do something incredibly foolish."

"It's not foolish," Sass protested, then immediately winced. "Well, not entirely foolish. Look, Val, I know Florin better than anyone else here. I understand how her mind works, what she values, what might persuade her to leave Wayside alone." She drummed her fingers on her arms. "If I can present myself voluntarily, offer to return the amulet, and give some explanation of why I left, then she won't tear the village apart looking for me and she might not insist on retribution against my clan."

Val considered this, nodding thoughtfully. "That's actually not a terrible plan, but I still can't let you go alone."

"Val—"

"No, hear me out." Val held up one hand to forestall Sass's protests. "You're right that going alone might put you in a better negotiating position. But what happens if Florin decides she doesn't want to negotiate? What if she's more interested in making an example of you than she is in recovering her amulet?"

Sass's stomach clenched at the thought, but she forced herself to keep her voice steady. "That's a risk I have to take. And that's exactly why I want to go alone. If Florin gets even a whiff of how much I care about this place, about the people here, about..." She left the word unspoken but held Val's gaze until the guard touched her arm gently. "She'll use it against me. She'll threaten Wayside, threaten my friends, you, anything to get what she wants."

"I've considered that," Val said. "Which is why I'll go as your bodyguard." She gestured to her quilted guard uniform, the leather armor that marked her as a member of the local laird's defense. "I'm dressed for the part, after all."

Sass opened her mouth to argue further, but Val's reasoning

made sense. Florin would respect her coming with a guard. It wouldn't signal personal attachment so much as prudent caution.

"Aye, all right." The relief that flooded through her at the thought of not facing Florin completely alone surprised Sass. "But you have to promise me something, Val. When we're there, you can't let on that there's anything between us. Not even that we're friends. Be completely detached."

Val bobbled her head. "Then maybe you shouldn't have kissed me like you did last night."

Sass's jaw dropped. "Me? What about the way you..." She stopped when she noticed Val's wicked grin and realized the woman was teasing her. She sighed. "If this doesn't work, this could be the last time I ever kiss you."

The playfulness immediately drained from Val's expression, and she bent down so that their faces were even. She cupped Sass's jaw in one hand, tipping the dwarf's face up so that their quick breaths mingled. "That would be a true crime."

Sass lost the ability to breathe as Val held her gaze, finally feathering her lips across the dwarf's slightly agape mouth so briefly that Sass was sure she'd imagined it.

Then Val straightened and snapped her heels together. "I promise to keep it completely professional. No one will suspect a thing."

Sass wasn't sure if either of them could manage that, but it would have to do. Val pivoted so she could fall in step with Sass as they headed away from the tavern, throwing waves to Rosie.

The gnome sat on the back step of the brandy wagon, polishing a red apple to a high shine with the corner of her apron and giving no indication that she'd witnessed anything. She waved back cheerfully, apparently unbothered by the early hour or the loud snores coming from inside the wagon. "Mind how you go, girls."

As they walked through the village, Sass thought about how different Wayside looked in the aftermath of the Harvest Festival.

The orange and gold pennant streamers that had draped between the storefronts still hung across the main road, but they were now sagging and gap-toothed.

Apple cores and scraps of paper littered the dirt road along with the odd lost hair ribbon or dropped coin. It wasn't messy so much as well-used, like the tavern after a busy night.

Fenni was already at work in front of his cheese shop, vigorously sweeping the walk with a bristle broom. Despite the early hour and the late end to the festival, his hair was primly combed to one side, and the apron tied around his tweed three-piece suit was spotless.

"Morning, ladies!" he called out cheerfully as they passed, pausing in his sweeping to lean on his broom handle. "There's nothing like fresh air and exercise to clear the head after a proper celebration."

"I couldn't agree with you more," Val said.

It took all of Sass's self-control not to wander toward Pip's bakery as they passed, and she tipped her nose into the air in anticipation of catching a citrus sugar breeze. But even the usually bustling bakery was quiet this morning, the glass door closed and only a faint glow that suggested Pip was preparing for the day's baking without the energy to open the front door or welcome customers just yet. Tin's haberdashery shop wasn't open either, its colorful window display of ribbons and buttons and fine fabrics looking somehow forlorn without the gnome bustling around inside.

They reached the town square with its weathered stone pillar, glanced at the empty market stalls that had been so busy the night before, and then cut across toward the woods that bordered the village on the eastern side.

The morning sunlight, which had been bright in the village, became dappled and suffused as they crossed the tree line. Ancient oaks and towering pines filtered the light through their branches, creating a mosaic of golden patches on the forest floor. The air smelled of damp earth and decomposing leaves, moss and wild herbs, with the faint underlying scent of wood smoke that suggested there was a camp not too far away.

Their footsteps made satisfying crunching sounds as they walked through the carpet of fallen leaves, and Sass marveled at the hush. For a band of well-armed dwarves, they were remarkably silent. No booming voices echoed off the trees, no hiss of axe blades being sharpened on stone, and no clang of ladle against cauldron. The only indication that they hadn't fled entirely was the faint prickling of the ring on her finger.

"They must be hiding well," she murmured to Val. "Dwarf camps aren't usually quiet."

Just as the words left her mouth, the ring burned as if it was on fire, startling Sass so much that she went rigid.

Val's hand had moved instinctively to rest on the pommel of her sword. "Maybe they're—"

The sentence was cut off abruptly as Sass felt the cold kiss of steel against her throat. A blade—broad and sharp enough that she could feel its edge even though it wasn't quite breaking skin—pressed against the exposed curve of her neck.

Sass slid her eyes sideways enough to see that Val was in an identical predicament, an axe blade pressed against her throat. The tall guardswoman had gone completely still, her palms up in the universal gesture of non-aggression.

"Don't take another step," growled a voice behind her, deep and raspy and unmistakably dwarf.

Thirty-Seven

SASS CAUGHT Val's eyes and gave her head the slightest shake she could manage without drawing blood from her own throat. The last thing they needed was for Val to be a hero.

"I'm here to talk to Florin," Sass said, her voice steady even though she could taste the metallic tang of fear in her mouth.

"Who says Florin wants to talk to you?" the dwarf behind her rasped.

Sass swallowed slowly, feeling the blade's edge whisper against her skin as the ring seared her finger. "Since I'm the dwarf she's looking for, I think she does."

There was a long moment of silence broken only by the rustle of wind through the forest canopy and the call of a morning lark. Sass could hear her own breathing, slightly too fast, and the creak of leather as a dwarf shifted position.

Then, as abruptly as they had appeared, the axes lowered.

Sass and Val spun around immediately, but the two dwarves who had ambushed them were still holding their battle axes at the ready, and behind them stood twice as many warriors, all brandishing axes. Val's hand twitched toward her sword hilt, but she didn't draw the weapon, clearly recognizing that they were outnumbered.

Sass studied the dwarves, noting their unfamiliar faces. She didn't recognize any of them, but that wasn't surprising since they wore the distinctive leather and chain mail of the Trollbane clan, with the twisted mountain peak emblem worked into the breastplate. As a member of the Thornshield clan, she wouldn't know most of Florin's people by sight, which also explained why they hadn't immediately recognized her.

The sound of footsteps on dried leaves made them all turn, and Sass's breath caught as a figure emerged from behind one of the massive oak trees. Even at a distance, there was no mistaking the dwarf.

Sass stiffened as Florin Trollbane stepped into the dappled morning light.

The dwarf with hair the color of forge fire wore leather armor reinforced with steel plates, sturdy boots made for long marches, and a sword at her hip. But she still looked utterly regal. Long braids coiled around her head, making it seem like she wore a circlet of flames.

Sass thought, with a mixture of admiration and fear, that Florin still looked striking. She always had. That was one of the many reasons everyone thought the dark-haired Thornshield princess and the flame-haired Trollbane heir made a perfect match. But Sass knew all too well that, despite her fiery hair, Florin's beauty was cold.

The dwarf's lips curved into what might charitably be called a smile, though it looked more predatory than welcoming. "I've been searching for you for a long time, my love."

Sass couldn't quite suppress the flinch that ran through her at the endearment, and she sensed Val bristle beside her. Before Florin could notice Val's reaction, Sass stepped forward.

"I've come to negotiate," she said firmly, drawing Florin's attention to herself.

Florin studied Sass with cool detachment. "You mean you've come to surrender."

Sass swallowed hard, her mouth suddenly dry even though the ring's prickling had waned. "No. I'm willing to return the amulet, but I can't marry you, Florin. I won't."

The smile slipped from Florin's face, and for a moment Sass remembered why the Trollbane clan had such a fearsome reputation throughout the Ice Lands.

"You know," Florin said, her voice taking on a deceptively conversational tone, "I had that amulet designed especially for you. The stone was mined from the deepest tunnels of our mountain, cut by our finest craftsmen, and set in silver by artisans renowned throughout the Known Lands." She paused, letting her gaze caress Sass's bare throat. "It breaks my heart that you aren't wearing it."

Sass thought privately that Florin had no heart to break, but she kept her tone even. "I don't have the occasion to wear such fine jewelry anymore."

Florin's smile returned, but it twisted and morphed into a sneer. "I heard you were working as a common tavern wench. How the mighty have fallen."

Sass didn't correct her, though every instinct she possessed was screaming at her to defend the tavern she now loved. But she wanted Florin to think she was nothing but a common laborer, someone whose connections and influence were negligible, someone who posed no threat and commanded no loyalty that could be leveraged.

Florin shook her head, though her eyes remained as cold as winter ice. "Your family would be so disappointed to see what you've chosen over a life as a queen under the mountain."

The words found their target, and Sass had to push aside thoughts of her family. Florin was right; there was no use denying that her family would be devastated to see how far she'd fallen from what they'd wished for her. But she also knew that she'd never been happier than she was here in Wayside, and that thought straightened her spine and strengthened her resolve.

Instead of dwelling on family disappointment, Sass stepped forward, close enough to see the flecks of gold in Florin's eyes. "I wouldn't make you a good wife, Florin. You know that as well as I do."

Florin opened her mouth as if to argue, but then she stopped, staring hard at Sass with an expression that was difficult to read. The ring circling Sass's little finger blazed hot for a moment then went quiet.

Florin jerked her gaze away and muttered, almost too low to hear, "Maybe you're right."

When she looked back at Sass, any shadow of emotion was gone. "Very well. I'll relinquish my claim on you if you return to these woods tomorrow with the amulet. Bring it to me, and I'll consider our engagement dissolved."

Sass didn't dare release the breath that felt lodged in her throat. "And you won't take retribution against my clan?"

Florin's nostrils flared as if scenting weakness. "It will be enough for me to see the faces of your family when I tell them how far their precious princess has fallen. The humiliation of that should be punishment enough for the Thornshields."

Sass had to bite the inside of her lip to keep tears from blinding her. But she nodded, recognizing that this was a far better agreement than she'd hoped to get. "Aye, you have a deal."

Florin held up one finger, and something in her expression made Sass's newfound relief evaporate. "On one condition, my love. When you bring the amulet tomorrow, I want you to wear it. I was not lying when I said that it hurts me not to see you wearing the gift I had designed especially for you. If I can see you wearing it one last time, I will be content to let you go."

It seemed like such a wee thing, but something about the request made Sass's gut churn and the ring heat her finger. Florin loved one thing more than shedding blood, and that was mind games, and this was clearly one of hers. Still, weighed against the alternative of forced marriage, it was a price she was willing to pay.

"Fine," she said simply, spinning the ring with her thumb as it continued to sting her skin.

Florin stepped closer, close enough that Sass could smell the leather of her armor and the faint scent of forge smoke that seemed to cling to all children of the Ice Lands. Her gaze flicked briefly to Val, as if finally registering the tall guardswoman's presence, before she leaned in to Sass.

The kiss she pressed to Sass's cheek was soft and brief, but it felt as cold and brittle as the burn of ice itself.

"Until next time, my love," Florin murmured against her ear, the words more a threat than a farewell.

Then she stepped back and, with a snap to her guards, disappeared into the depths of the forest. Within moments, it was as if the dwarves had never been there at all, the lingering scent of leather, steel, and smoke the only evidence of their presence. That and the pricking ring she wanted to wrench from her finger.

Sass stood frozen for a long moment, one hand unconsciously lifting to brush the spot where Florin's lips had touched her cheek. She was marveling at how well things had gone, how easily Florin had let her go, when she realized Val was staring at her.

"That," Val said quietly, "went almost too well."

A chill slithered down Sass's spine as she realized with growing unease that Val was absolutely right.

"I CAN'T BELIEVE you went to find Florin without us," Lira said, one toe tapping rapid-fire against the tavern's wooden floorboards.

Cali had uncoiled from the upholstered chair and was wearing her quiver of bows slung across her back again. "You should have at least asked me to follow at a distance. I'm very good at moving unseen."

Sass had every reason to believe her and every reason to cringe at the look of betrayal on the Pantheri's face.

"I can't believe you're planning to go back," Thrain mumbled as he gave Sass a slightly wounded look that was marred only by his grogginess.

Val cleared her throat as she and Sass stood in the great room surrounded by the friends they'd woken up when they'd returned from the forest. "She didn't go alone, and she won't be alone when she goes back."

"That's right, she won't." Lira's toe-tapping paused long enough for her to brace her hands on her hips. "It's too dangerous for her to go with only one person as backup." She tipped her head to one side as she acknowledged Val. "Even if that one person is a trained guard."

"The elf is right." Thrain dragged a hand through his tangled black hair and then down the length of his beard. "Two are no match against Florin's hunting party."

"Half elf," Lira and Sass said quietly at the same time.

Lira caught Sass's eyes, and her scowl melted into a grin. "You know we're just worried about your safety."

Sass walked toward the freshly stoked fire and held her hands to it, grateful the ring had finally stopped prickling. Even though it wasn't cold in the tavern, she was still fighting off the shivers that had been wracking her since she'd seen Florin. The dwarf's proposal, while seeming fair, made her feel cold all over. "I know, but seeing Florin myself was the best way to keep all of you safe."

Lira made a noise in the back of her throat that said she didn't fully agree, but it was Korl who surprised Sass by speaking.

"I understand why you went and why Val went with you, but I don't understand why the dwarves let you go so easily."

"You wish they'd held them captive?" Lira asked, snapping her gaze to the orc with surprising heat.

Korl rocked back on his heels. "You know I don't, but from what I heard about this dwarf hunting party, I expected them to put up more of a fight."

Thrain stood and joined Sass at the fire, but he stared into it, wrinkling his brow. "I'm with the orc. It makes little sense that Florin would go to all this trouble to find you and then agree to let bygones be bygones."

Sass thought back to Florin's cold eyes and tenderly worded threat. "That's not exactly what happened. She wants me to return the amulet."

"And she wants to see Sass wear it one last time," Val added in a low voice.

Lira swung her head to Val. "What?"

Vaskel and Iris had walked over from the bar to join the group gathered around the hearth, and the Hellkin's tail slashed behind him. "She wants Sass to wear the amulet when she returns it? Why?"

Sass shrugged. "Some kind of power play, I guess. It's typical Florin to want to make others jump at her say-so."

Thrain grunted at this. "Typical Trollbane."

"And that's all she wants?" Cali asked, the fur on the back of her neck fluffed up. "To see you in some necklace one last time?"

Vaskel scowled, and his devilish features morphed from sultry to terrifying. "It seems oddly sentimental for a dwarf warrior of her reputation."

"Never try to predict what a Trollbane will do," Thrain said with a grumble that told everyone precisely what he thought about the Trollbanes.

Sass knew Thrain was right, but her other friends weren't wrong. Florin agreeing to release her from their bond without more penance had startled her, especially since Thrain had been sure the dwarf wanted to punish her clan. Instead, Florin had been reasonable and almost kind. Sass shivered. It was unsettling.

"Could I see the amulet in question?" Iris asked as she absently twirled one curl around her pointer finger.

Sass didn't mind showing the apothecary the piece of jewelry, and she made quick work of going upstairs and retrieving it from under her mattress, exhaling with relief that it was still there. Not that anyone but her friends knew of its existence, and only she knew where she'd hidden it. Still, she wouldn't have put it past Florin to demand the return of the amulet while simultaneously plotting to steal it back.

Sass felt the jewel through the velvet pouch as she hurried back down the stairs, and she poured it into her palm once she reached Iris. Everyone gathered closer to her, even though most of them had seen it before.

The center stone glittered, even in the muted firelight, and Sass marveled that the metal didn't show any signs of age. It was as bright and shiny as it had been the night she'd received it. Sass swallowed hard. A night she'd rather forget.

"Do you mind if I hold it, love?" Iris asked, extending her own hand.

Sass gratefully tipped the amulet into Iris's palm, rubbing her own on her skirt as if dislodging whatever lingering connection she had to the piece.

Vaskel leaned closer, squinting at the amulet as Iris turned it over in her hand, one thumb brushing across the stone as she hummed contemplatively.

Finally, Vaskel straightened, growling without speaking. The Hellkin was clearly unsettled by something.

Iris looked up at Sass. "It's a lovely piece, and the craftsmanship is remarkable."

"Dwarf metalworking is unrivaled," Thrain said, his chest puffing up as he pulled himself to his full height.

"Reminds me of that cursed necklace we recovered near Craigmire." Vaskel shot Lira and Cali loaded glances.

"Only because both are silver," Cali said. "If this necklace was like that one, we'd all be speaking in tongues and hallucinating."

Vaskel mumbled something about giving the hex time as he eyed the amulet warily.

Lira pivoted away from Vaskel and focused on Iris. "Can you tell us anything else about it? Anything suspicious?"

Sass swung her head to Lira and then back to Iris. "Is that why you wanted to see it? You think it's hexed?"

Pink splotches mottled Iris's cheeks. "Lira knows me too well, but even if I have suspicions, curses and enchantments were never my strength." She gave Lira an apologetic smile. "That was your gran's domain. If she were here, she could probably use a spell to detect any curses."

"Should I get her book?" Lira asked, nibbling the bottom corner of her lip. "I'm not sure which spell would work, but maybe if we all worked together—"

"And end up with this amulet turned into an enchanted platypus and nothing to return to Florin?" Sass shook her head. "No, thank you."

"The bookwyrms were a one-off," Iris muttered. "And that never happened again."

Sass gestured toward the kitchen. "What about Crumpet?"

Iris twisted her lips into a prim bow before sighing. "I'm pretty sure Elia meant to do that and didn't want to admit it."

Sass thought about the vanishing powder Lira had attempted, but she didn't mention it. The fewer who knew about that near miss, the better.

"If you want to know if your amulet is enchanted, I can tell you that, my dears."

They all pivoted to see Erindil, who'd slipped into the tavern through the back door and was standing on the outskirts of their group, his long, jewel-laden fingers steepled in front of his chest.

Sass could have kicked herself. Of course, the elf could tell them. Aside from having certain magical powers of their own, most elves possessed the ability to detect enchantment or magic in other creatures or things. It was one of the many traits that made the species so superior and insufferable, if you asked Sass—or really any dwarf.

But at the moment, she'd never been so happy to see an elf.

Thirty-Nine

"YOU MUST BE ERINDIL." Iris stepped forward, continuing to hold the amulet in her outstretched palm.

The elf's eyes twinkled at the woman's ruffled skirt and wild mane of curls. "And you're the apothecary. I remember hearing about the rogue turned potion-maker."

Iris blinked rapidly as she took in the regal elf in a green velvet tunic over snug brown pants, all the components edged in gold cording. "You do?"

Erindil bowed his head to her. "My brother told me all about

Wayside and the people surrounding my niece. It's how I could track her down."

Lira stiffened at this, but Erindil was already taking Iris's hand in his own, bending low to examine the amulet. "Yes, yes," he murmured, more to himself than to any of them. "Very intriguing."

Vaskel folded his arms over his chest, and Korl followed suit, as if silently objecting to the proceedings. Both could be overprotective, especially of Lira, but Sass noticed Val grinning at the male posturing and Cali rolling her golden eyes.

After a few moments, Erindil tipped the amulet from Iris's hand into his, making more contemplative sounds as he brushed delicate fingers over the gemstone in the center and whispered elvish words.

Thrain had edged his way around the group to stand alongside Sass, and he nudged her in the ribs. "You put stock in this elf sorcery?"

Sass twitched a shoulder, careful not to let Erindil catch her and fully aware that he could hear each of Thrain's rumbling words. "You and I both know that elves have powers we don't."

Thrain harrumphed at this. "If we're so powerless, how is that amulet supposed to be hexed?"

"Not by dwarves," Sass said, which made Thrain's scowl deepen.

"She must have found someone to do it for her," Val whispered.

Sass had never thought about that, but Val was right. The Trollbanes dwelled beneath the mountains, but that didn't mean they'd never ventured away from them or that they'd never summoned others to their underground palace. Sass remembered hearing that Florin's father swore by gnomes for developing the contraptions that made his forges the best in the Ice Lands.

She cut a look at Thrain, who seemed to remember the same thing she had.

"Gnomes," they said simultaneously.

A grin split Thrain's face, and he nudged Sass again.

Erindil tipped his head up and shook it. "Oh no, my dear dwarves. This trickery has nothing to do with gnomes."

Thrain looked on the verge of complaining about being called a dear dwarf, but Sass had snagged onto something else Erindil said. "Did you say trickery?"

Lira took a step back. "Are you saying the amulet's cursed?"

Even Iris looked alarmed as their group exchanged nervous glances.

Erindil let out a high, melodious laugh that seemed completely ill-suited to the moment. "I didn't say that." Then his laugh died out. "Although I can't rule it out."

Vaskel glowered at the elf, seemingly unimpressed by Erindil's regal bearing or whatever powers he might possess. "Then what are you saying?"

Erindil eyed the Hellkin as if just registering him for the first time, his eyes widening at Vaskel's red horns and the tail that quivered behind him like a coiled spring. "I suppose I don't know exactly what I'm saying."

Sass stared at the elf. She'd never expected him to admit that he didn't know. From what she'd heard of elves, they possessed more knowledge than most because of their long lives, and they were more than happy to let everyone else know it.

He handed the amulet back to Iris, who gaped at the piece as if it might come to life and devour her. "I sense some sort of enchantment surrounding the amulet." He fluttered his fingers toward the jewel. "Whether it's a charm to make the stone appear bigger," he winked at Iris and chuckled, "which seems to be a popular charm for more than just jewelry, or whether it's something more nefarious, I cannot know for certain without further study of it."

Lira took the velvet bag from Sass and then held it open so Iris could drop the amulet inside. "But you're certain it's enchanted?"

Erindil bobbed his head. "I am certain of that, my dear."

Sass put a hand to her throat as if remembering the one time she'd worn the necklace. "That explains why I hated wearing it and why it made me feel so...unsettled."

Val crossed her arms and set her legs wide. "And why you're absolutely not wearing it again to return it to Florin."

"Agreed," Lira said before Sass could argue. "There's no way we can let you wear an amulet that could be cursed."

"Or charmed," Erindil said with a raised finger.

A shiver went through Sass. "I wonder why it didn't affect me when I wore it the first time."

Erindil tapped a finger on his chin. "It's very possible that the curse is only activated by proximity to the one who controls it or a trigger word."

"Which is why Florin needs you to wear it and why you absolutely cannot," Val said.

Thrain grunted. "I'm with the lady guard. Just because you wore it once and lived to tell the tale doesn't mean you will again. There's a reason Florin wants that around your neck, and it isn't because she likes a pretty throat."

Sass threw up her arms in frustration. "Then what do you suggest we do, because I'm not willing to bring retribution upon my clan or be the reason anyone in Wayside gets hurt."

"Simple." Lira held up the velvet pouch and let it swing from her finger. "First, we find out how the amulet is enchanted, and then we have the charm or hex or what-have-you removed."

Cali tipped her head. "Good plan, but how do we do either of those without a mage?"

"And do not say we use your gran's book," Sass said. "You and I both know that's as dangerous as my winging it with the amulet."

Iris swiveled her gaze back to Erindil. "I suspect Lira's uncle is being modest about his powers."

Forty

"HOW'S IT GOING IN THERE?" Sass sidled up to Vaskel behind the bar and jerked her head toward the kitchen.

Lira and Korl had disappeared through the half doors, and Sass didn't dare follow the two. Not when Lira was clearly unsettled about the appearance of her uncle and using him for his magic.

Vaskel made a low, raspy sound in the back of his throat. "Lira will come around."

Sass sighed. She couldn't help feeling that all this was her fault. "Learning that she has an uncle and a father who's missing is a lot to absorb, and now we want to enlist her uncle as part of our solution? I get why she stormed off."

Vaskel quirked a dark, peaked brow at her. "You might not have known Lira before she was happily baking in a tavern, but she can take a lot in stride."

Maybe when it came to quests, thought Sass. But family was different. She should know.

"I do hope I haven't caused problems."

Sass and Vaskel swiveled toward the elf who'd glided up to the other side of the bar. To his credit, Erindil's face was pinched and his forehead furrowed. He tapped his two pointer fingers together just below his chin. "Perhaps I shouldn't have mentioned the amulet's enchantment."

"You were only trying to help."

Erindil beamed at Sass. "That's kind of you to say, my dear."

Sass returned his smile, glancing beyond him to the tavern's great room, which had emptied considerably. Thrain had dragged himself up to his room to have, as he put it, "a proper lie-down," and Cali had left with Iris to open the apothecary.

Erindil's companions had taken up residence in the camp behind the tavern, evidenced by the lilting lute music wafting through the windows. Only Val remained near the hearth, and not even the lute could drown out her soft snoring as she half sat, half lay in her chair with her long legs stretched in front of her.

Vaskel seemed too wired for sleep, which didn't surprise Sass. As a rule, Tielfings required little rest, which was why he looked alert, while she fought to keep her heavy eyelids from drooping. Lira's elf uncle also looked as fresh as if he'd woken from a restorative sleep, but she chalked that up to elf immortality. Who had ever heard of an elf looking bedraggled? Sass couldn't imagine Erindil appearing anything less than pristine.

Erindil gave the Hellkin an appraising look. "You were one of Lira's crew when she was a rogue, correct?"

Vaskel nodded. "I was."

The elf cut his gaze to Sass. "But you...?"

"I was not," Sass told him. "We only met when we both arrived in Wayside."

She didn't bother explaining the entire story. Somehow, she suspected he already knew.

"And our crew first met Lira in this very tavern many years ago," Vaskel said, his gaze wandering to one of the long tables. "And now we've all reunited here again." His blue eyes darkened. "Almost all."

Erindil cocked his head to one side. "It seems like your crew has expanded here."

Sass liked the sound of that and enjoyed thinking of herself as part of a crew.

"When you find a good crew, you stick together." Vaskel winked at Sass. "Even if you go your separate ways for a while, friends that are like family always find their way back to each other."

Erindil eyed the Hellkin as if sizing him up and finding him worthy. "I couldn't agree more."

Korl emerged from the kitchen, his face giving away nothing.

"How's she doing?" Sass asked.

"She'll come around," the orc said, mustering a weak smile.

Erindil wrung his hands. "Oh dear. Maybe I shouldn't have come."

There was no turning back time, as Sass knew all too well. That didn't mean that she didn't feel for Lira and everything that had been thrown her way.

She touched the elf's arm. "Let me talk to her."

SASS PUSHED through the kitchen doors, expecting to see Lira humming as she mixed up her usual cinnamon scones. Instead, the woman stood staring into the earthenware mixing bowl with Crumpet perched on her shoulder and also focused on the contents of the bowl.

"Is everything okay?" Sass asked.

Lira glanced up quickly, and the flutterstoat chattered indignantly as he took flight and landed on the rack overhead that held the copper pots and pans. "Only if you consider ruined scones okay."

"How did you ruin them?"

Lira sighed and blew a strand of auburn hair off her forehead. "I was explaining to Korl why it's not so easy to welcome Erindil with open arms, even if he is my uncle and even if he did gift us the tavern."

"I think he knows that," Sass said.

Lira's shoulders sank. "I know he does. I might have taken out my frustrations about this whole situation on him, which wasn't fair."

"I think he'll forgive you."

Lira met the dwarf's eyes and released a breath. "It's not his fault that I suddenly have to deal with a missing father, and it's not actually Erindil's either. My uncle isn't the one who left me when I was young, and he did buy us this tavern. He's been nothing but kind and helpful. I shouldn't be so conflicted about him or about him helping us."

Sass recognized the independent woman she'd encountered that first fateful night at The Tusk & Tail—and the stubborn one. She also recognized that independence and stubbornness in herself, so she couldn't give Lira too hard of a time. Not when she understood her so well.

"Trust me, I get it." Sass crossed her arms over her chest. "Sometimes we all take out our frustrations on the people who least deserve it. No one blames you for being overwhelmed by Erindil's appearance and his news. Not even him."

Lira's shoulders drooped. "Did I really flounce from the room when he offered to help?"

"I wouldn't say flounce. Now your uncle might flounce. You stomped."

Lira put a hand over her mouth to stifle a giggle. "Despite whatever I might feel about my father, I should give Erindil a chance. Especially if he can help figure out the amulet."

"If you don't want him involved, just say the word."

Lira shook her head. "I want to learn the truth about the amulet as much as anyone. If I'm being honest, I'm ready to know more about my elf family too."

"Truly?" Sass asked.

Lira gave her a genuine smile. "Truly."

Sass returned her attention to the mixing bowl. "Now how did you ruin the scones?"

Lira released another long breath. "I was so busy trying to explain my point of view that I ended up dumping the chai spices into the bowl instead of just the cinnamon."

Sass stepped closer, getting up on her tiptoes to peer into the mixing bowl. "That's it? You didn't add salt when it should have been sugar or maybe add magical ingredients by accident?"

Lira gasped and gave Sass a horrified look. "I only did that once. What kind of baker do you think I am?"

Sass shrugged one shoulder. "The kind who can rescue this batch of scones and make them delicious, anyway."

The woman scrunched her lips to one side as she looked at Sass, then looked at the bowl, then looked at Sass. "You're right. This isn't a lost cause. I was always good at adjusting on the spot during missions. That was usually about picking locks and not adjusting spices, but it's still pivoting."

Lira spun around and snapped her fingers as she spotted something on the counter. "Crumpet brought me these pears he foraged earlier. I'll bet if I add some chopped pear to the chai spices, it will be delicious."

Crumpet glided down to the counter and picked up one of the bumpy, green pears, his white paws prodding at the fruit. He pushed it aside and grabbed another, going through the same motions. Finally, he chirped happily and held out the chosen pear.

"This one?" Lira took it from him, her own thumb pressing gently near the stem before she smiled. "You're right, Crump. It's perfect."

"So we're serving pear scones today instead of cinnamon ones?" Sass asked.

"Chai pear scones," Lira corrected as she efficiently peeled the pear with one of her rogue daggers and chopped it into small bits. She paused after dropping the fruit into the bowl. "Thanks, Sass. Usually baking calms me, but I think I've been so worried that even mixing and measuring hasn't worked."

"Worried about your missing father?"

Lira splashed some cream into the bowl and folded it into the dry ingredients. "No. I don't know enough about that to worry." Then she leveled her batter-covered spoon at the dwarf. "I've been worried about you, Sass."

Sass blinked a few times, as if this made no sense. "You've been so worried about me that baking won't calm you?"

"The thought of you leaving—having to leave—after all we've built together and all we've been through…" Her words faded as her voice cracked. "You've become such an important part of my life, of all our lives, that I can't imagine losing you."

Sass's throat tightened as tears stung the back of her eyes, but before she could find her voice, Lira closed the distance between them and pulled her into a fierce hug.

"You're as much a part of The Tusk & Tail as the beams in the ceiling," Lira whispered.

"Or the troll smell in the cellar?" Sass croaked.

Lira laughed and hugged her tighter. "Exactly like that."

Tiny feet landed on Sass's shoulder, and wings enveloped both her and Lira's heads as Crumpet joined the hug, his chittering soft and soothing.

Sass reached up and patted the tiny flutterstoat's back, marveling at his silky fur. "Thanks, Crump."

Lira pulled away and squeezed Sass's shoulders. "I'd better get these scones in the oven so we can get to work figuring out that amulet."

And how to defeat a dwarf princess, Sass thought.

Forty-Two

"YOU'RE SURE this is a good idea?" Sass cast a longing look back at The Tusk & Tail.

"Iris, Cali, and Erindil are already at the apothecary researching possible enchantments." Lira put a reassuring arm around Sass's shoulders as Thrain, Korl, and Val walked ahead. "We won't be gone long. Besides, I have every confidence in Rog and Rosie. If the gnome can peddle apple brandy the way she does, she's more than capable of handling afternoon scones and chai."

Sass bobbled her head back and forth. Part of her thought she should stay behind to help the gnomes pass out scones and pour chai, but there was also no way she was going to miss learning what enchantment had been placed on the amulet Florin gave her.

She slipped one hand into her skirt pocket, touching the velvet pouch as if to reassure herself that the amulet was there. Then she remembered it was charmed and snatched back her hand.

"Don't you worry about me and Rosie." Rog bellowed to them from the front door of the tavern with a pear and chai scone in one hand and crumbs speckling his blue beard. "We've handled rowdier bunches than the folks in Wayside. Doling out scones and mugs of that spiced tea won't make me and the missus break a sweat."

Sass wanted to say that there was more to it than that, but she pressed her lips together. Lira was right. She was being overly territorial about the scone service she thought of as her innovation. It would survive without her for one day, just like their usual customers would be fine with a different flavor of scone.

"See? Nothing to worry about." Lira gave her shoulders a squeeze before running to catch up to Korl.

Sass sighed and picked up her pace to join the rest of the group headed toward the village. The midday sun eased down the sky, the morning mist long since burned away as Wayside had finally roused itself from its post-festival slumber. Hooves clopped on the dusty road, the blacksmith's hammer clanged against steel, and the waterwheel splashed in the stream.

When she caught up to Thrain, he took a sizable bite of the scone he'd grabbed on the way out the door. "These are quite the treat."

Lira swiveled her head to grin at him. "They turned out well, didn't they? Sass was the one who saved them, you know. I thought the batch was ruined when I mistakenly put the chai spices in the scone batter, but she reminded me that every misstep is still a step forward, and possibly even in a better direction."

"Even the errant swing of a pickaxe cuts a tunnel," Thrain said.

Lira fell back so she could walk in step with Sass, dropping her voice to a whisper. "Sounds like your mum isn't the only dwarf dispensing mining wisdom."

"Thrain spent a lot of time at my house growing up," Sass told her. "Trust me, he got all of his wisdom from my mum."

Lira laughed at this, giving Sass a nudge of her hips and taking a few long strides to catch up to Korl and Vaskel as they strode past Pip's bakery.

Val slowed her pace so that she walked alongside Sass, smiling down at the dwarf. "You ready to figure out how Florin enchanted your amulet?"

Despite the humid gusts of sugar-dusted air coming from the bakery, a chill slithered down Sass's spine as she recalled the feel of the cool stone pressed to her neck. "It's not my amulet, and the sooner I'm rid of it, the better."

Before another memory could make the dwarf shudder, Val's hand enveloped Sass's smaller one, comforting and solid. "Don't worry. I've got you."

Ahead, the door to the apothecary shop jingled as it was opened.

"I know you do," Sass said as they followed the rest of the group inside the dimly-lit shop. She drew in a deep breath, the air thick with the scent of herbs and fragrant oils that had become familiar and comforting.

There wasn't more time for talking or even exchanging sweet looks, as Iris was standing behind the counter with Erindil beside her. Books were sprawled open and stretched down the length of the glass. Sass had thought they'd be in the back room, but as she glanced at their number, she understood why they weren't crowding into the cozy space.

"Lock the door,' the apothecary requested as she flicked up her gaze.

Val paused to snap the bolt into place behind them, flipping over the "open" sign so that the gold letters on the black paper read "closed." Luckily the windows of the shop were already darkened, so there was no chance of villagers peeking inside.

Cali emerged from the back. "Oh, good. Everyone's here." She cut her eyes to Iris. "Have you told them?"

Iris shook her head, and her curls jiggled. Then she lifted her gaze and smiled. "I thought I'd read about enchanted jewels somewhere, and I was right." She tapped a finger on one of the open pages. "*The Traveling Chronicles of Verendel the Gray* talks about encountering a charmed jewel. In this case, the jewel was hexed to slowly poison the wearer."

Lira gasped and her gaze found Sass, who swallowed hard.

"Not that we believe your jewel is poisonous, my dear." Erindil beamed at Sass, holding out his hand. "But if you'll pass it to me, I can start the process of determining the charm or curse."

Sass pulled the velvet bag from her pocket and passed it to the elf, glad to be rid of it.

Iris pointed to a line in the book. "The chronicles detail how Verendel the Gray used a simple spell to reveal the magic."

"Which I feel confident I can perform," Erindil said. "Revealing spells can rarely go wrong or inflict harm, and as an elf, I have the power to survive magic if it happens to rebound."

Despite the elf's reassuring smile, that only sounded mildly comforting.

The elf poured the amulet into a black bowl that Iris produced. Then he held his hands over the bowl, whispering, "Arcana Revela."

The room was so quiet Sass could hear her own quick breaths, as Erindil paused before repeating the incantation. After a few more rounds, Val slid Sass a look and a shrug.

Before Sass could return the shrug, the bowl started to shake and Erindil's hands glowed as he gripped the edges. The elf's eyes were closed and his head tipped up, and Sass wondered if the spell was as harmless as he'd believed.

Then as quickly as the bowl had started rattling and glowing, it stopped. Erindil opened his eyes, and a satisfied grin stretched across his face.

"Well?" Lira asked, her voice a hush.

Erindil locked his eyes on Sass. "It's most certainly enchanted, and whoever cast this spell meant to use the amulet to control you, my dear."

Sass tried to steady her scattered heartbeat but failed miserably.

Forty-Three

SASS STOPPED SHORT when she walked back into The Tusk & Tail.

She'd expected to see Rosie overwhelmed by the task of passing out scones and pouring chai. She hadn't expected the merry din that greeted them. The chai and pear scones appeared to be going over well, and even more than the usual number of customers crowded around tables and bellied up to the bar.

Rog stood in place of Vaskel and was obviously standing on a stool so he could clear the bar. Now that she looked more closely, it seemed that Rosie was splashing brandy into the chai mugs as she made her way around the tables. That explained the louder than usual laughing and the lute player who'd gone from strumming lilting melodies to rollicking dancing reels.

"Are Tin and Pip dancing the halfling two-step?" Cali muttered from behind Sass.

"Looks like Rog and Rosie have rolled out the gnomish hospitality," Vaskel said.

"Looks like she's rolled out the brandy," Lira added, with a nudge to Sass's ribs.

Erindil peered down his long nose, his lips pursing when he spotted his lute player perilously perched on a stool by the hearth and strumming with abandon. "And it appears my musician is about to tumble onto the floor."

Thrain's belly laugh was deep and loud. "This is just what I need."

When Rosie spotted their group, she threw up a wave with the hand that held the brandy. She scooted around a table with a tray of scones held high over her head with the other hand.

"This crowd might just spill right into dinner," Lira said with an amused shake of her head. "I'd better get in the kitchen and start cooking. I'm surprised the scones I made lasted this long."

"And I'll lend Rog a hand," Vaskel said, as he and Thrain both headed for the bar.

Sass followed Lira to the kitchen, still stunned by the goings-on in the great room. But that was nothing compared to what greeted them in the kitchen.

Instead of a chaotic mess of baking gone awry, the scone-making was humming along courtesy of Crumpet. The flutterstoat was in the middle of the large wooden worktable, dancing along the rolling pin to flatten the dough. He glanced up and chittered something that sounded slightly like scolding.

Sass made a sound that was akin to a squeak before she found her voice again. "What in Grognick's beard is going on in here?"

More chittering from Crumpet, but this time some of it was directed at the raccoon who'd popped his head through the window and rolled two pears onto the counter.

Sass's knees wobbled, so she found the stool before she sank to the floor. "Don't tell me that one flies too?"

Crumpet gave her a withering look and returned to his work.

"Sorry it took so long, Crump," Lira said as she watched the enchanted creature roll the dough into a perfect circle by skipping on the wooden pin as if he was in a log roll competition, "but it looks like you've got things well in hand."

"Well in hand?" Sass rubbed a hand across her forehead. "The kitchen is overrun with wee beasties."

"I'd hardly call one flutterstoat and a raccoon being overrun." Lira patted Sass' arm as she passed her to join Crumpet at the wooden table. "Besides, he's only rolling out the dough I left. Anyone could do that."

Sass wasn't so sure that was true.

"I don't know which is most alarming," Sass muttered. "Discovering that Florin put a controlling spell on the amulet, or seeing Crumpet and crew running our kitchen."

Lira took over the rolling from Crumpet, who flew to her shoulder and sagged against her as if worn out. "I assumed full elves would have more powers than me, but I had no idea he could perform spells."

The rules placed on magic did not apply to the elvish island kingdom of Lananore or to elves in general, since their powers were innate and not artificially created. Sass remembered the powers Lira had displayed to save their friends, and she thought that her friend gravely underestimated elf magic.

She was just relieved that they now knew the amulet's power, although that didn't mean she was any closer to ridding herself of the dwarf who'd given it to her. That thought made her pulse jangle.

"I'm going to pop upstairs since it looks like things down here are under control," Sass told Lira, who was already cutting out a new batch of scones.

Tenuous control, she thought, as she left the kitchen and trudged up the stairs to her room. She gladly divested herself of the amulet, shoving it under her mattress once more. But instead of sinking onto the bed, she climbed out the window and onto the thatched roof.

On the roof, she could only hear snatches of the lute music, which had now returned to its previous repertoire of soft, ethereal melodies. On the roof, the air was crisp and clean with only the faintest whiff of peat smoke drifting to her from the chimney. On the roof, she could be alone and think.

Sass wrapped her arms around her bent knees and settled herself on the prickly thatch. Her mind still raced from what she'd learned. Erindil's revelation that the amulet carried a controlling enchantment should have shocked her, but considering that Florin was the gift-giver, it hadn't.

Now everything made sense. Florin had given her the amulet precisely because she wanted to control Sass. Sass's gut roiled at the thought of what Florin might have made her do and the even more undeniable fact that no one would have known a Trollbane was behind it. It also explained why Florin was so eager to retrieve the powerful amulet and why she insisted on Sass wearing it one more time. What did Florin intend for her to do then? Most crucially, what was Sass going to do now that she knew?

Sass's friends had been full of ideas on the walk back from the apothecary. Cali was in favor of an ambush of the dwarf campground, while Lira had suggested they confront Florin with the news and use what they knew to force her to leave. Unsurprisingly, Vaskel's suggestion had been the most diabolical, as he wanted to sneak into the dwarf camp and slip the amulet around Florin's neck.

But it was down to Sass to decide what to do, and her thoughts were as much of a chaotic buzz as the crowd downstairs. Not for the first time since she'd left home, she wished she could access her mum's dwarf wisdom.

"You would know the answer," she whispered. "You would know what to do."

As she blew out a breath and tried to summon some mining wisdom that might apply, the thatch crackled behind her.

"I thought I might find you out here."

Forty-Four

"DID you have your fill of spiked chai?" Sass asked, shifting on the thatch to make room for Val, who had scooted onto the roof without standing. Her heart fluttered at the press of the guard's shoulder into hers, but she kept her voice steady.

Val made a face. "Rosie's apple brandy will cure what ails you —and polish the tarnish off a dagger."

Sass muffled a snort. "Or your insides."

Val laughed, the sound low and throaty. "That's what I'm afraid of."

Sass curled her arms around her knees again and rocked back, as the two sat in quiet and observed the comings and goings of the village below. "I like to come out here to get away from all the hustle and bustle downstairs." She cut her eyes to the guard. "Don't get me wrong. I love the tavern, and I even love how busy it's gotten, but sometimes it's nice to come up here and get a little perspective."

"Perspective, eh?"

"Lira was the one who taught me that rooftops were the perfect place to escape. Sometimes, seeing your world from a distance helps you understand it better."

"Makes sense. Things seem less intimidating from up here." Val inclined her head toward the blacksmith shop and the green figures shuffling outside it to hitch a cart. "Even Korl's dads don't seem so big."

Sass wasn't sure she agreed with that. Even from the roof, the orcs looked big to her.

"I hope I'm not ruining your peace and quiet," Val said as she stole a glance at Sass, "but I wanted to make sure you were okay after everything that happened."

Sass slunk a smile in the woman's direction. "I'm okay. Overwhelmed, I guess. I'm not sure of the best way to handle Florin."

Val nodded. "Everyone has a different idea of what you should do, and they're all certain their way is the best way."

"I can see advantages and disadvantages with every plan, but I keep thinking about what will keep everyone here safe. It's no good if she attacks our group when I confront her, and it's even worse if we convince Florin to leave but she comes back and wreaks havoc on the village when we least expect it."

"Is there anything I can do to help?"

Sass felt the tightness in her chest melt as she leaned into Val. "Your being here and asking helps."

Val gave her a shy smile and leaned into Sass, almost knocking over the dwarf with her bulk. Sass caught herself with one hand before tipping over completely.

"Sorry!" Val reached for her and yanked her back, sending both of them flailing to the other side.

Sass dissolved into giggles as they thrashed on the thatch for a few moments, finally wiggling themselves back to sitting. Despite having been in some actual danger of rolling off the roof, their laughter had lightened the heaviness of her worries.

Val plucked a bit of thatch from Sass's braid. "That would have been embarrassing."

"Sliding off the roof and landing on a departing tavern patron?" Sass teased. "I think we would have had some explaining to do."

Val put a hand over her mouth as her shoulders trembled with laughter. "Imagine poor Pip or Tin if I'd landed on *them*."

"Bless the stars!" Sass imitated Pip's higher voice, which sent Val into another fit of laughter, which Sass joined in on.

When the pair finally stopped laughing, Val grinned at Sass. "It's not everyone who can make me laugh." She nudged the dwarf gently with one elbow. "I'm very particular about who I spend my time with, you know."

"Aye, I've noticed. You and Korl are thick as thieves, but until Lira turned his head, it was always the two of you doing everything together." Sass ventured a questioning look. "For a long time, I wasn't sure if you wanted more friends."

Or something more than a friend, she thought, but didn't say.

Val's expression turned serious. "You're right. For the longest time it was just Korl, because I had known him for so long and I could trust that he cared about me. With other folks, I could never be sure. Too many had walked away from me for me to trust my own judgment. My parents didn't have time for me. I think my mother's giant lineage didn't give her much in the way of maternal instincts. It wasn't until Korl's dads took me in that I knew what it was like to be cared for. I guess I learned young not to hope for too much, and to be happy with what I had." She sighed. "Which until I met you and Lira and the rest of the gang, I was."

Sass's heart twisted as the guard kept her gaze on her own hands. "It isn't only Korl and his dads who care for you, Val."

Val tilted her head to meet Sass's eyes. "I know that now, but it took a bit of time for it to sink in. If I've been hard to read, that's why."

Sass understood more than Val could know. For most of her life in the Ice Lands, she hadn't felt seen, although she could never claim that she'd been cast aside like Val.

Sass put a hand over Val's. "Home isn't where your axe hangs, but where your heart feels light enough to set it down."

Val released a breath. "I like that. More dwarf wisdom from your mum?"

Sass's throat was thick as she nodded. "I've been missing her advice lately, but I just realized something."

"That you don't need your mum to be here for you to hear her wisdom?"

Sass scrunched her lips to one side and quirked a brow at Val. "When did you get so smart?"

"You've been quoting your mum since I met you. It seems like the part of her you miss is already inside you."

Sass's eyes burned with unshed tears, but she blinked them away. "If she were here, she would tell me that a dwarf isn't measured by the notches in their axe but by the warriors by their side."

Val put an arm around Sass's shoulders. "Just like the best hearth isn't the one with the biggest fire, it's the one that's surrounded by your friends."

Sass tipped her head back to look at Val, wondering if she'd picked that up from Vorto and Klaff. "Orc wisdom?"

The guard winked at her. "Val wisdom."

Forty-Five

THE LUTE PLAYER had long since left the tavern, and even the rowdiest patrons had drunk their fill and devoured the last of Lira's meat pies. Only Pip and Tin rested on a back table, their heads cradled in their folded arms and their snuffling snores wrapped up in the hiss and sigh of the dying fire. Even Rosie and Rog were tucked away in their wagon, and Iris had returned home in the moonlight with a sleepy Cali accompanying her.

Sass stopped swiping at one of the dirty wooden tables and put her hands on her hips. "I've made a decision."

Vaskel glanced up from where he was swabbing the bar, and Thrain woke with a start, jerking so straight he fell off the barstool.

"Orc's blood!" He caught himself before he landed on his face, snapping to his feet and swiveling his head as if searching for an incoming attack.

Val stopped knitting by the fire, and Korl's mouth gaped into a yawn.

"What was that?" Lira emerged from the kitchen, untying her apron as she walked.

Vaskel cocked a thumb at Sass. "She's decided what she wants to do."

"About Florin?" Lira's face brightened. "Whose plan are you choosing?"

Vaskel's blue eyes flashed heat. "Should I prepare to sneak into the dwarf camp?"

"And attempt to get the amulet onto Florin without her or any of her guards hearing you?" Sass shook her head. "Absolutely not. I'm not sending you on a suicide mission."

Vaskel braced his hands on the bar and leaned forward. "You have no idea how stealthy I can be."

"I have never doubted your ability to be sneaky, Vaskel."

The Hellkin frowned, not sure if he was being flattered or insulted by the dwarf—or a bit of both.

"I'm not ignorant of everyone's talents and skills," Sass continued. "I know Lira can pick any lock, and Cali can shoot a fly through the wings at fifty paces. I'm vague on all the things Vaskel can do, but I have no doubt it's an impressive list."

The Hellkin preened at this, and Thrain cleared his throat.

Sass tipped her head at the dwarf. "And I know all too well that Thrain can swing an axe with the best of them."

"Too right," he rasped, sleep still blanketing his voice.

"It doesn't matter if we can defeat Florin," Sass said, her gaze meeting Val's for a beat. "I can't risk losing any of you in the trying."

"Let us defend you," Lira said. "Don't think for a moment that we'll let you do this alone."

Sass crossed to Lira and took her hand. "I'm not suggesting I go alone. I'm suggesting I don't go to meet Florin with battle on the mind."

"Florin knows nothing but fighting," Thrain reminded her.

"Then maybe it's time she learned something new." Sass held Lira's hand while she turned to face her friends. "We've uncovered Florin's duplicity and her scheme. We can prove that I wasn't the one who broke the agreement by running away. She broke it first by giving me a charmed amulet. If she doesn't want me to reveal all, she'll leave and release her claim and her threat of retribution."

"That's it?" Thrain blinked at her. "That's the plan? You're going to tell her she broke the rules and needs to go home?"

Lira squeezed Sass's hand. "Being direct and honest is never the wrong answer."

"It is if it gets you killed," Thrain said, but mostly to himself.

Korl rose from his chair by the hearth and rubbed his dusky green hands together. "Doing the right thing is never the wrong thing. Reasoning with an enemy and attempting to broker a fair peace in order to save lives could never be a mistake."

Thrain rubbed his forehead. "Am I losing my mind, or is an orc casting a vote not to fight?"

Lira beamed at Korl and winked at Thrain. "He's not your typical orc."

"I'm starting to think that none of the folks around these parts are typical," the dwarf said as he sank onto a bench, muttering to himself about peaceful orcs and dwarves who'd rather talk than fight.

"I'm going to take that as a compliment," Sass said.

Thrain pressed his brows together. "Then I must not have said it right."

Vaskel huffed out a breath that actually produced steam. "When are we leaving on this diplomatic mission?"

Sass swept her gaze around the cozy great room and the friends who were putting their trust in her. "Tomorrow morning. I don't want to give Florin the chance to get impatient and attack first." Everyone eyed Sass without speaking, and the dwarf sighed. "I promise not to sneak out and go on my own."

Lira gave her hand another squeeze before releasing it. "Then it's agreed. We leave in the morning, which means we should all get some rest tonight. This might not be a battle, but we'll need to be on our toes."

"Tomorrow?" Thrain dragged a hand down his beard. "I suppose that's enough time."

"Enough time for what?" Sass asked as everyone pushed chairs under tables, and Korl stamped out the last embers of the fire with his boot.

Thrain's eyes went wide before he cleared his throat roughly. "Enough time to think of a backup plan if Florin doesn't go along with yours, of course."

That made sense, Sass thought as she watched him shuffle off to bed. Then why did Sass suspect that her oldest friend was hiding something?

Forty-Six

SASS POPPED her head into the kitchen the next morning, expecting to see Lira in her usual spot behind the worktable with a pot of chai bubbling on the stove and Crumpet chattering on her shoulder. But the flutterstoat slept soundly in his nest of dishrags, only sparing her a barely opened eye and a contented sigh before snuggling deeper into his bed.

"I suppose she doesn't want to start her baking if we're headed out," Sass reasoned to herself as she backed from the kitchen and headed for the great room.

But that was empty too. The hearth yawned cold and dark, the tables were barren, and not even Vaskel was at his usual post behind the bar. Was everyone having a lie-in before heading out to deal with Florin?

Sass reached a hand into the pocket of her pants, her fingers brushing the velvet pouch she'd tucked safely away. She had no intention of wearing the amulet, but she didn't want to keep it either. Something with such ill intent had no place in her new life.

She cocked her head and absorbed the quiet of the tavern, which was something she rarely experienced anymore. Even before they opened, Lira or Vaskel or both were usually around. It was never so silent.

Her ears pricked at the sound of voices, familiar voices. But they weren't coming from outside the front of The Tusk & Tail. They were coming from the back.

Sass walked to the back door and pushed it open, blinking at the wash of sunlight splashed across the horizon and a sight she'd never imagined she'd see.

"Your powers don't come from your hands, my dear." Erindil held Lira's hands in his own. "Your hands merely direct them."

Lira had donned her old rogue's clothes for the occasion, with a cloak draped over her brown pants and leather waistcoat. Boots replaced the slip-on shoes she'd taken to wearing around the tavern, and the glint of a dagger's steel flashed at her waist.

Lira turned when she noticed Sass, her mouth quirking when she saw the dwarf was also wearing the outfit she'd had on when they first met. A cloak covered Sass's shoulder armor and hid her blades, but it was a far cry from the dresses she now favored.

"Good morning." Erindil flashed a bright smile her way. Although his attire was as ornate as usual, Sass didn't miss the fact that the colors were more muted and an exquisitely carved bow was hooked to his back.

"Getting in an early morning lesson on elf magic?"

Lira hitched one shoulder. "Learning what it means to be part elf."

Erindil put a hand on Lira's arm. "I don't believe in part this and half that. You're as much an elf as I am. Besides, we all contain multitudes."

Sass wasn't sure what that meant. Then again, she had spent little time talking to elves.

"Where's Vaskel?" Sass asked. "Or Korl?"

"Vaskel was coming with Cali and Iris, and I told Korl that we'd swing by and get him and Val on our way."

Erindil swiveled his head around as if searching for something. "Are we going then?"

"You're joining us?" Sass tried to keep the surprise from her voice, but failed.

The elf touched a hand to his chest and bowed his head at her. "I wouldn't miss it, my dear."

Lira gave her uncle a grateful smile, and Sass had the feeling that she'd pulled in a favor. It wasn't the time to ask, though, and she wouldn't say no to the help. The sight of an elf might just make Florin think twice about choosing violence.

Erindil busied himself untethering his ostrich, but he didn't mount the creature. "Come along, Glen."

"You aren't riding him?" Sass asked.

"Good heavens, no. Not until we're ready to do battle," the elf said, as he patted the creature's lavender plumage and then dropped his voice to a conspiratorial whisper. "To be completely forthcoming, Glen's experience in battle is limited."

If the ostrich understood a word the elf said about him, he gave no indication. Lira, however, slid Sass a wry wink.

Their group proceeded around the tavern and onto the dirt road with Sass on one side and Erindil leading the ostrich on the other. Sass walked briskly to keep up with their longer legs, but they soon slowed as Korl and Val approached them from the direction of the blacksmith and wheelwright workshops. Behind them were Klaff and Vorto, each dressed in head-to-toe leather and brandishing smithing hammers.

"What are—?" Sass started to ask before Val held up a hand.

"Don't argue with them," she said. "They won't have it any other way."

Korl nodded, glancing back at his dads and giving them a small smile. "We're all coming."

Sass managed a peek at Val through glassy eyes as the group headed down the road into the village. Just as Sass registered the lack of yeast and sugar in the air, she spotted Pip and Fenni walking toward them.

Instead of wearing a liberal dusting of flour and an apron around his waist, the halfling baker's clothes were clean, his apron was gone, and there was no dough in his hair. He did wield a rolling pin as if it were a cudgel, though.

His brother Fenni was more casually dressed than usual and had a row of cheese knives tucked into the waistband of his tweed pants. If he hadn't sported a pocket square in his vest, he might have appeared mildly threatening.

"We're coming with you," Pip said as Fenni bobbed his head in agreement.

"So am I, so am I!" Tinpin cried out as he rushed from his shop holding a pair of fabric shears with the blades pointed out before shrieking and flipping them around. "Sweet simmering cauldrons, I was running with scissors."

"What...you can't...How did you know?" Sass stuttered.

Pip bounced on his toes. "We heard you last night in the tavern."

The haberdasher's cheeks flushed. "We weren't sleeping the entire time. Not the entire time."

"And don't say we can't come because you need all the bodies you can get against a band of dwarves." Fenni whipped out one of his wee, curved knives.

"That's right, love," Iris said as she, Vaskel, and Cali walked up with Rosie and Rog arm-in-arm and at least half the village behind them. "You're part of the village now."

Pip leaned forward, his large eyes sparkling. "You're one of us."

Sass's eyes burned, and her throat was so thick she could barely swallow.

"What did I tell you?" Val whispered, slipping a hand around hers. "You've found your hearth."

'Thank you," Sass said, even though her voice cracked. "You don't have to do this, but I couldn't have picked a better crew than all of you."

Pip's smile was incandescent as he elbowed his brother. "Bless the stars! Did you hear that? We're finally part of a crew."

As the group shuffled toward the village square, Thrain hurried up and fell in step, still shaking off sleep.

"Where have you been?" Sass asked.

"Late start," her friend said with his gaze fixed ahead. "I overslept."

Vaskel gave the dwarf a once-over. "Glad you joined us. We need our whole crew on a day like today."

Thrain gave a brusque nod to the Hellkin, his cheeks reddening with pleasure. "I never miss the chance to fight alongside friends."

Sass hid her smile, but Thrain considering the motley villagers his friends might have been one of the more surprising parts of her morning—and that was saying something.

AS HONORED as Sass was to have so many of her friends and villagers joining her, she hadn't fully appreciated the sound of so many people walking through the forest. Even with Vaskel and Cali moving in front of the group with considerable stealth, Klaff and Vorto couldn't help crushing the dry leaves beneath their massive orc feet. Surprisingly, Erindil's battle ostrich made almost no sound as he walked alongside the elf, delicately placing each two-toed foot on the ground.

Not to mention, Tinpin was seemingly powerless to suppress his nervous muttering.

"It's quite shady in here, isn't it?" he said in a stage whisper to Pip. "Quite shady indeed."

"We aren't supposed to talk," Fenni hissed, putting one of his cheese knives to his lips and nearly slicing into himself.

Even though Val was clearly on high alert, Sass caught the twitch of a smile at the corner of her mouth. "Not you too."

Val flattened her lips and regained her solemn expression. "Say what you will about our group, we have the element of surprise."

Sass stole a look at Glen, who boasted a harness that looked more like a jeweled headdress. "If you mean the dwarves will be stunned by the makeup of our armed party, then I agree."

Vaskel held up a clenched fist, and Cali whispered, "Almost to the camp."

This only made Pip bounce more and Tin drop his scissors. Sass touched her thumb to the ring, which was prickling just like it had the first time she'd come searching for Florin. The dwarves were there, she was sure of it, but maybe their group had the element of surprise.

The trees thinned as they approached the outskirts of the clearing, but it was instantly apparent that they hadn't snuck up on the search party. A full complement of armed guards waited with battle axes at the ready, and Florin stood in front of all of them.

"I didn't expect you to bring company, my love."

Her gaze sought Sass, who stepped forward with Val close at her heels. "You never said to come alone."

Florin's jaw ticked, but she mustered a smile. "But I asked you to wear the amulet I gave you."

"About that—"

"The deal," Florin interrupted with a swish of her hand, "was that you would wear the jewel I gifted you one final time in exchange for me leaving in peace and not demanding retribution from your clan."

"That deal was based on the lie that you wanted everyone to believe."

The redheaded dwarf flinched, and her guards shifted angrily. "What lie?"

"That you gave me a beautiful amulet crafted by your clan as a token of our bond, and that I broke that bond by running off with the amulet."

Florin crossed her arms over her chain mail. "I hear no lie."

Sass reached into her pocket and produced the velvet pouch. "You forgot to mention that you had a powerful mage or dark wizard cast a spell on the amulet. You never wanted me to wear it because it symbolized our bond. You needed me to wear it so you could control me."

Florin's left eye twitched, and her lips became a tight, white line. "Ridiculous."

Sass let the pouch swing from one finger. "What's ridiculous is my ever thinking that you cared about anything other than power. What was your plan, Florin? What were you going to make me do once I wore the amulet and you could control me?"

Florin's jaw clenched, but she forced a smile. "You can't prove anything."

"Actually, I can. My elf friend used a revealing spell on the amulet to determine the magic in it."

Florin's hands twitched, but she curled them into fists, as if she was keeping herself from lunging for the pouch. "It doesn't matter what you know or think you know. I'm still going to return to the Ice Lands and tell everyone that you broke the arrangement. Then the Thornshield clan will pay."

Thrain pushed through the crowd to stand next to Sass. "Not if I tell everyone at home what really happened."

Relief coursed through Sass at her friend's courage, and she scolded herself for ever thinking he could be anything but loyal.

Florin's eyes flashed malice but then she laughed. "One

dwarf?" She narrowed her eyes at Thrain. "You'll never make it back alive."

As if moving as one, the villagers and friends closed in on Thrain and Sass.

"You'll have to go through all of us," Val growled.

Florin bared her teeth in a menacing grin. "With pleasure." She flicked a finger at her guards, who assumed battle stances.

Cali's arm was a blur as she whipped out an arrow and notched it, and Vaskel suddenly held a throwing dagger in each hand. Even Erindil swung himself onto Glen's back with the grace of a seasoned warrior, and the ostrich narrowed his eyes, emitted a terrifying scream, and extended his neck as if ready to charge.

"You take the dwarves on the left, and I'll take the ones on the right," Vorto said to Klaff, his burr of a voice loud enough for the dwarves in question to exchange wary glances as the orcs shifted their grips on the smithing irons.

The ring on Sass's pinky finger burned, but instead of spurring her to violence, it reminded her that Iris had given it to her to keep her safe. Iris, who'd become like family to her, just as so many of the villagers had.

Sass held up her hands. "This isn't the only way, Florin. You're the future ruler under the mountains. You have the power to choose another way, just like I have."

"You ran." Florin spat out the words.

"I did, and I should have chosen a better way." A breath hissed from Sass's chest. "I should have told you that my destiny wasn't to rule. Maybe that would have saved us both a lot of trouble."

Florin choked back a bitter laugh, but some of the rage drained from her eyes. "It would have saved me a trek through these hot, godsforsaken lands."

Sass took a tentative step forward, even as Val and Vaskel tensed beside her. "I don't know why you gave me a cursed amulet, but you don't need to control me to be a powerful leader. You don't need to start a war to have your name recited into dwarf lore. You don't need to be brutal to be a legend."

Florin swept her gaze across the motley villagers. "As if you know anything about making a mark."

Sass shrugged. "I've chosen to make my mark here. I've discovered that I don't need to fight epic battles or sit on a throne to matter. What matters to me is forging friendships and being loved. That's my legacy."

Florin's expression flickered, and something like regret flashed in her eyes before they hardened. "And you never intend to return home?"

Sass twisted to smile at her friends. "This is my home."

Erindil nudged Glen forward, the ostrich's ornate harness jingling. He leveled a severe gaze at Florin. "And I suggest you return to yours. Unless you think the Trollbanes would welcome a delegation from Lananore."

It clearly wasn't lost on Florin that the warning came from an elf or his steely implication that the delegation from the elf kingdom would not be a friendly one. Doubt wavered her haughty gaze, as she cut her eyes across the orcs brandishing irons and the Hellkin's fiery glare and slashing tail. She clocked the Pantheri archer pointing an arrow at her head and Val with her broadsword ready to strike. Finally, the dwarf princess lifted her chin. "It would be a waste to battle an unworthy opponent. If this is what you choose, Sass, so be it."

Sass sensed bristling outrage from her battle-trained friends, but they quelled whatever urges they had to protest Florin's insults. Relief, instead of outrage, coursed through her, but she didn't dare show it.

Instead, she touched a finger to the now-still ring and gave a curt nod. "This is what I choose. I wish you luck in ruling under the mountains." She pulled the amulet's pouch from her pocket. "As promised, here is your amulet."

Florin stomped closer, snatched the velvet pouch from Sass,

and turned on her heel. She motioned to her crew. "Let's go. There's no need to stay in the Ageless Lands a moment longer than we must."

Sass didn't wait to watch the dwarves pack up their campsite or tromp off through the forest. She didn't want to linger around Florin or give the dwarf a chance to change her mind.

Pivoting toward the village, Sass waved for her friends to follow, still in a state of shock that her plan of reasoning with Florin had worked—with the added assistance of Erindil's threat and several fierce fighters at her back.

As Sass and the villagers walked back through the forest, she thought that maybe Florin had truly decided her ragtag bunch of friends wasn't worth the effort to fight and Erindil wasn't an elf worth crossing, but she hoped the dwarf had rethought what mattered in life. Knowing Florin, it was probably the former, but Sass could always hope.

When they cleared the forest, Sass stopped and turned to the group who continued to look shell-shocked by the encounter. Pip's knuckles were white where he clenched the rolling pin, and TinPin's blinking was such a blur she feared he might lift off the ground.

"We did it," she told them with a tentative grin. "We scared off the hunting party."

Then the group erupted in cheers as weapons were dropped to the ground and everyone danced and hugged. Vorto and Klaff trembled the ground with their exuberant jumping, and Pip and Fenni broke into the halfing two-step.

Val swept Sass into a tight embrace, whispering in her ear, "*You* did it."

Sass's feet dangled in the air, and she shook her head even as it nuzzled in the guard's neck. "I couldn't have done it without having my friends behind me—literally."

Val laughed and lowered Sass so that her feet touched the grass. "We will always be here for you. I hope you know that."

Sass bobbed her head as tears clouded her vision. "I do now."

A screech pulled her attention from Val, and she blinked rapidly as she searched for the source. For a beat, she thought it might be Glen, but no ostrich was that loud. Besides, the sound that shook the trees came from overhead.

"Is that a…?" Pip tipped his head as he walked backward and straight into Fenni.

"Impossible." Vaskel shook his head, as if to dislodge the image of the enormous wingspan blocking the sun.

"Please tell me that's not a dragon," Lira said.

"Oh, it most certainly is." Her uncle's voice was almost cheery. "I haven't seen one in centuries, and never in the Known Lands. This is unprecedented, my dears."

Sass's stomach dropped as the beast circled lower, letting out another terrifying screech. "Lucky us."

Forty-Eight

THE VILLAGERS SCATTERED as the sky darkened and the dragon swooped lower, its massive black wings stretching so wide they brushed the treetops on one side. Everyone in their party aside from Erindil backed away as the beast landed, its tree-trunk legs trembling the ground beneath their feet.

"What a beauty." Erindil slipped off the back of Glen and rubbed his hands together with barely contained glee at the sight of the ebony, scaled dragon.

Sass's attention was no longer riveted to the long-necked creature huffing steam from flared nostrils. It was on the figures sliding off the dragon's back.

"Mum?" Sass squinted at the dwarf who descended first and was busy brushing off her moss-green travel gown. The woman's dark braids wound intricately around her head, making her appear taller than she was, although she didn't need to be tall to command attention. Everyone gaped at her.

The female dwarf looked up, the wrinkles on her brow smoothing when she spotted Sass. "There you are, Sarsaparilla!"

Despite running from her home, despite fleeing the Ice Lands, despite every reason she'd ever had for staying away, Sass ran to her mum and straight into her arms.

"Now, now." Her mum patted her hair as she held her. "No need to fuss. We're here now."

At that, Sass pulled back and saw that her father was dismounting from the dragon's back, landing in a crouch and straightening with a grunt. His gray fur cloak swung around his legs and matched some of the gray streaks in his black beard.

"It's been a while since I've ridden on a dragon and never for so long," he said under his breath as he knuckled the small of his back.

Sass forgot all her reasons for running from home as new questions flooded her brain. "How are you here? And where did you get a dragon?"

Her father stroked his wiry black whiskers as he gave her a quick once-over. "That's not important, Sarsaparilla. Are you hurt? You didn't wear that amulet, did you?"

"I'm fine." Sass cocked her head. "But how do you know about the amulet?"

Her father's expression darkened.

"He knows because of me," Thrain said, stepping forward and giving both Thornshields a bow. "I used the rookery at Castle Greyhelm to sent a raven to the Ice Lands. It was the only way to ensure they knew what Florin had done, but I also knew you wouldn't want me to alert your family, so I didn't tell you. Sorry, Sass."

Sass gawked at her friend. If it were possible to feel even worse for doubting him, she did.

Val tapped a finger on her chin as she eyed Thrain. "That's why you wanted the tour of the castle and lingered so long looking at the ravens."

"Thought you just liked birds," Korl said, more to himself than anyone else.

Thrain gave the guards an apologetic grin. "It was a backup plan of sorts and a bit of insurance in case Florin tried to spread untruths."

"A backup plan I didn't need," Sass said to Thrain in a low voice.

Thrain appraised Sass. "No. Turns out you didn't. How was I to know you'd have the entire village behind you? Also, I didn't know your parents would come here themselves or commandeer a dragon to do so."

Sass's father cleared his throat, cutting a brief look at his wife. "Lady Thornshield insisted."

Sass's mum had inherited the crown through her mother, which meant they had the only unbroken line of female leaders who had ruled under the mountains. Sass swallowed hard, knowing what her rejection of the match meant.

"How could we not come after not knowing where you were for so long?" Her mum brushed a loose strand of hair from Sass's face then shot a look at her husband. "We've both been worried sick."

Sass's skin crawled, hot shame making her drop her gaze. "I'm sorry I left without telling you, but I couldn't marry Florin. She wasn't right for me, and neither was ruling under the mountains. It was never the life I wanted."

Her father made a rough sound in the back of his throat. "If I'd known that the Trollbanes would resort to treachery to seize power, we never would have agreed to the match."

Sass's mum sketched a shrewd gaze over Sass and her friends. "Where is Florin?"

Sass drew herself up to her full height, which almost matched her mum's. "She left. She decided not to take retribution, after all."

"Because Sass was brilliant," Val said from behind her. "She convinced Florin to leave."

Sass's mum slid a smile to Val then back to her daughter. "Maybe you were meant to be a diplomat."

Sass grimaced. "That was enough politics for me for a lifetime." She drew in a breath. "I was never meant to be a ruler or stay in the Ice Lands. It wasn't my destiny. Not like it was yours."

Her mum took her face in both of her soft brown hands. "I always knew you were destined for something more. You never took to my mining wisdom."

"You'd be surprised," Lira muttered from where she was tucked next to Korl.

"That doesn't mean it isn't hard to let you go," her mum continued with an amiable glance over Sass's shoulder. "Although it looks like you found a brave crew."

Sass turned to her friends and smiled. "They may not be dwarves, but they've become like family."

Her father narrowed his eyes at the group but nodded. "It takes courage to meet a band of dwarf warriors armed with only..." He tilted his head at Pip.

"A rolling pin," Pip offered with a flickering smile.

"And are those tiny daggers?" Sass's father asked Fenni.

"Cheese knives, your dwarfliness," Fenni said with a courtly bow.

Sass stepped forward before the cheesemonger could explain the unique cheese-slicing benefits of each one. She made cursory introductions of every last villager, saving Lira and Val for last.

"This is Lira, who saw something in me even I didn't, and made me her partner in the tavern." Sass then reached for Val's hand and pulled her close. "And this is Val."

She wasn't sure what to add since she and Val hadn't decided what they were. Even Sass knew that a couple of kisses didn't mean everything had changed. "My very close friend."

"Very, very close," Val added, with a tentative glance to Sass.

Bubbly happiness made it impossible for Sass not to grin and nod, squeezing Val's hand and enjoying the tingles racing up her arm when Val squeezed back.

Sass's mum watched the pair with a content smile, while her father clasped his hands behind his back. "You all would make fine dwarves."

Sass smiled, knowing that this was the highest compliment her father—or any dwarf—could bestow.

"I take it this means you aren't returning home," her mum said with a heavy sigh, "even if marriage to Florin is off the table?"

Sass shook her head. "Leaving was the hardest thing I've ever done, but finding a place that welcomed me for who I am and didn't care about my lineage made it worth it."

Her mum's eyes shone as she nodded. "All we have ever wanted is for you to be happy, Sarsaparilla. Even if it didn't always seem that way. Sometimes parents become blinded to what we think you could be, and we forget to see you as you truly are."

"A dwarf should never be so enchanted by the gold that *might* be in the rock that they forget to be grateful for the gold in their bucket," Sass told her mum.

Lady Thornshield threw back her head and let out a belly laugh that shook her entire body. Finally, she swiped at her eyes. "So you have been listening to me."

Sass blinked away tears. "Your dwarf wisdom has been a faithful companion all this time. Every time I got stuck, I remembered something you'd told me."

Her mum elbowed her husband in the ribs. "I told you she was listening."

Sass's father rubbed his side. "You're as clever and capable as we always knew you could be, and you don't need us to tell you how to live your life."

Sass knew how hard it was for her father to say this. "That doesn't mean I don't need you at all."

A grin flickered on his face. "You are always welcome at home, even if only for a visit. As are all your friends." He swept his arms wide and turned to the group. "Lady Thornshield and I would be honored to host you at our palace under the mountains." His gaze lingered on Erindil. "And we would be delighted to host you for another visit, Erindil."

The elf and his battle ostrich dipped into a low bow, as the rest of the group—and Sass—gawped. Erindil knew her parents?

"Anytime," her mum added, giving Val a special wink.

"Now we need to get this dragon back to the Ice Lands," her father said as he patted the creature's side. "Dragons don't do well in the south, and they technically aren't allowed in the Ageless Lands."

Before Sass could ask him again how he'd sourced a willing dragon, he was pulling her into a brusque hug and climbing back onto the dragon. Her mum lingered a bit longer over her hugs and goodbyes, waving at everyone and blowing kisses before joining her husband on the gilded saddle perched behind the dragon's long neck.

As the dragon slowly beat its massive wings and lifted off the ground, Sass tipped her head back to watch her parents fly away.

"I guess we're stuck with you good and proper now," Val said.

Sass smiled at her. "Aye, you are."

Forty-Nine

SASS STIFLED a yawn as she walked into the kitchen the next morning. As she'd hoped, there was a pot of chai bubbling away on the stove, but there was no Lira.

She rubbed her eyes at the flutterstoat dutifully stirring the aromatic tea. "Sweet simmering cauldrons! She left you in charge, eh, Crump?"

Crumpet chirped something, but didn't stop swirling the long wooden spoon. She supposed she could get used to Crumpet taking a more active role in the kitchen, but she did a double take when she spotted the raccoon sitting on the open windowsill. Sass eyed the pile of pears inside the window, along with a brown hair ribbon that looked remarkably like one she was missing.

"Oy." She walked past the wooden worktable to the counter, picking up the ribbon and giving the raccoon a stern look. "I have no objection to your bringing us things you've foraged, but no foraging in my room."

The creature rubbed his black hands together, his eyes luminous, and Sass was sure he understood her. The raccoon didn't look enchanted, but she couldn't be sure he wasn't magical, and she wouldn't chance being on the wrong side of an enchanted animal.

Sass pulled her thick braid forward and tied the ribbon around the end before grabbing a nearby mug. "Any chance I could get some chai before I start work?"

Crumpet bobbed his white, furry head, stepping aside so Sass could lift the pot and pour herself a cup of the spicy tea. She winked at him and backed out of the kitchen. "Thanks, lads."

Sipping her spiced chai, Sass walked to the great room, which was empty and quiet. She and Vaskel had done a good job of leaving the place tidy from the night before, so the tables gleamed and the air that drifted in through the open windows was cool and fresh. Even though the temperatures were dropping, she enjoyed the nip in the morning air and was in no rush to light up the peat in the fireplace.

She curled her hands around the earthenware mug, letting the warmth seep into her fingers as she walked out the back door of the tavern, where she suspected she'd find Lira again.

Sure enough, the woman was sitting beside her uncle as his various companions and attendants drifted around the ornate collection of tents that looked more like miniature palaces than temporary structures. The lute player sat on a purple tufted ottoman, strumming as he blinked away sleep, and what Sass could only assume was a strolling poet wandered around the perimeter speaking in verse. Glen stood next to the most impressive tent, grooming his feathers with his beak and sparing Sass only a cursory glance.

"You're awake," Lira said when she spotted Sass. "I haven't seen Thrain yet, but I assume he's having another lie-in."

"He does like his sleep." Sass also knew that he liked his late nights over ale and runes, and he'd lurched up to bed long after the rest of the tavern patrons had left the night before.

Erindil crossed his legs at the knee and draped his hands over the ornate armrests of his chair. "I take it he's not heading back to the Ice Lands anytime soon?"

"Rog promised to teach him the secret to making brandy, so he won't be leaving yet," Sass said. "That and he's made friends he'd miss. Not that he'd admit that, mind you."

Lira gave a knowing nod. "I did notice a bromance brewing with Vaskel."

"If and when he does return, I'd love for him to find out where your parents found that marvelous dragon." Erindil fluttered his fingers on the arms of his chair. "There's a story there, and I must hear it."

Sass wouldn't mind knowing either, since she'd never heard her parents speak of dragon-riding and had only ever seen one dragon before the one that had transported her parents to the forest. "After you tell me how you know my parents and how many times you've been to The Ice Lands."

Erindil chuckled. "That's a longer story, my dear. Perhaps best told over the course of a few evenings."

"You'll be staying for a while then?" Sass asked the elf, noticing that his encampment looked more and more permanent every day. They'd even erected a golden flagpole, and a colorful flag bearing the sigil of Lananore flapped in the breeze.

The elf smiled at Lira and then at Sass. "My niece and I have years of catching up to do."

Lira returned the elf's smile. "There's still a lot I want to know about the elven side of my family."

She didn't mention her father by name, but Sass suspected she wished to know more about him, as well, and where he might be.

Erindil squared his shoulders. "Plus, Lira has asked me to walk her down the aisle, and I would not miss that for all the jewels in the Known Lands."

"Your wedding!" Sass smacked her hands to her cheeks. "I almost forgot about the planning with everything that's been going on."

Lira waved a hand at her. "Don't worry. I have too, but there's no rush. Besides, Tinpin is adamant I wait for a special fabric he's ordered from Hearthorn, and I can't get married without a proper wedding dress."

Erindil's eyes sparkled. "There's nothing quite like a winter wedding."

The nip in the air whispered the coming of colder weather, and Sass knew that winter would descend before they knew it. "Has Pip had any more thoughts about your wedding cake?"

Lira laughed. "Only that it has to be the most extraordinary confection anyone in Wayside has ever seen." She held up a finger. "His words. Not mine."

Sass's stomach growled at the thought of Pip's creations. "Speaking of Pip, I should head to the village for supplies."

"I'm assuming those supplies include sweet rolls?"

Sass grinned at Lira's eager expression. "You assume correctly." She glanced around the camp. "How many should I get?"

"None for us." Erindil leaned forward and winked. "I'm going to visit the baker myself today."

"I might see you there then." Sass waved to the elves as she headed back into the tavern. "Don't forget that you left the chai on the stove with a flutterstoat stirring it."

"Hells and cinders," Lira said as she leapt to her feet. Clearly, she *had* forgotten that she'd left Crumpet manning the stove.

Sass was already halfway across the great room and snagging her market basket from behind the bar when Lira rushed in and ran straight to the kitchen. Sass shook her head as she walked out of the tavern, pausing under the swinging Tusk & Tail sign to take another deep breath.

Rog and Rosie's wagon squatted near the entrance to the tavern, the stairs folded up and the doors shut tight. Snoring and singing came from inside, both sounds muffled. Even when Rosie wasn't hawking her apple brandy from the back of the wagon, the tart aroma of fermented apples seemed to seep from the wood itself.

The basket swung from the crook in Sass's arm as she strolled toward the village, humming a sea shanty to herself. Once she could no longer smell apple brandy, every breath filled her lungs with the welcome scents of yeast and sugar. She picked up her pace and was about the turn onto the main road when her gaze snagged on something.

Val sat on the stone bridge with her feet dangling over the side and one of Pip's paper bags in her lap. Her gold hair was pulled up into a messy bun, and she wore casual pants and a blousy top instead of her guard uniform. She waved at Sass and held up the bag.

Sass didn't need more convincing than that. She quickly changed course and headed for the bridge.

"I thought I might catch you before you went to the market." Val held out the bag when Sass reached her. "And I decided to lure you over with sweet rolls."

"You don't need sweet rolls to lure me," Sass said, as she plunged a hand into the bag, her fingers meeting sticky icing.

"Then let's call this me buying you breakfast."

Sass pulled out a pumpkin spice sweet roll and sighed. "I'll never say no to a date that has pastry."

Val laughed and chose her own roll from the bag. "That's good to know."

Sass hopped onto the stone wall of the bridge and shimmied herself around so that she was pressed against Val with her legs also hanging over the side. "Now you know all my secrets."

Val chuckled and bit into her sweet roll. "I doubt that, but I have all the time in the world to learn the rest."

Sass hid her grin behind her oversized pastry swirl and took a big bite, savoring the burst of sugar on her tongue and the sweet moment with Val. After chewing and swallowing, she peered at the stream gurgling beneath them. "This is nice."

"It's a good place to come and think." Val nudged her gently. "Almost as good as rooftops."

Sass nudged her back just as gingerly. "It's a nice place for a morning date."

"I hoped you'd like it." Val slid her a shy smile.

"Especially since you're my very, very good friend," Sass teased.

Val rolled her eyes. "About that...I thought we might discuss upgrading our status."

"To very, very, *very* good friends?"

Val elbowed Sass, but took care to do it gently and not knock her off the bridge and into the stream. "To girlfriends."

Sass's heart tripped in her chest, as Val entwined her fingers with hers. "I like the sound of that."

"Me too." Val's voice was a throaty rasp that sent a jolt through the dwarf.

They sat side-by-side on the stone bridge holding hands and breathing quickly until Sass twisted to face Val. "I suppose we should make it official."

Val curled an arm around Sass's waist, pulling her closer as she lowered her mouth to the dwarf's. "I suppose we should."

Val's lips were as soft as sweet rolls and twice as sweet, Sass thought, as she let herself savor the kiss every bit as much as she had the pastry.

Epilogue

VASKEL STEPPED from the front door of the inn and stretched his arms overhead. He'd gotten a late start to the day, but yesterday had been more tiring that usual, between the encounter with the dwarves, seeing a dragon for the first time, and celebrating their victory late into the night.

He touched a hand to the pocket in his vest, remembering what he'd promised Sass before he'd finished tidying the bar.

"I won't need this anymore." Sass had held out the etched

silver ring. "I forgot to give it back to Iris, but you walk past the apothecary on the way to the tavern, don't you?"

"You sure?" he'd asked, eyeing the elvish ring that should warn of danger.

Sass had nodded, her smile wide. "Positive."

Vaskel had been happy to see the dwarf so sure of herself and her future in Wayside, so of course he'd taken the ring, promising to drop it off to Iris before heading into the tavern. Besides, he enjoyed a bit of harmless flirting with the apothecary.

Turning toward the heart of the village, Vaskel took long strides past the weathered stone monument in the square. Even from there, he caught the distinctive aroma of Pip's baking on the breeze, and his stomach growled.

He spied the black-and-white awning of the apothecary, pulling the ring from his pocket and rubbing the etched sides with his thumb. Even though it had been in his vest pocket, the metal was surprisingly warm to the touch.

Vaskel's steps slowed as he peered at the ring, twirling it in his palm before tentatively slipping it onto the tip of his smallest finger. It had been crafted to fit delicate elf fingers, not larger Hellkin ones, but he worked it over the first knuckle joint.

So, this was the ring that possessed elven magic? He held out his hand to let the silver catch the sunlight, admiring the intricate etchings in elvish.

The tinkling shop bell made him jerk his hand down and give a brusque shake of his head. Enough of this. He needed to return the ring to Iris and then head to the tavern. The village might be recovering from the Harvest Festival and the potential dwarf incursion, but that was all the more reason the tavern would be busy.

Vaskel resumed his determined strides toward the shops lining the main road and facing each other, giving a tug at the ring on his little finger. When it didn't slip off, he paused in front of Iris's shop windows to yank harder.

That was when the ring started to burn and prickle his skin so violently that he yelped in pain. He wrested the band from his finger and flung it to the ground, panting and pivoting on one foot as he looked around him.

The dwarves were gone, and the dark mage who'd once been a threat was safely subdued in the castle dungeons. Besides, the dwarves had never been a danger to him.

But the ring had alerted him to something. Something that was dangerous to *him*. The Hellkin steadied his ragged breath as he searched the quiet village and empty road for any sign of danger.

Who from his checkered past had come back to haunt him?

* * *

Thank you for reading Sorcery, Swords & Scones! Stay tuned for Vaskel's cozy adventure.

Would you like to be a member of my VIP Reader list and get bonus recipes and sneak peeks of future books? Click below to join:

https://broadmoorbooks.kit.com/3b6c0e21ec

* * *

This book has been edited and proofed, but typos are like little goblins that like to sneak in when we're not looking. If you spot a typo, please report it to:
hello@tlstoneauthor.com

Acknowledgments

Orc-sized thanks to Cristina, Sav, and Len for being brilliant and on top of everything, Frauke at Croco Designs for the fabulous cover, Illustrated Page Book Design for the fantasy world map, Emma for beta reading, Gloria for proofing, my lovely husband for helping design the recipe cards and printed swag (again). Cozy hugs to the real-life Crumpet and to my dear friend Kate for generously sharing her adorable dog's name with me.

Special thanks to the amazing members of my Cozy Crew, who have helped share the word about my cozy fantasy novels. You are AMAZING! Thank you Wendy, Jen Miller, brynna.reads, Jenn Adams, Rozanne Visagie, Sadie Young, Annie, Ashley, Taylor Parker, Andrea Wooten, Melinda Trimble, Sammy Taylor, Bianca, Katherine Ramos-Thompson, Cambria, Steph Barker, Jessica Rose, Kate Kempster, Layne, Simon Howard, Nicole Parsons, Danielle Gant, Melissa Wilson, Jacklyn Furlong, Velishia, Tiffany S., Kate Brasington, Stephanie Lewis, Mindy Woolf, Kallie Street,

Sabrina Kaeder, CinnamonBunReads, Madison Schroeder, Ericka Guernsey, Sarah Donaldson, Sabie, Marisela Lopez, Harley Grenier, Jessica Booth, Teah, Madeeha Idrees, CJ Jones, Jamie, Jada La Belle, Ashlie Hakes, Emily Buchanan, Leora Gulkarov, Jess Moran, Kayla Sibley, Dianne Lebold, Chelsea Pawer, Tarasbookrecs, Brie Starkovski, Maggie Jatzlau, Heather Close, Mott Foxdene, Jessica Steed, Emma M Castiglione, kimthebookishbaker, Amber Spiewak, Annette Palma, Hollie Lake, Jaime Katz, Kelsey Warren, Jamie Brandenburg, Nash Wood, Shannon LeBoeuf, Kaitlyn Rautine, Danielle Hardie, Sarah Robinson, Gilli, Trisha Thompson, Kendra Hart, Ivy (@readwivy), Emily Denton, Hannah, Amy Hausey, Madi Johnson, Maddie Rice, Genna Godley, Nicole Garcia, Cecilia de Alvarado, Kaitlyn Cohen, Erin Sherman, Holly Mayes, Jessica White, Shelby Martin, GinnyB, Morgan Crum, Steph Serrano, Susan (@Ravenbooklover), Cali Kavanagh, Sara Allison, Amber Mars, AmyzBookNook, Liz Stathakos, Molly Palmer Masood, Erin Shea, Tanvi, Nadia Gardner, Maggie Haley, Veronique Lessard, Megan Tauber, Cinnamon, Kelsie Jelsema, Lauren Beauchamp, Elizabeth Kinlaw, Amanda Hanson, Tiffany Weinhold, Sarah McGee, Ashlee Donley, Ed Wiscombe, Arizona Parrett, Sarah Blakeley, Maria-Zoe Massonne, Alexandra Shaw, Stephanie Conroy, Amanda Wright, Shelby Alexis Paige Marek, Amanda Meyer, Calista Wielgos, Ashley Colon Reyes, Tara White, Amanda Stout, Amber Maner, Hannah Lyn Gjovik Grudzinski, Amber Vance, Shannon Emerick, Kimber Freund, Claire Wilband, Catriona Anderson, Christopher G, Rebecca Doyle, Natasha Leighton, Tommi Key, Charlotte Kane, Nichelle Shields, Aura Clark, Elyssa Davis, Cindy Crivellone, Dindi Doward, Kirsty Gudmundsson, Katrina Ingram, Amanda Mace, Tara White, Sierra Rhines, Yael Levy, Zoey Wheeler, Amanda Hanson, Ashley Ellis, Haley Shea Jordan, Amy Scoville, Christine Manning, Gillian Parker, Christina Smith, Becky Lee, Samantha Coonrad.

Also by T.L. Stone

Tusks, Tails & Teacakes

Sorcery, Swords & Scones

Solstice, Spice & Everything Nice (A Tiny Tale from the Tavern)

Cauldrons, Charms & Chai

Potions, Pirates & Pie

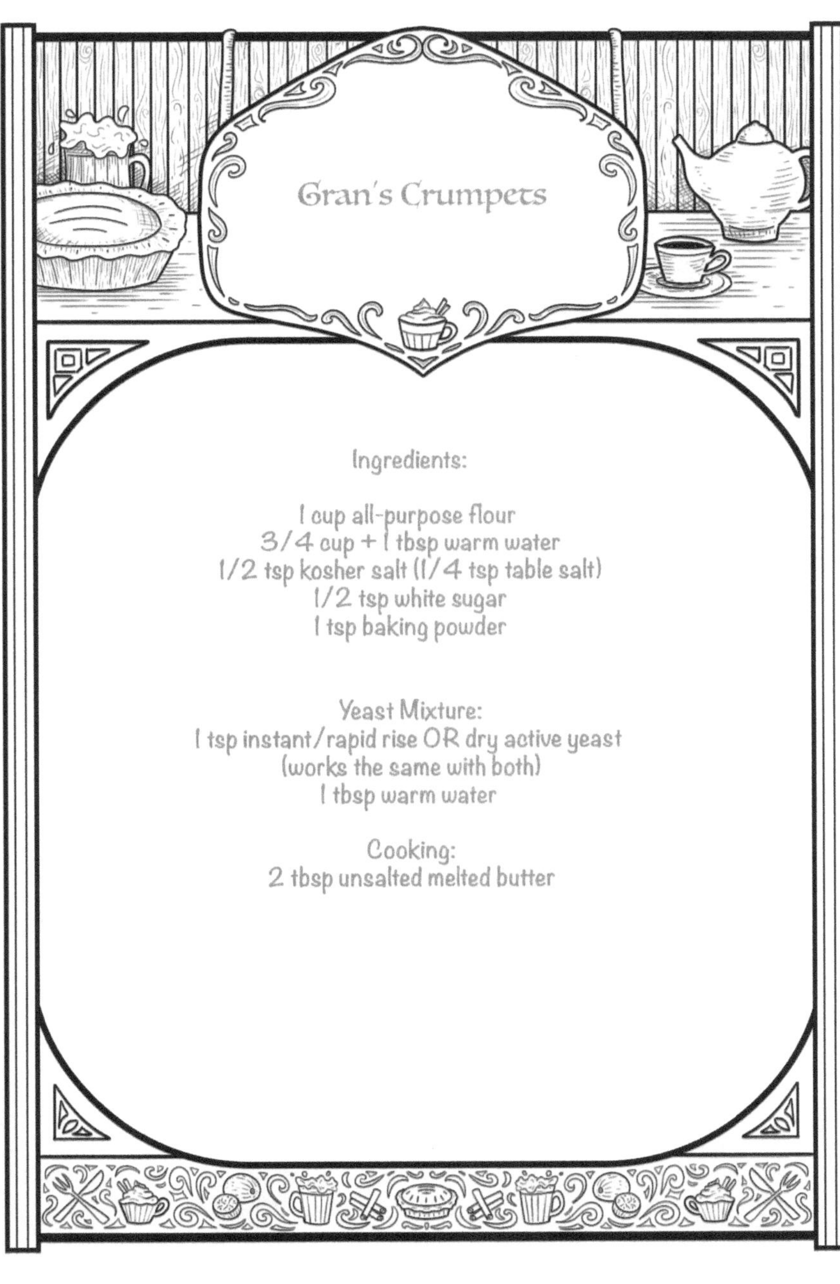

Gran's Crumpets

Ingredients:

1 cup all-purpose flour
3/4 cup + 1 tbsp warm water
1/2 tsp kosher salt (1/4 tsp table salt)
1/2 tsp white sugar
1 tsp baking powder

Yeast Mixture:
1 tsp instant/rapid rise OR dry active yeast
(works the same with both)
1 tbsp warm water

Cooking:
2 tbsp unsalted melted butter

Instructions:

Crumpet Batter:
Place flour, water and salt in a bowl and whisk for 2 minutes.
Yeast Mixture - Dissolve Yeast into 1 tbsp warm water in a small bowl.
Add Yeast Mixture, sugar and baking powder into bowl, then whisk for 30 seconds. Cover with plastic wrap, then place in a very warm place for 15 to 30 minutes until the surface gets foamy. It will only increase in volume by about 10-15%.

Cooking Crumpets:
MGrease 2 or 3 rings or metal shapers with butter
(TIP: Nonstick rings - brush with melted butter. Everything else - smear with butter)Brush nonstick skillet lightly with melted butter then place rings in the skillet.Turn stove on medium high and bring to heat.
Pour 1/4 cup batter into the rings about 1cm / 2/5" deep (will rise about 60%).Cook for 1 1/2 minutes - bubbles should start appearing on the surface (but not popping yet).
Turn heat down to medium, cook for 1 minute - some bubbles should pop around the edges.

Turn heat down to medium low, cook for a further 2 1/2 to 4 minutes, until the surface is "set" and it's clear there will be no more bubbles popping! (At this stage you can help the final bubbles pop with a skewer.)
Remove rings (you might need to run knife around to loosen).
Then flip and cook the other side for 20 to 30 seconds for a blush of color.Transfer to write rack (golden side down) and fully cool.
Can be eaten once cool, but they're even better the next day.

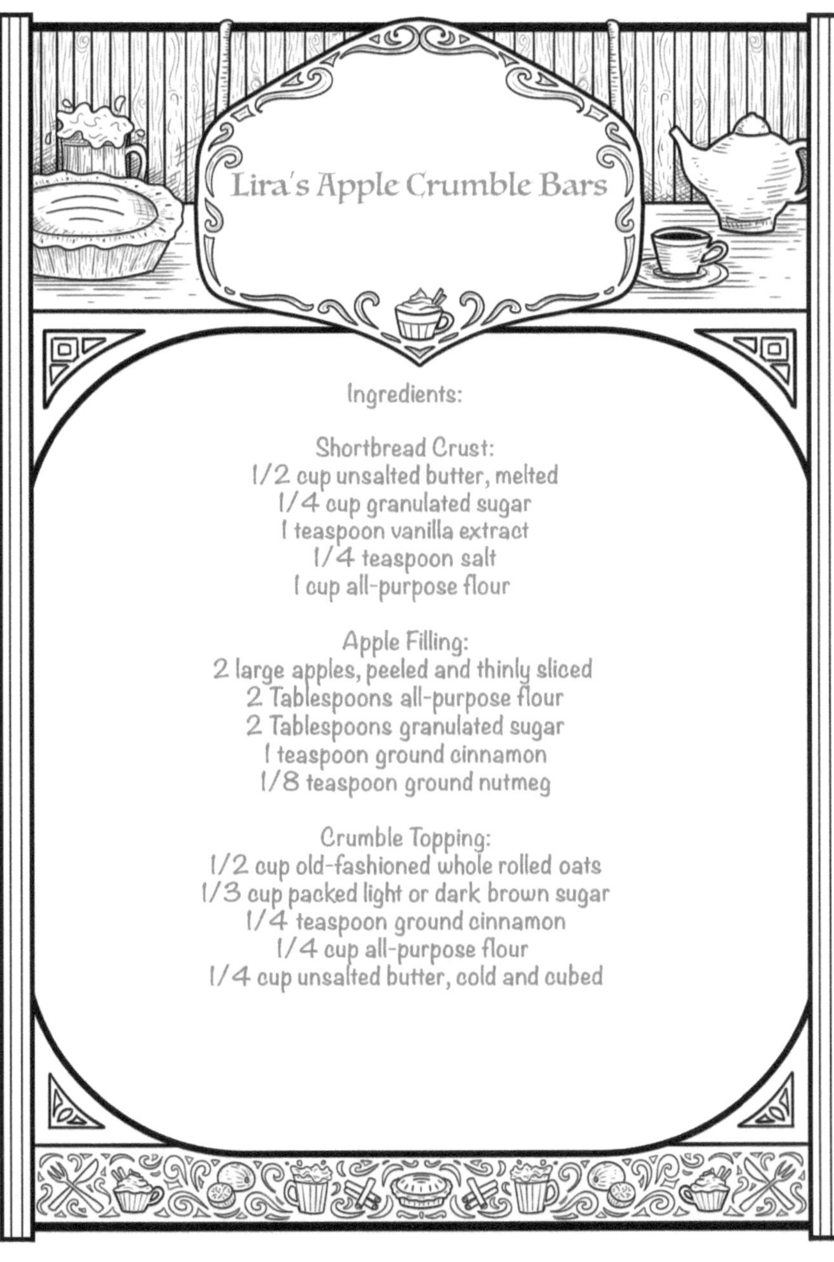

Lira's Apple Crumble Bars

Ingredients:

Shortbread Crust:
1/2 cup unsalted butter, melted
1/4 cup granulated sugar
1 teaspoon vanilla extract
1/4 teaspoon salt
1 cup all-purpose flour

Apple Filling:
2 large apples, peeled and thinly sliced
2 Tablespoons all-purpose flour
2 Tablespoons granulated sugar
1 teaspoon ground cinnamon
1/8 teaspoon ground nutmeg

Crumble Topping:
1/2 cup old-fashioned whole rolled oats
1/3 cup packed light or dark brown sugar
1/4 teaspoon ground cinnamon
1/4 cup all-purpose flour
1/4 cup unsalted butter, cold and cubed

Lira's Apple Crumble Bars

Instructions:

Preheat the oven to 300°F. Line the bottom and sides of an 8-inch square baking pan with parchment paper or aluminum foil, leaving enough overhang on all sides. Set aside.

Make the crust: Stir the melted butter, granulated sugar, vanilla, and salt together in a medium bowl. Add the flour and stir until everything is combined. Press the mixture evenly into the prepared baking pan. Bake for 15 minutes and then remove from the oven.
(As the crust bakes, you can prepare the filling and streusel.)

Make the apple filling: Combine the sliced apples, flour, granulated sugar, cinnamon, and nutmeg together in a large bowl until all the apples are evenly coated. Set aside.

TMake the streusel: Whisk the oats, brown sugar, cinnamon, and flour together in a medium bowl. Cut in the chilled butter with a pastry blender or two knives until the mixture resembles coarse crumbs. Set aside.

Turn the oven up to 350°F. Evenly layer the apples on top of the warm crust. Layer them tightly and press them down to fit. Sprinkle the apple layer with streusel and bake for 30-35 minutes or until the streusel is golden brown.

Remove from the oven and allow to cool for at least 20 minutes at room temperature, then chill in the refrigerator for at least 2 hours. Lift the foil or parchment out of the pan using the overhang on the sides and cut into bars. They can be eaten warm, at room temperature, or even cold.

About the Author

T.L. Stone is a cozy fantasy author who loves writing and reading about friends who become family, fantastical realms, and cozy moments where everything is right with the world. She likes her books and sweaters thick, her drinks sweet and hot, and her pastries buttery.

She's on a quest to make the perfect brownie, and her almond pound cake is swoonworthy. When she's not writing, you can find her cozied up to a crackling fire with a good book or planning her next travel adventure.